PENGUIN BOOKS

EMPORIUM

Adam Johnson teaches creative writing at Stanford University. His fiction has appeared in *Esquire*, *Harper's* and *Paris Review*, as well as *Best New American Voices*. He lives in San Francisco with his wife and son.

Praise for *Emporium*

"Adam Johnson's funny-sad-bizarre stories take place in a world located somewhere between Kurt Vonnegut's sci-fi empire and that wild and crazy land of weirdos limned in T. Coraghessan Boyle's stories. It's a place where strange things happen and stranger things threaten to occur; a place recognizable, in its lineaments, from our present-day reality, but exaggerated, italicized or stretched out to the point of distortion like Silly Putty. Mr. Johnson uses his keen sense of the absurd and his magpie's feel for language to create some wonderfully antic black comedy. But running through his tales is also a melancholy of longing and loss: a Salingeresque sense of adolescent alienation and confusion, combined with an acute awareness of the randomness of life and the difficulty of making and sustaining connections. Mr. Johnson delineates these lives with a mixture of wry amusement and genuine sympathy, satiric glee and elegiac compassion, seemingly contradictory attitudes that combine to create an idiosyncratic and compelling voice."
—Michiko Kakutani, *The New York Times*

"Masterful . . . beautifully crafted . . . achingly poignant . . . cleverly funny. . . . All the wildly inventive stories in the collection are told in fist-person narratives so evocative that we slide effortlessly under each individual skin. 'Teen Sniper' . . . [a] paradoxically tender coming-of-age story most clearly displays Johnson's skill with representing unforgettable voices. Johnson often blends the past, present and future to create a searing juxtaposition between scientific progress and its futility in the face of mortality. With pulsating energy and seemingly endless imagination, this collection pushes that irony to its exciting limits."
—*San Francisco Chronicle*

"[A] striking debut collection . . . the stories are filled with feeling but retain an eccentric satiric edge. The terrific first story establishes Johnson's distinctive blend of futuristic fantasy, cultural parody, and emotional depth. What makes so many of these stories resonate is their tenderness." —Daniel Mendelsohn, *New York*

"Adam Johnson is the most exciting young writer I've ever read. He not only has dazzling verbal skills but his work has pitch-perfect authenticity—of landscape and weather, of hand tools and police procedure—indeed, of *all* the day-to-day details of the human endeavor. And he writes with a profound authenticity of the human heart. He knows how we live, how we yearn, and in *Emporium* he gives us extraordinary fictions that are at once universal and dazzlingly original. Ladies and Gentlemen, Adam Johnson is the real deal." —Robert Olen Butler

"Like a squall moving in on a dead-muggy day, Adam Johnson's audacious work blows the covers off the short story and leaves the genre newly invigorated. The nine stories in his debut collection, *Emporium*—some of them filling fewer than 20 pages—triumph on scales small and large. All of the virtues of the short story at its conventional best belong to them: the deft, economical sketching of character, the planting of resonant little epiphanies among the minutiae of everyday life. But these stories go even further, whipping up a whole askew fictional universe that exerts an unrelenting centripetal force on the reader." —*Chicago Tribune*

"*Emporium* leaves you reeling, dizzy from twisted visions and punch drunk with admiration." —*San Diego Union Tribune*

"Johnson is a masterful writer, the type who makes you feel a mood with all five senses and who goes so deep inside characters that you can't even remember what you were thinking about before you started reading." —*San Francisco Bay Guardian*

"Adam Johnson's prose has an unforgettable radioactive thrum, and *Emporium* will likely have a shelf life equal to plutonium's." —Bob Shacochis

"The stories in Adam Johnson's *Emporium* capture youth's torque, its weird braid of exhilaration and loneliness. Except there's nothing humdrum here. Each of Johnson's fantasies, each peculiar landscape, glows hot with imagination. Johnson's ear is pitch perfect. The ache of isolation finds beautiful expression all over the *Emporium*. Johnson's prose recalls the inventions of Barry Hannah, his wild setting bring George Saunders to mine, and he's as funny as both."
—Esquire.com

"The force and reach of these stories is startling, every sentence something new. Johnson can be darkly funny or disturbingly serious, but what his work reflects most is a fresh and powerful take on the human predicament. Originality and imaginative muscle meet in the worlds of his stories. This is a writer who's going to rock the boat."
—Ron Carlson

"A short story collection is often a lot like a rock 'n' roll record: you can expect two or three cuts to be good and the rest to be just filler. Adam Johnson's debut collection, *Emporium*, is better than that. In fact, as the kids say, it rocks balls-out. Johnson's work is wry and smart, but also very powerful, very moving. His language can make your hair bristle, like a cool hand on the back of your neck. If you enjoy the work of George Saunders, Martin Amis and Donald Barthelme, this book will thrill you."
—*Square Books*

"Adam Johnson reports from a world that has quietly seeped into our groundwater; it's poisonous, alien-made and familiar-tasting. His characters carve life lines in their palms seeking hope. You'll remember them vividly and their resolve to live in the newly ruined future coming our way."
—Mark Richard

"Adam Johnson's *Emporium* first grabs you when you scan the titles of its nine short stories. The stories themselves give you a good shake. Johnson roams a fictional terrain where reality is ramped up to near absurdity. His characters, groping toward understanding and sympathy for each other, then trump that absurdity. His settings, as a commentary on America, are intellectually thrilling. But his characters are fully realized human beings, not props as they often are in satires. The settings

are not the point; it's how people deal with them. Throughout these stories there's plenty of that all-purpose human defense mechanism—humor. The stories here are straightforward and chronological, yet laced with dazzling prose and metaphors."
—*The Kansas City Star*

"Adam Johnson unleashes a big, thrilling and fully realized talent in *Emporium*. These richly atmospheric stories quiver with humor, danger and complete authenticity as their protagonists—a discredited pilot, an angst-ridden zookeeper, salesmen of bulletproof vests—struggle to steady themselves in a landscape of ex-urban sprawl and mysterious beauty. For all the irony and sophistication of these tales, an undertow of sadness and menace sucks at them from someplace very deep, lending them urgency and gravitas that are rare in contemporary fiction and impossible to forget." —Jennifer Egan

"Full of robots, zoo animals, stray bullets and stranded astronauts, Johnson's affecting story collection is unabashedly bizarre. These uncanny pieces are not all dark humor and glib fatalism, however. Despite their absurd circumstances, Johnson's lovingly crafted characters are sometimes distinguished by hopefulness, making this debut collection seem vital and familiar." —*Book*

"Sharp and original." —*Esquire*

"A wildly imagined first collection that manages to be simultaneously terrifying and good-hearted. *Emporium* overflows with intelligence, wit, and a kindness-in-the-face-of-disaster that suddenly seems very relevant." —George Saunders

EMPORIUM

EMPORIUM

Stories

ADAM JOHNSON

PENGUIN BOOKS

to the boxy loop of youth

PENGUIN BOOKS
Published by the Penguin Group
Penguin Putnam Inc., 375 Hudson Street, New York, New York 10014, U.S.A.
Penguin Books Ltd, 80 Strand, London WC2R 0RL, England
Penguin Books Australia Ltd, 250 Camberwell Road, Camberwell, Victoria 3124, Australia
Penguin Books Canada Ltd, 10 Alcorn Avenue, Toronto, Ontario, Canada M4V 3B2
Penguin Books India (P) Ltd, 11 Community Centre,
    Panchsheel Park, New Delhi – 110 017, India
Penguin Books (N.Z.) Ltd, Cnr Rosedale and Airborne Roads,
    Albany, Auckland, New Zealand
Penguin Books (South Africa) (Pty) Ltd, 24 Sturdee Avenue,
    Rosebank, Johannesburg 2196, South Africa

Penguin Books Ltd, Registered Offices: Harmondsworth, Middlesex, England

First published in the United States of America by Viking Penguin,
a member of Penguin Putnam Inc. 2002
Published in Penguin Book 2003

10 9 8 7 6 5 4 3 2

Acknowledgments to the original publishers of some of these stories appear on page 245.

THE LIBRARY OF CONGRESS HAS CATALOGED THE HARDCOVER EDITION AS FOLLOWS:
Johnson, Adam.
Emporium : stories / Adam Johnson.
p.   cm.
ISBN 0-670-03072-4 (hc.)
ISBN 0 14 20.0195 3 (pbk.)
I. Title.
PS3610.O3 E47 2001
813'.54—dc21   2001026804

Printed in the United States of America
Set in Fairfield Light
Designed by Nancy Resnick

CONTENTS

EMPORIUM

TEEN SNIPER

When I reach the rooftop, I pull the dustcovers off my rifle scope and head for a folding chair leaned up against an air-conditioning unit—right where I left it the last time I was up here. Sitting down, I have a clear view across a courtyard of lawns and fountains to Hewlett Packard. I line up a couple breakfast burritos on the parapet wall, in case this is a long one, and I crack a can of Nix. Most of us drink Nix because of how other sodas make you twitchy. I dial in my optics by focusing on flowers in the distance, impatiens and pansies, mostly, and I'm tuning the rangefinder when I get the go-ahead from Lt. Kim.

"Blackbird," Lt. Kim says over the radio, "at your leisure," which is code for the fact that the hostage negotiations are failing and it's time to get to work. There's a tone in her voice, though, that kind of sounds like my mom when she gets on my case to join the private sector, where the "real money" is. I'll admit I sometimes daydream on the job, but I'm trying to better the community, so it's like, get off my back already.

I sweep my scope along the flowers a little longer—there's a giant H formed from orange poppies and a P of velvety petunias.

One of the perks of being a police sniper in Palo Alto, aside from the satisfaction you get from serving the public, is the serious commitment these software companies show toward floral displays, toward making the world a more beautiful place. I shoot over flowers every day.

I fix the bipod of my Kruger Mark VI and chamber a round. The Kruger's an old South African rifle, made in the gravy days of long-bore ballistics, but the scope is state of the art, a fully digital Raytheon with cellular live-feed, so that it's a camera, phone, and radio, all in one. That means Lt. Kim can see and hear everything on a bank of screens in her command van down the street, but it's my shoulder she's usually looking over. I'm one of the best shots in the world—I mean, I have the gift. I've been lead sniper for over a year, but Lt. Kim can't get past the fact that I'm only fifteen.

The target is a Pakistani guy over in HP's think tank. He's wearing a tie-dyed T-shirt that says "Cherry Garcia," and he's pacing back and forth in a cubicle decorated only with an *Aladdin* movie poster. The guy's pretty worked up, yelling into the phone, probably to Gupta, our communications officer. In the poster, Aladdin's hauling ass on his magic carpet with his little monkey friend, and there's an evil genie hot on his tail.

There's no hostages that I can see, only about 475 meters of open courtyard between me and Cherry G. The shot will be a tricky one: the bullet will become wobbly and transient as it moves through different temperature zones—bucking in the heat waves above the hot parking lot, diving as it crosses cool, shady lawn, and finally tumbling through the rising humidity of a man-made lake.

To the west, Cedric and Henry are dragging their heavy, water-cooled magnum into position atop a Jamba Juice, while across the way, Twan climbs a cellular tower, a sleek rifle equipped with satellite-assisted targeting dangling behind him on a rope. The satellite rifle is essential when the fog rolls in, and Twan is just the man to operate it—he's got the cool, the confidence, to fire on faith into a blanket of white. That dude is smooth, and it has nothing to do with the color of his skin. Lt. Kim tends to only hire African Americans for my team. I think it's because they had it bad for a long time, and we need to make it up to them. Snipers in general take pride in not discriminating.

I'm calculating the crosswind when Lt. Kim calls back.

"Tell me how you're feeling about the shot," she says.

I don't answer right away. I can hear her sipping tea in the command van, waiting for a response, while in the background, Gupta is negotiating his ass off in Urdu, though I do make out the word *pizza*.

"Maybe let's talk about it later," I tell her. I know the guys are listening, and I'm gonna get some razzing about "my feelings" in the locker room.

"Do you want to try a few visualizations?" she asks.

"Just leave me alone, all right?" I radio in, trying not to let my voice crack, which is a problem lately.

Lt. Kim's one of those sniper commanders who also has an MSW, so she's always all over my emotions. I've been having some dreams, I'll admit, and we've been working on replacing bad images with good ones. Flowers are supposed to be my replacement images.

I ease my eye back into the scope. Even when Cherry G's standing still, his figure warps like a mirage at this distance, and the crosshairs, flinching with my pulse, skip across his body. The only way to get closer to him would be to belly crawl through a hundred meters of flowers, but I don't think I could handle sneaking through bed after bed of what's supposed to be my positive imagery.

"Yo, homies," I say into my scope. "Who's calling the shot?"

I try to talk cool to the guys, you know, to work on our unity.

From his perch on the tower, Twan just grunts.

Henry is huffing and puffing when he calls in. "We've got a decent shot," he says, running out of breath. "Probably seventy percent." He's working the foot pedals of the huge twenty-millimeter magnum while Cedric aims.

Like me, Cedric and Henry came out of the target-match circuit, with Cedric riding a full sniper scholarship to BYU and Henry touring Asia for Team Adidas. But Twan is different. He's self-taught, on the rooftops of Oakland, and like they say, the Lord looks out for left-handed snipers. Twan's an ayatollah with a rifle, completely composed, but he's touch-and-go as a police officer because he refuses to shoot women.

Any of us could probably make the shot, but I don't want to look like a puss in front of the guys. Besides, not that I'm stuck up or anything, but I'm the one with the gift. I won the Disney Classic at age eleven, scored a perfect one thousand at the North Hollywood Open, and took gold in the summer Sniptathalon in Bonn, all before thirteen.

I flip down my clip-on shades and take aim. Sometimes, when I look through my scope, I am overwhelmed by the illusion that I know this stranger in the crosshairs in an essential way, like we're old friends, like you can see their soul. This effect is known as "flash empathy." The LAPD has conducted a lot of field studies and found that "flash empathy" is a leftover from the reptilian part of our brain and can't be avoided. You just got to turn a cold shoulder to it. Luckily, we have these new Raytheon scopes, which make it so you're not actually looking at the dude—it's just a video image. Sunglasses help.

"Blackbird has the shot," I announce and begin my positive visualization, which Lt. Kim says gives my mind a newer, more optimistic vocabulary for violence. A slug to the chest resembles a dwarf rose blossom, for example, so I would try to think of that. The head produces a pink mist of baby's breath. If you've ever seen the maroonish-green bloom of a chocolate beauty, then you'll know when you clip the liver. Exit wounds in general are trailing vines of red, kind of tangled and groping, like the new chutes of a spring hibiscus.

Finally, I do the math. At this distance, the slug will drop thirty centimeters, and the way the poppies are leaning suggests a slight breeze. So, I'll need to train my crosshairs above Cherry G and to the right, making it look like my target is really the skinny monkey with the fez on the *Aladdin* poster.

Then it hits me, this feeling that I really know this guy. In the rinsed color of my video scope, I study the tinsely lines of sweat coming from his brow, the flush of anguish in his skin. In a flash, I see a guy who left his culture and traveled around the world, only to become a hopeless outcast. His words are always a little off, and maybe the people make fun of him because he looks different and can't dress so good. Forget about the girls. It's like, because of your job, you have to leave your old friends behind, and then your new friends are always saying things to keep you down. You work side by side with them, and you're really trying, but it's like you're not even there. They never ask you to lunch or anything. Sometimes you eat alone at a restaurant and spot one of them, but they don't even see you. You overhear them talking about some new movie, and it's a movie you want to see, and—I stop myself, try to get a grip. Like the LAPD says, this isn't real.

I shift my aim toward the little monkey, and start my countdown.

Here's where the gift comes in: the secret to being a world-class sniper is knowing how to stop your heart. I exhale, my chest goes quiet, and there's a ghostly feeling of serenity in my limbs. The rifle seems to just settle into its purpose, and things feel clear and flat in the scope. There's a hollow crack, and for a second, the time it takes for the spent shell to spring and glint to the ground, Cherry G and I will both be lifeless.

Duck, you fool, I can't help whispering.

The slug goes, connects—a neck shot, my trademark, the wound lapping like the tongues of orchid petals. The target's knees go out, and he falls from view, dropping into the beige of his cubicle.

"Morning has broken," I radio in.

"Copy that, people," Lt. Kim announces. "Blackbird has spoken."

Back at the police station, I slip in through the side door and take the back way, around the squash courts, toward the locker room. I'm supposed to debrief with Lt. Kim after every assignment, but I'm just not into talking about it today. She's been worried about my "problems with intimacy," which she always drags back to the fact that my mother's a classic "sniper mom" who shuttled me around to every child firearms contest there was. And I'd be on psych leave for a zillion years if I ever told Lt. Kim about the shrine my dad built out of all his second-place shooting trophies.

I run into my team in the hallway. They're standing next to a soda machine, working on some song lyrics. They've got a band but they don't get many gigs because they all play bass. Eyes closed, Cedric holds two fingers to his ear while Henry and Twan sing backup, snapping their fingers. It's an old love ballad.

"*Pardon, mon cheri,*" Cedric sings. Snap. Snap. "Why you rebukin' me?"

Twan jumps in with the chorus; he's a large man with a booming voice.

"*Ce soir, ce soir,*" Twan sings. "Girl, you're having me."

I never thought much of French, but it sounds tough coming from these guys.

"Word up," I say.

Twan stops mid-snap when I say this.

"That French is phat," I say. "Bet the lady friends go for that smooth talk."

That's when ROMS rolls up. ROMS sniffs us, then lifts a claw in greeting.

"Yo, holmses," he says, which is something I taught him. ROMS is the only one around here who's geekier than me, and he's a bomb detection and disposal robot. He's got some basic hostage negotiating programming, so I've been trying to teach him to talk cooler.

"Hey, ROMS," I say. "The posse and me was thinking about grabbing some chow. Wanna chill with us?"

"Let's eat and make friends," he announces. "Food is the first step in peaceful resolutions. Pizza, burger, baba ghanoush."

"Shit," Twan says and just walks away.

"Maybe another time, sir," Cedric says, and Henry looks like he wants to bust a stitch something's so funny.

"It's a date," ROMS says to them as they walk away.

ROMS is clueless to how the guys are always avoiding him, and I try to shield him from that. You see, ROMS and I are both Cancers, which means we're sensitive and a little moody, but with a lot to say. For his birthday in July, I'm planning on getting him an update—Negotiator 5.0, with the latest Black English Converters—because ROMS wants to express himself, but he just doesn't have the programming.

For now, ROMS and I decide to eat lunch without those guys. I have a learner's permit, but there has to be someone in the car with me, and technically, ROMS doesn't count, so we walk across the street to grab a Sony burger.

Generally, people don't like to see a bomb robot enter the building, so ROMS and I use the drive-thru, which is a little humiliating. The ugly truth is, though, robots are way looked down upon in our society. Just because some people are different doesn't mean they're not the same as you or me. That's why, when we're working at a playground or day care, I tie a "Barney" mask on ROMS's display panel—purple and humorous, it helps ensure the next generation won't have to live in fear.

I order a double Sony dog with a large Nix. For ROMS, I get a water, no ice—you have to wet his sponge reservoir every once in a while to keep his sniffer from drying out.

The girl at the drive-thru's kind of cute. She's about my age, with some skin trouble, though I like the cock of her headset. When it's our turn in line, I can't think of anything to say, but she's the one who speaks first.

"Nice rifle," she says when she hands me the bag.

I want to make my move, but ROMS won't quit sniffing her, and he's ruining everything! I kick him on the sly. When I do open my mouth, all that comes out is "extra ketchup." Then I go and add, *"s'il vous plaît."*

She shakes her head and hands me two packets, like there's a ketchup shortage or something.

The car behind us starts honking, so ROMS and I move along.

The only place to eat outside is the kiddie area, so I sit in a dinky seat, and ROMS parks on the rumpus pad. The play area's really just a giant food recycler dressed up to look like a jungle gym, and the thing's loud as heck. I look past the little rope that's supposed to keep kids out of the heavy gears, but I don't see a muffler on the thing, a total code violation.

I sift through the fries for my instant game card, while ROMS pulls out a really long straw. I get excited when I scratch off a bikini and then a martini, but it turns out I'm one machete short of winning the trip to Haiti with the Sony Girls.

I throw the game card on the ground. What's the use, anyway?

ROMS can see my disappointment. "Why the long face?" he asks

"Thanks, ROMS, but I don't want to talk about it."

"We can resolve this crisis together. We're friends. First let's start with some small talk. What do you think of the Raiders this year?"

That puts a smile on my face. ROMS is my friend. Some bomb robots, every time you turn them on, you're a new person to them. You have to reintroduce yourself and everything. But ROMS is different. We're like a team—both of us dedicated to saving people, though I do it indirectly, of course.

"Okay," I say. "Tell me this—you ever find a bomb, and when you touch it, you get a feel for the person who made it, like, who they really are, and suddenly you're connected to them?"

"All the time," ROMS says, though it's a little hard to hear him over the gnashing blades of the recycler. "I'm versed in the signature detonation devices of most major terrorists."

"No, man. I mean, like, see their soul."

ROMS slurps. "Is this about the Sony Girls?" he asks.

"Don't even talk about girls. This problem is way different. Say I'm about to resolve a crisis, okay? I go to pull the trigger, and I get this weird sense of connection with the target, like we're old homies. But then, as soon as I shoot them, that closeness goes away, and I'm left feeling sort of mechanical."

"I know where you're coming from. I've been there."

"Really?"

"I love you, man," ROMS says.

I chew a mouthful of hot dog, and looking at ROMS, wash it

down with Nix. Because of his hostage skills, he always has something good to say when you're down, but this surprises me. This is not in his programming.

"Are you feeling okay?" I ask ROMS.

"Love makes the world go round," he says and sniffles.

I reach out, and his instrument shield is cool to the touch. When I check his power light, it's flashing. He gets pretty emotional when his batteries are low, and his bomb sniffer resets to default, so that it sounds like he's sniveling, like he's about to cry.

"Can't we all just get along?" he asks me, his voice slow and slurred.

Poor guy. I use my scope to call Maintenance to come pick him up.

"Hugs," ROMS mutters before all five of his arms droop, and he finally goes out.

In the afternoon, there's a brief rampage at Oracle and then a standoff at an upstart called crepes.com, but tactical ends up handling it. It turns out that a crepe is a sort of pancake, except you roll it up like a breakfast burrito. I don't get to try one, though. All those bulls on SWAT snarf them down. Online crepe sales must be good, though—the parking lot's solid BMW.

The last shot of the day is a disgruntled so-and-so at Sun Microsystems, and as the news choppers begin to circle overhead, my heart stops for the longest time ever. I can't even tell if I stopped it or if it just shut down on its own. I've never been hooked up to a monitor or anything, but you can feel your chest tighten and know when something's not working, so this is not in my head, like Lt. Kim says. Above, the hovering reporters are already trying to hack into my scope's video feed for the evening news, and all I can do is sit on a gray, stinky roof, feeling nothing.

After work, Gupta and I ride the CalTrain to his gym.

Lt. Kim says one of the keys to being a healthy sniper is not taking your job home with you, so I agreed to find a way to unwind after work. That's when Gupta invited me to join him a couple nights a week for a little Brazilian jiu-jitsu.

At rush hour, the train is packed. Most of the people are just guys hunched over their Porn Pilots, though there's a couple tough-looking characters, too. I don't get worried. Even though I only weigh 110 pounds, people don't mess with me. They see my rifle and know I'm a peace officer, that I'm here to help.

The Transit Authority painted yellow happy faces on the fronts of their trains to discourage all these suicides, and as a northbound commuter races past in a smiley blur, it makes me wonder if Lt. Kim doesn't have it all wrong. Maybe when you put a good image over a bad one, it's the bad that wins out. I wonder if the happy face helps the guy driving the train.

I ask Gupta, "Hey, who's Cherry Garcia?"

"Ah, this is Ben and Jerry," he says. "A very fine flavor of ice cream. Every bite is cherries."

I think of cherry blossoms, see their peeling pink bursts.

"Well, at least all those hostages made it safely out of HP."

"It was data he was holding hostage," Gupta says. "He threatened to erase all of HP's bar codes. Talk about bringing a company to its knees."

"So no one was in danger?"

Gupta shakes his head.

"What were his demands?"

"He wanted a magic carpet ride back to Karachi."

We shake our heads over the tragedy of this, over the needless waste.

"Why not just jump on a plane, then?" I ask

"Why not just jump in front of a train?" Gupta says.

"He really said 'magic carpet ride'?"

Gupta shrugs. Beyond him in the window, California bungalows flash their pastel backs at us. "I don't know about exact words," he says. "This is a popular saying."

When we get to the jiu-jitsu gym, there's a beautiful girl waiting for Gupta. She's about sixteen, bay-leaf skin against the blue of the mat, warming up with knee twirls and neck bridges.

"What a daughter," Gupta says to me. "Why couldn't she stick with debate? Keep your distance from this one," he adds, but I can't tell if he thinks I'd be trouble for her, or the other way around.

When she comes over, she's still loosening up her arms.

"Nice rifle," she says. "Rhodesian?"

She talks a little funny because of her mouthguard.

"South African," I answer. "It's an early model Kruger."

"Didn't the UN ban those?"

I shrug. "Technically."

She lifts her eyebrows, impressed. "I'm Seema," she says. "Wanna spar?"

"Okay," I tell her, even though she's got ten pounds on me and "Mission: Submission" is embroidered on her gi.

We start to circle each other, with Seema faking a couple lazy leg chops. Her ankles, when they flash from her gi, are strong and cut.

Jiu-jitsu is based on the notion that people need distance to hurt you. Instead of keeping away, you pull your opponent closer, so that your bodies are touching, so their arms and legs are too close to strike. Then you have to learn to feel at home in the grasp of a stranger.

Seema rushes me, clinches, and sweeps a leg. On the ground, I endure a couple ankle cranks. I roll out of a double heel hook, then surprise her with a wrist crucifix.

That gets her attention. "You new here?" I ask.

Seema's keylocks are savage, and she keeps a constant knee in my kidneys.

"I beat all the guys at my old dojo," she says, "so here I am."

From behind her hot pink mouthguard, she flashes me a wicked smile.

Her legs are around my hips, feet interlocked, and when I try to pass her guard, I almost eat a triangle choke. Even though she's wearing a full gi, her ta-tas are *right there*. I've never grappled with a girl before, and I'll admit I'm concentrating on not farting or anything.

"You're the Blackbird, aren't you?" she asks, sneaking her legs up to my shoulders so she can set an arm bar.

"My real name's Tim." I block her arm attempt, but the distraction suckers me into a side-mount, and before I know it, I'm breathing some serious shoulder blade. Suddenly, I've got gi burns on my face. This girl is wriggly.

"So, do you shoot women?" she asks.

This question is probably just a distraction so she can reverse me. I entangle an arm and work an elbow lock. She winces enough that I know the joint is getting pretty hot. "Justice is blind," I tell her.

"What's that supposed to mean?"

I don't really have an answer for this. It's just what they taught us at the Academy. Under me, I can feel her ribs undulate as she breathes, the graceful arc of her sternum, and to answer her question, my mind's drifting back to an old sniper ethics course, when Wham—she flips me with an elevator.

"I'd shoot a woman," Seema says. "If she was asking for it."

"Really?"

She sets her hooks, improves position, and then Bang—rear naked choke.

"That was a joke," she says, knowing I can't talk anymore. To really sink the choke, she arches her back, which makes my vision go sparkly. Then she gives me a little lecture. "You know, in Switzerland, you need a court order to shoot a woman, and in Brazil, they teach women jiu-jitsu, so there's way less violence."

I can't tell if her dark hair has fallen in my face or if the lights have gone out. All I know is I feel relaxed all over and warm, the opposite of when your heart stops and your blood's just loitering. I picture Brazil as a green country filled with colorful talking birds and mangos maybe, where beautiful women walk around in white gis, and whenever one person tries to hurt another person, a woman appears and pulls you down, wraps her arms around you.

The next morning, I cruise the hallways looking for Gupta so I can gather some intel about Seema. I check the whole police station, practically—the lockdown, motor pool, all the tanning beds— before I see the red light flashing outside the interrogation room.

Through the one-way mirror, I see Gupta doing an interrogation: a "suspect" is blindfolded and strapped—for his own safety—to a reclining medical table next to the truth machine. What I can't believe is that behind Gupta, at the toolbench, is Seema. She's wearing a crisp labcoat, hair up in a little bun, and she's stripping wire with a set of black cutters, trying to make clean connections for the electrodes.

The interrogation room kind of gives me the willies. Not that I'm against the judicious use of electricity, in the name of Protection and Service; it's just there's something a little claustrophobic about the place. I admit Lt. Kim's done wonders with the decor, throwing in a few plants and inspirational posters—she even invested in a new kind of oral shunt, which not only keeps a "suspect" from biting his or her tongue, but also forces the mouth into the shape of a gentle smile.

I put on my mirrored sunglasses, and as I open the door, remember to watch my language—all "suspect" conferences are taped on closed-circuit, which means the reporters hack in every once in a while, so we try to keep a lid on the cussing.

"What are you doing here?" I ask Seema.

"I'm soldering," she says when she sees me, "for justice." She holds up the smoking iron like the Statue of Liberty.

"No, I mean here, at the police station."

"It's national Take Your Daughter to Work Day," Seema says, though we can barely hear each other over Gupta's "suspect."

"Oh, right, sure. Hey, I had a great time yesterday."

"You hung in there longer than most," she says, and without a mouthguard, you can see she's got a chocky set of braces. Wearing her hair up also reveals some cauliflowered ears from grappling. But her eyes are deep brown, rifted with gold.

Behind us, Gupta's really going after it. "Where did you stash the dang PIN numbers?" he demands. "And no more of your darn lies."

The "suspect" keeps confessing, but it's lame, and Gupta hates to reward insincerity. Plus, you can barely understand him with that oral shunt.

"Not so fast this time," he says, and the grinding buzz of the truth machine starts again. The whole thing unnerves me—you know the sparking zap is coming, followed by a little blue smoke ring and that ozone smell. The suspect's blindfolded, so he can't see when the next jolt is coming, and his skin keeps wincing in anticipation.

Look out, I whisper, feeling a wave of flash empathy coming on, strong enough that the "suspect" begins to resemble a normal person, a neighbor you might know or some guy walking in the park. The LAPD says this is when good cops make mistakes.

I throw my sunglasses on the bench—they aren't working at all. I feel a little woozy, and I'd look like a total puss if I fainted in front of Seema.

"Hey, Gupta," I call, which makes him stop and smile, surprised to see me.

"Take five," Gupta tells the "suspect," then comes over to grab a clean towel.

"Blackbird," he says, "what the heck are you doing here?"

"How about we give the technology a rest," I tell Gupta. "What say I bring Twan in here so the two of us can play a little 'good sniper–bad sniper,' see if that works?"

"Sorry, Blackbird. This is kind of a father-daughter thing."

"As if," Seema says. "This is so unfair. That guy doesn't even have a fighting chance."

"I'm sure the world would be a better place," Gupta tells her, "if everyone settled their differences with hand-to-hand. Until then, aren't you forgetting how angry you got when someone stole your PIN number last year?"

"At least in jiu-jitsu there's rules," she says.

Gupta sops his forehead and turns to me. "Kids," he says, shaking his head.

We follow him back to the silver table, careful to stand on the rubber mat, and looking at that poor fool all strapped down makes me want to amscray out of there. I look at Seema's large eyes, at the way she bites the tip of a finger, and I get the feeling she's waging her own battle with empathy. I've got some techniques that could help, but it's something everyone, finally, has to do on their own.

Gupta adjusts the truth machine's dial past "candid" and "frank" to "gospel," the highest setting. Then he tests the new electrodes by swiping them together, and an arcing flash of light leaves us all blinking a moment.

"That's not really a truth machine, is it?" Seema asks.

Gupta throws her a stern look.

Seema points at the machine's fancy display panel. "I mean, behind those lights and buttons is some kind of pain machine, right?"

"Hush now," Gupta says, lowering the rods, and I can't tell if he's speaking to his daughter or the "suspect." Our eyes follow Gupta's hands to the man on the table, who lies there flinching. There's a point in sniping when the bullet's away, when someone's fate is sealed. The Kruger bucks in my hands, and for the moment or two it takes the slug to find its home, the target still thinks life is A-okay. They're so clueless in my scope, so lost, I can't help whispering, *hit the deck.* This is the dream I keep having: It's always a nice day. I'm raking leaves. Sometimes washing my dad's car. Ghostly, from far away, I hear my own voice call, *duck.* I don't scramble for cover in these dreams; instead, I just stand there, holding the hose, searching the roofs and trees for the part of me that's sure everything's about to go wrong. This is the voice that Lt. Kim always wants to talk about, the voice in my head that believes anything can end, suddenly and without warning.

There's a flash of light, and my knees go weak. I must look like one of those old snipers who's gone soft, the kind you see living in the street in his dirty uniform, selling daisies for a buck. All I can do is head for the door, steadying myself as I go.

In the hall, I lean over and breathe deep as a team of chirpy cadets passes.

Then Seema is by my side. "Hey, are you okay?"

"Yeah," I tell her, hands on knees.

"I don't know how you do it," she says. "I mean, I only have to come here one day a year."

I stand straight, try to arch my back, snap myself out of it.

"That room's just a little claustrophobic," I tell her.

"Let's get some fresh air, then," she says. "I could use some fresh air."

I'm feeling pretty shaky, so I'm thinking of what a cool sniper might say. I lean against the wall, try to stand all smooth. "Yo," I tell her, "we could maybe grab some lunch."

Seema casts a weary glance through the one-way glass to her father, hunched over the metal table. "Sure," she says, and it's that easy, we're going to lunch.

We start walking together, debating tostadas or vindaloo, but before we even decide on a restaurant, ROMS comes cruising by, obviously headed out on a bomb disposal run. He's pushing an asbestos supply cart and wearing his shiny Mylar blast suit.

He stops when he sees me. "What up, peoples?" he asks.

I pretend I don't see him, even though he's waving his claws in big *hellos*.

"Do you know this robot?" Seema asks me.

"Sure, we're home-slices," ROMS says.

It knots my gut, but I cold-shoulder ROMS. "This geek?" I ask Seema. "No way."

ROMS pulls off his shiny hood. "Hey, homie, it's me!"

"Shove off, drone," I tell ROMS, who puts his hat on all wrong and slumps away. To Seema, I say, "That robot used to help carry equipment for our band."

"You're in a band?" Seema asks.

"Yeah, I play bass," I tell her. "Most of our numbers are in French, though, so you probably wouldn't understand."

My hands are all shaking, I feel like such a fake.

"*Quel chance,*" she says. "*Je parle français aussi.*"

Then I hear this voice in my head. *Get out of there,* it says.

"Sorry, gotta go, see you," I say and head back down the hall, beating it through the lockdown and central processing. I race past rows of booking tables, then stumble through the gift shop—knocking over all kinds of souvenir shot glasses and nearly killing the bail blonde—before finally ducking into the Sniper Lounge.

Inside the lounge, I'm so wound up I pace back and forth, trying to get hold of myself.

"Easy, there, Blackbird," Twan says from his recliner.

Cedric and Henry look up from the couch—they've got the new Monsanto catalog, and they're checking out the centerfold. Everyone's trying to relax and clear their heads before the America Online convention this afternoon. They'll need their best, if last year was any indication.

I go to grab a Nix, but the fridge's empty. "Crap," I say. "Someone came in here and stole our sodas again."

I slam the cooler shut, but no one even looks up, nobody around here seems to give a turd. So much for unity. No weekend retreat to Team Mountain will fix things this time.

"I bet it was those asswipes on SWAT," I say, furious. "They're doing it just to laugh at us. Everyone knows the guys on SWAT all drink Buzz."

Normally, Twan won't give me the time of day, but he comes over and puts a hand on my shoulder. "Hey, Blackbird, get some focus. Save it for AOL," he tells me. "What say you sit in my chair, put your feet up, check out the Monsanto Girls?"

"I don't think so," I say in total defeat. "I'm only into the Sony Girls."

"There you go," Twan says. "You're sounding better already."

"Oh, come now," Cedric says from the couch. "The Monsanto Girls are it."

"What are you talking about?" Henry asks him, laughing. "You're Mormon."

"The Monsanto Girls are kosher with the hive," Cedric answers. To Twan, he asks, "Where's Muhammad stand on the Monsanto Girls?"

"Twan likes 'em natural," Twan announces. "I don't speak for the Prophet."

I pull Twan aside, steering him over to the fireplace.

"Twan," I say, quiet enough that the guys can't hear. "I need some advice."

He leans against the humidor, considers me. "Yeah?"

He looks very fatherly, with the bookshelves behind him. I feel I can trust him.

"There's this girl, and she's not like other girls. She's different, but I keep screwing everything up."

"Different how?"

"She's got these big eyes. Man, when she looks at you, she knows the real you."

Something I say contains a certain gravity for Twan.

"This girl," he asks, "she a friend, or you talking love?"

"I just met her," I say. "How do you tell?"

"Look at her," Twan says. "Really look at her. Not just check out her body. You need to see the real her. Then you'll know. You can't help but know."

After work, I grab a sixer of Buzz, to work up my nerve, then I head to the old Iridium Satellite Tracking facility near Stanford. The company went belly-up, but its tower is the tallest fixed object in sight. At the padlocked gate, the dish above is mongo, a sniper's dream. I sling my rifle, hop the fence, and start to climb the huge frame, monkey footing it up the diagonal struts.

When I reach the lip of the giant white dish, high above Palo Alto, I swing a leg over and slide through the dust to the center, where I find the remains of an old campfire. There's like fifty cigarette butts strewn around and some used condoms, so I watch where I step.

At the leading edge of the dish, I dangle an arm off the side and assume a Thompson side cradle stance, which keeps your legs from going to sleep during prolonged situations. After my scope calibrates, I crack the six-pack and begin scanning the neighborhoods for Seema's house. It's funny, but when I finally drink my first can of Buzz, it tastes just like Nix.

Combing the storybook neighborhoods and canopied streets for her house, I guess I've got it in my head that I'll find Seema in some perfect state—wearing a flowing gold and pink sari as she swings in a hammock, reading one of those really long novels, in French maybe, and she has a foot dangling, just sweeping the grass as she rocks. She's probably eating a crepe, very elegantly.

On my third can of Buzz, I spot a guy washing an old-timey station wagon, and when I see he's wearing generic white sneakers with blue dress socks, I know this must be Gupta. I dial in the focus, careful not to start my countdown or anything—I mean, Krugers don't come with safeties.

Sweeping to the backyard, I spot Seema. She's wearing khaki pants and a khaki polo with the insignia of the local animal shelter, and she's doing a pretty weak job of cleaning the barbecue. She scrubs for a while, stops to look around, accidentally wipes a dark smudge on her cheek.

I know what it's like getting stuck doing chores no one else wants to do, and I get this urge to tell Seema she's not alone, that I'm here, too. I want to place my crosshairs on an apple or pear above her, to shoot through the stem and have it land perfectly in her hand, so she'd know someone's looking out for her. It's a pretty stupid thought, I guess. Gupta doesn't have any fruit trees, and there's only so many ways to show affection with a rifle.

I crack another Buzz, and even though it's warm, there's something really snappy to it. I don't even down my first sip before I start to get the sense that I know Seema in a special way. It doesn't hit me in a flash, but sort of grows on me. I'm doing what Twan says, really looking at her through my scope—the way the splashing water makes her feet glimmer, how she squinches her face when she works a gross spot on the grill—when I get this sense that she's ahead of the kids her own age, a little smarter, more mature. She doesn't really have friends who know the real her. So she has to pretend she's someone she's not, acting older, tougher. Then her father's trying to make her follow in his footsteps, shoving French classes down her throat, steering her toward debate, toughening her with jiu-jitsu. Through my scope, I watch her hose the spider webs out of the burner, and it's clear that Gupta's trying to make her the world-class negotiator he never was. It's like she has to live someone else's life. Maybe all she really wants to be is a UN monitor, to travel to other countries on peacekeeping missions, wear cool uniforms, and try to make a difference. This is the real her, without any poses, a girl who really likes to help animals, who just wants to go out and make the world a better place without having to shoot anyone.

Suddenly my legs have a mind of their own. I jump up, and I'm balancing on the edge of the dish, and if I fall, I'm like, *whatever*. I feel that light.

I grab the tower's guy-wire cables, and in a slow-motion jump, rappel all the way to the ground, a move that leaves my crotch and one armpit black. Before I know it, I'm over the fence and heading down the street. I find myself jogging, and it's like I'm wearing headphones that only play static. There's a silver fire hydrant, and for no reason, I go up and kick it. I'm running along, turning into her neighborhood, and have you ever taken a good look at your hand, I mean really stared at it?

"Howdy, Gupta," I say as I trot past the mist of his hose. At the door, I ring the bell, and I'm kind of jogging in place. I ring it again. At my feet, there's a flower bowl of puffy-faced dahlias and aster, all purple and trippy. Normally I'd get sort of queasy, and my ribs would be tightening. But I feel great, like I'm ten years younger.

It takes long enough, but Seema finally answers. She's sort of smiling at first.

"Look, Seema, wow," I say. "I am so into peace. And animals."

"Blackbird? What are you doing here?"

"I'm a Cancer, you know," I tell her. "So it's hard for me to talk. And I have all these weird dreams, not the ones with the Sony Girls—ha-ha—but mostly where I mow the lawn. Sometimes I just wash the car, like Gupta! But there's this voice in my head, and Lt. Kim thinks that once we get it to go away, I'll stop worrying that the good things in life are destined to fail, like you and me. But I'm up in this satellite dish, and I'm thinking: what if this is the voice that still believes things can be okay, that believes in good and warns me away from bad? It wants to protect me, just like the United Nations."

"Dad," Seema says.

"You win a lot of awards, you know," I say. "And you think you're Aladdin, cruisin' on that carpet, showin' off with some loop-the-loops, but the real question is—what about the evil genie? Honestly, Seema, I'm no Aladdin. I'm more like the little monkey."

Gupta comes up the driveway, wielding a soapy brush.

I admit I've been gesturing kind of wild with my rifle. I pull the last Buzz from my back pocket, all hot and shaken. It goes everywhere when I open it, and I lift a finger to say *gimme a sec* while I suck the overflow.

"*Pardon moi,*" I say with foam on my face.

"I think it's time to leave, Tim," Gupta says.

"Okay, that was a lie, I admit it. I don't really speak French."

"Dad, let me handle this," Seema says. "Get lost, stalker-boy," she shouts and goes to slam the door.

"Hey, wait," I tell her. "I really have to use your bathroom."

I still need to explain how I don't like to shoot women, but Seema assumes a jiu-jitsu stance, so I decide I'll maybe just down my Buzz and go.

The next morning, I wake on the lawn of the police station with a blistering case of dry mouth. The sprinklers have run, and I'm clueless how I got here. My rifle's gone. When I sit up, it's like there's rock salt in my joints, and maybe I cracked a couple floater ribs—sure signs I've been on the losing end of some grappling. Wringing the water out of my shirt, flashes start coming to me from last night—tank tops, cutoff shorts, and lots of mustaches, all broomy and stiff—evidence I tangled with SWAT. I'm pulling my sneakers off to shake them out when I spot a rifle barrel sticking out of a Dumpster beside the station.

My poor Kruger. I shake a banana peel off the scope and try to clean coffee grounds out of the breech with a wet sock. Can I sink any lower? I decide right there to lay down my pride and squish out back to the bomb shed to see ROMS.

The bomb shed's really just a nickname for a complex series of bunkers behind the station that house all the equipment we don't want the media to know about. The walls are three feet thick and the ceiling is satellite proof, so this is where ROMS goes to hide out when his feelings are hurt.

When I reach the bottom of the stairs, ROMS is parked alone

in the middle of a dark corridor where we store the blanket cannon, a device that fires sheets of steel wool at incredible velocities. The protesters call them "drapes of wrath," but most everyone agrees there's no faster way to induce good citizenship.

The air is damp and smells faintly of rust. ROMS has his screen saver on.

"Hey," I say to him.

"You must be lost," he answers. "Your new, cool friends aren't here. Why don't you check the SWAT Rec Room?"

"You know I don't have any cool friends. I'm here to see you, man."

This cheers ROMS up enough that his green light comes on. He smiles a bit, and I know it's cowardly, but when he doesn't say anything about the way I dogged him, neither do I.

"Heard you had quite a night last night. Tried to fight the whole SWAT team?"

"I keep screwing everything up," I say.

"You know, Tim, turning to sodas and martial arts never solved anything."

I hang my head at the truth of ROMS's words. "Look, I need your help."

ROMS grows serious. He points his dish at me.

"Okay. Tell me about it."

"There's this girl, and maybe I'm in love with her. But every time I try to talk to her, I turn into an idiot."

ROMS starts to pace the room, rolling past bushels of finely wound laceration wire. He turns suddenly to face me.

"I have much experience in the realms of amour," ROMS says. "My years in demolition and negotiation have taught me firsthand about the effects of love, with my specialties being rampages, revenge bombings, and murder-suicides."

I sit on an empty canister of laxative gas. "Go ahead," I say.

"Here are a couple tips. First, love and firearms don't mix. That also goes for drugs, alcohol, or artificial stimulants."

"Too late for that one."

"Next, when making decisions in matters of love, avoid ledges, bridges, rooftops, towers, and open windows."

"Strike two."

"Most important," and here he pauses. "Never, ever diss a friend over a girl."

"Ouch," I say. "Point taken. But those are all don'ts. I need the dos, man."

ROMS thinks on this. He sniffs the vacant air as if for wisdom, then continues.

"To begin with," he says, "She might be hungry. Supply her with pizza. People need food to make good decisions. Sharing food is also an ancient ritual of trust and friendship. Next, show your good faith—give her something, a gift perhaps, no strings. Then, open the lines of communication and be prepared to listen. Finally, give her space and time to make up her own mind, without any pressure. If all else fails, offer yourself in exchange."

"In exchange for what?"

"Um," ROMS says, "the hostages?"

"Hostages? There aren't any hostages. You don't know anything about love, do you? You don't know the first thing."

My voice cracks when I say this, and I tromp off.

The rest of the week is hard to take. Cedric and Henry quit the force to start snipers.com, a private "consulting" firm that provides just-in-time sniping to Silicon Valley companies. Because they do all their shooting in-house, everyone's spared the media attention. Henry leaves me a note that reads, "He who hesitates, masturbates," which is what the SWAT guys are always saying, and only too late do we realize that Cedric copied all our training videos and gave them to *America's Zaniest Sniper Bloopers*.

Twan and I put in lots of overtime, which means I have to shoot all the females, and it gets to where I'm barely able to focus on the targets in my scope. Forget about replacement imagery— it's everything I can do not to set the Kruger on autosnipe mode. Gupta gives me the silent treatment, and the Sniper Lounge is like a ghost town. My mom buys stock in Cedric's IPO.

Then ROMS is killed in a blast at Ikea. It's one of those savage detergent bombs. The explosion is broadcast live, and the video has the same color-leaked quality as my scope. ROMS lets out this sad little moan when he realizes he's snipped the wrong wire, and knowing what's coming, he turns himself off. He mutters something as his arms droop, his screen blips green, and all that's left is a halo of static. Then his video feed stops. Flowers, I think. Flowers, flowers.

I'm a zombie, I'm so sad—I find myself eating breakfast burritos morning, noon, and night, and I about OD on Nix. But no one seems to care. Hewlett Packard digs up its poppies, and rebeds with snapdragon. CalTrans installs speakers on the fronts of its trains that blare "Ode to Joy" all day. And each shift, after I hang up my Kruger, is nothing but another star next to my name at the detail desk, and I don't even care about the perfect attendance award anymore. You know, when a K-9 is lost in the line of duty, he gets like a twenty-one-gun salute, but ROMS is simply swept up with an electromagnet so they can recycle his parts.

To try to cheer me up, the guys on Narco invite me out for a Buzz after work, and the bail blondes bake some awesome cupcakes—the girls are sweet, and they laugh at all my jokes, but I wish I could say they made me feel any better. The funny thing is my shooting just gets sharper and sharper. It's like I've got my heart working on remote control, my accuracy is that good. I go where Lt. Kim tells me, fire at a dot on the horizon, and a kilometer away, a neck goes pop.

Then our new ROMS arrives. I'm chitchatting in the gift shop when the maintenance guys drag a big crate into the station. They tear it open right there in the lobby, cardboard going everywhere, and I figure I could use a new sidekick—I know it would be dissing the memory of ROMS to chill with a new robot, but I've been feeling pretty low, and then there's this dream that won't let up. Cruising over for a closer look, I decide that I won't teach this ROMS to talk cool, that I'll just accept him for who he is.

When the shrink-wrapping comes off, this robot's the spitting image of ROMS, though it looks pretty pathetic all covered in foam peanuts. The bar code says it's a Virgo, which means it's finicky and needs to be needed. The guys boot up the operating system and wet the sniffer reservoir. Suddenly everything comes online. Arms lift and hover.

"Hi, I'm ROMS," it says to a maintenance guy. "Let's eat and make friends."

It turns to me. "I'm ROMS. Let's make some small talk."

I kind of back up, and the robot advances. "Food is the first step in peaceful resolutions," it says. "Pizza, burger, baba ghanoush?"

But I keep moving, across the marble floor, and out the glass doors of the station. In the parking lot, it's raining lightly. There is a chill in the air, the magnolias looking a darker green against a sky that's roof-sealant gray. Hearing that robot say the exact things as ROMS makes me feel duped, like I've been best homies with a parrot.

I shoulder my rifle and wander the wet streets of Palo Alto. I'm like, who cares if my gun gets wet? The Kruger saw a dozen hard years in Angola before it ever met me, so I suppose it can take a little rain. I follow the CalTrans tracks, tromping through gray shale. Rows of eucalyptus trees hem the rails, which alternate between silence and the shock of commuter cars. The smile-faced engines have taken a beating. The yellow paint's chipped and dingy, and the insistent smile on these bruised faces makes me philosophical, gets me thinking about the big sniper in the sky and what he has in mind for us.

I stand among trees whose leaves shiver green for the northbound trains and silver for the south. Did ROMS know the real me? Was he my friend, or just a machine programmed to say whatever I wanted to hear? To find out, I decide I will believe in him and try his advice.

I detach my scope from the old Kruger. I notice how scuffed the stock is, touch the spots where my fingers have worn away the varnish. Then I hang my rifle in a tree, where it slowly turns with the wind, and start the long walk toward the foothills of Stanford to Seema's house.

When I knock on her door, my hair is wet on my face.

Seema answers in baggy sweats. She's holding a can of Sass.

"Hey, it's freak boy" she says, but she doesn't slam the door.

I hold up my hand. "Please."

"You're a freak. You know that?" She puts a fist on her hip, and leaning against the door, considers me.

"Please, I only wanna say three things."

"Number one?"

That fizzy scent of Sass is on her breath, but I don't let it intimidate me.

"I would like, when it's cool with your dad, to take you out for some pizza."

"How about, *I'm sorry I went freako whack-out on you.*"

"Here's the second," I say and hand her the scope.

She looks at me like I'm an idiot.

"It's a Raytheon," I tell her. "Top of the line, unavailable to civilians."

"A rifle scope. Just what I've been needing."

"Well, it's also a telephone and a radio, so you can reach me anytime, at work or home. If you ever want to talk. Or maybe if you just need someone to listen."

Seema looks at me skeptically, then walks out in the driveway with me.

"Hold my Sass," she says and lifts the scope. Suddenly, her iris is amplified in the lens, a ring of iridescent chocolate with green rifts and pits of oily gold. When she blinks, it stuns me. She roams the neighborhood with a slow scan.

"Here's the rangefinder," I say. "And this switches it to thermal. Thermal's so sensitive you can see the heat signature of a pumping heart. If someone looks normal, but you can't see the strobe of their heart, then you know they're concealing body armor."

"Cool," she says. *"Thermal."* A smile, greedy with amazement, crosses her face.

Real quick, she lowers the scope to look at me, like this is some kind of trick.

"What's the third thing?" she asks.

"If you ever need a friend, I offer myself."

She squints one eye, staring at me, like she's trying to figure me out.

"So you just came over here to give me this, as a friend?"

"Look, I think you're cool, and if you wanna hang out sometime, call me."

She keeps looking at me like that, and it makes me nervous.

"Dad says that robot on the news was your little friend, the one from the band."

"His name was ROMS," I tell her. "We lost one of the good guys."

Seema doesn't say anything to this, which is one of Lt. Kim's tricks to get me to talk more. I take a step backward, toward the street. "ROMS was a friend, and I'm not sure I'm ready to debrief yet. But I'm ready to listen, if you want to talk. Cool?"

Seema sort of shrugs and smiles. There's possibility in the gesture, which means I haven't been totally shot down, and I don't want to push my luck.

That's when I turn and start walking. I make my way down the middle of the street so Seema has a perfect line of sight—if she decides to lift the scope and watch me go. Maybe I look like a dork to people driving by, a kid walking all slow down the yellow line, but if you're looking at someone through a scope, they become large, filling the whole field of view, and there's nothing in the world but them.

I don't puff up my shoulders or anything. I want her to see the real me. If she trains her lens on me, she'll know me, and she'll call. If she calls, that means the LAPD is wrong, that empathy is real. Even if Seema uses thermal, she'll see a kid who looks pretty skinny, but is glowing red as he walks into the blue-green of a relatively cold world.

YOUR OWN BACKYARD

It is the oily tang of tiger fur that startles me awake, and the first thing I do is look for my son, whom I dreamed of at top speed. The scent is gone before I even open my eyes, but a quick pulse still pants in my wrists as I sit up to see my boy watching *CHiPs* reruns with the sound off. Ponch and John ride their motorcycles on the beach while wearing mirrored sunglasses.

I have taken to sleeping on the couch because it is summer, and Mac is a boy with too much time on his hands and a day sleeper for a father. Last week I woke to find his hands on my belt, lightly twisting off the key to handcuffs I hadn't even noticed were missing. We looked at each other. "I have the right to remain silent," he volunteered, *for the record,* and I watched him roll out into our south Phoenix neighborhood, headed toward wherever my handcuffs might be. But today, he seems satisfied with *CHiPs*. I pull off my khaki security guard shirt from the zoo last night and rub my eyes against the midday sun through the windows. Today he's just a normal boy again, a little Indian on shag carpeting, legs crossed, shoulders hunched, reading Ponch's lips.

Sue says he's been telling kids in the neighborhood his father's a police officer again, that they better look out, which only adds to her theory that my quitting the force made things even worse for him. It's hard to know what to do about this. She is at the end of her rope with the board exams and a boy like Mac. She is reduced these days to studying with a stopwatch and speaking in two-word sentences: Room, *now*. Toys, *away*.

I see Sam moving under the carpet and watch him slowly cross our living room. He's a Mexican boa, five foot, that I inherited from the zoo one night. There's a hole in the carpet behind the couch where he gets in, and in the summer heat, he roams the whole house, a prowling shape between the cool padding and shag. The other pets are unsure of him, including my Dalmatian, Toby, so things work out. Sam runs into the side of Mac, who doesn't move, who's gotten used to this dark-roaming shape. Sam is also indifferent to what might be out there; he turns and swims off toward the television set, where Ponch and John now appear in a five-lane freeway. With their white bikes and round helmets, they are like bowling pins, a seven-ten split. "You think that's really them riding those bikes?" I ask.

Mac knows how I feel about this show. He doesn't even take his eyes off the screen. "I want my shoes back."

"Those bikes have never even taken a real turn. There aren't even scratches on the footpegs, and those sidecovers are spotless. They've never been down."

"They catch a lot of bad guys," he says.

"They catch old movie stars, has-beens."

"At least they're out there riding," he says, "and not code nine at home."

I try not to escalate this, especially over a show Mac usually says is for "dildoes," a term whose meaning, at nine years old, he seems sure of. "What makes you an expert on code nine?" I ask him.

He turns back to me for the first time, a little too proud that I can now see he has picked up yet another black eye from somewhere. "You," he says with enough drama to make me think he's heard the term somewhere and assumes it means more than merely off duty.

I try not to be coplike about all this. I watch Ponch and John pull over a limo with a Jacuzzi full of bikini-clad women. The girls bounce and throw handfuls of bubbles on Eric Estrada, who feigns a mock defense, and I tell you I'm really trying.

"Come on," I say. "Let's cut that hair."

"For the shoes."

It's dangerous to give him too much leverage here. "One day. No more, okay?"

"Affirmative," Mac says. "Roger that."

Aff-erm-tive, I hear from the kitchen. It took me a year to teach that bird to say that. But you can't unteach them once they've learned.

In the kitchen I grab Sue's veterinary shears and open a pack of hot dogs she's left on the counter to thaw. Taped to all the cabinets are her anatomy lists and dosage scales. On the fridge hangs a chart of the parasitic cycle. I snap off a half-frozen hot dog and crunch on it while I wonder how much animal science Mac has picked up the last four years I was on night patrol. Only now, as a rent-a-cop, do I think about how many times he's reached for the cereal, the bowl, the milk, and read the secrets of animal husbandry. Slowly, unknowingly, he must have picked it up.

When he comes in the kitchen I get my first good look at the shiner, a deep purple-brown that swoops and fans out to his cheekbone. He doesn't say anything about it and neither do I, which is our version of life after the bomb. The first black eye was last year, and he learned the worst possible lesson in the world for an eight-year-old: it didn't hurt nearly as bad as he'd expected.

Next time, I knew, he would punch first. The boy's been pun-ished, rewarded, tested, and medicated, and here we are, *post-bomb,* as Sue says, *stealing our son's shoes.*

We had long ago made a deal, and it was supposed to go like this: she'd do most of the child-raising work while I made it through the academy and the first three years on Traffic, then I'd watch Mac while she made it through vet school. Well, Mac is nine now, Sue's exams are here, and I am no longer a cop. I am no longer the same kind of father that once thought Mac was a good name for a boy, who used to describe motor-throwing car crashes to his son over dinner each night, who referred to hurt people as occupants and ejections and incidentals.

He snaps one of the cold hot dogs off the pack and sticks it in his mouth like a cigar. Though chewing frozen hot dogs on hot days is a habit he inherited from me, I am confronted with a por-trait of him in what seems to be his natural state: bored, bruised, and sullenly indifferent to anything an afternoon with me might bring. I take a breath, open the door, and step out into the sum-mer heat.

Out back, I set him on a stool so he can watch his haircut through the dog slobber and paw prints on the sliding glass door. I hook up Sue's grooming shears and then stand behind him, a sweating father and his black-eyed son reflected in a patio door. He is too large for his age, with bully sized shoulders and thick hands that already have a hunch about how to get their way.

"I hear there's been some trouble in the neighborhood," I say and flip on the shears.

He simply shrugs and bends his head forward, chin to chest, waiting for me to start. I palm the curve of his head and roll it side to side as I run the buzzer up the back of his neck. Toby trots up with the desert tortoise in his mouth, an object he carries every-where, and he shows it to Mac and me as he eyes first the buzzer and then the half a hot dog in Mac's hand. The tortoise has long since resigned itself to this fate and even lets his legs hang out, which serve to funnel the slobber.

"Mom says you've been telling the kids I'm back on the force." I say this and I'm suddenly unsure if I'm going about this the right way, but his head feels loose and pliant in my hand, the hair soft and short like when he was young.

"So."

"So, is this true?"

"Mom told me you didn't turn in your badge. She says you can go back anytime you want." As easily as he spoke, he waves the hot dog back and forth before Toby, who sways and drools but can't figure a way to eat without letting go of the tortoise.

"You know that's not true."

He shrugs.

I spin his head halfway round, so he can see me out the sides of his eyes. "I'm not going back there, so it doesn't matter. You listening to me? Believe me on this. That's over." But even as I say this I see he's messing with the dog. He's shaking Toby by the nose, pinching the nostrils so its cheeks puff out around the tortoise. "Let go of the dog."

He does this and then I let go of Mac's head, which rolls back down to his chest.

"Brad's dog. You can hit it with a brick and it won't even blink."

"I'm serious. I'm not going back on the force. You hit a dog with a brick?"

"I'm just sayin'," he says and scratches the dusting of stubble on his arm.

"Did you?"

"What?"

"Throw a brick."

"Mom says you're lazy, says you want to be code nine."

Code nine, he says and I can feel his lip curl, sense the slouching indifference of his shoulders, and suddenly I don't want to keep shaving him. Suddenly, I can see him in a not-too-distant future, a tattoo on his arm, an earring maybe, wearing a black concert shirt with a wallet on a chain, and I don't even want to touch him, because for a moment I know this kid. I have arrested him a hundred times.

I flip off the buzzer and tell him to go hose off.

"What about my hair?" he asks, but it is not a question. "This sucks."

"Hose, *now,*" is all I can say as I point him away, toward the hose and the algae-green dog pool beyond.

You'd be surprised how many animals get killed at a zoo. We cull old ones, young ones, sick ones, extra ones. I cull them. Yesterday I spent most of the night scooping baby scorpions out of Desert Dwellers. They'd gotten out of their glass enclosure through the vent tube and were all over the atrium. I used a fishnet to scoop them up and drop them into a bucket of water, where they sank like dull pennies. The night before that, I fished all the newly hatched alligators out of Reptile Land with a long-handled pool skimmer. I dumped them in a feed tub and then placed it in the big cat meat locker till they were hard as tent stakes. I cull the overbred carp and the pigeons that swoop in from the capitol. I'm the one who harvests the ostrich eggs, and unless you've entered a dark pen of nine-foot birds, armed only with a pole and a flashlight, to try to take their eggs, you don't know what I'm talking about. An ostrich can put a man's ribs out his back, which is something I've seen, though not from a bird. Last week I shot a tiger.

But tonight is the kind you find only in Phoenix, only in July.

The moon is rising over the Papago foothills like some distant drive-in movie, and I will forget about black eyes and roughed knuckles, will swing wide of the empty tiger pen as I roam the zoo's dark paths in my zebra-striped golf cart. I have tonight's list of the animals I'm to cull stuck to the cart's visor, and beside me on the seat are my son's dirty Converse sneakers, a temporary measure I know, a faint hope that tonight at least, he won't get too far from the house while I'm gone. It would be dangerously simple to get in the habit of daydreaming on a job like this, to let myself ponder life amid a sleeping zoo, to speculate on the animals on that list, to keep looking at those shoes. I know that trap already, and tonight, I have decided, there will be nothing in the world beyond the cart, nothing but the luft of stale, warm air up my shirt-sleeves and four more hours of dark. I will hum through the exhibits, roll through my list, and later, I hope, remember nothing.

In the distance I can hear a big cat scratching against chain link. From somewhere come the soft thumps of a great owl hovering in its small aviary, and I sink into the kind of feeling I used to get back when I was a police officer and would cruise through residential neighborhoods. I could meander through dark cul-de-sacs for hours, head back, one thumb on the wheel, only using cruising lights, as I passed homeowners' neat lawns, their sprinklers snapping on to hiss in the dark, their security lights occasionally sensing my patrol car and shocking an upturned Big Wheel in the drive or an empty swing set. There would be nothing at all but the green glow of my dash gauges; beyond my windshield, the world became a series of dark houses that blended, and my mind would go blank.

I keep my headlights off now as I did then, but tonight, it's because of the rabbits. They make their way down the empty Salt River bed from the city dumps, and the zoo is overrun with them. Pink eyes are everywhere, ears swiveling in turn, and the sudden sight of me racing through the zoo is enough that they can throw themselves into the bright lights of trouble. You can't believe what they're capable of. When they get into the Oasis, they'll eat whole flats of hot dog buns at a time. They end up in trash cans, air ducts, gummed up in water pumps, or zapped in electric fences, and even if they find their way into a place like Sonoran Predators, it's not good because they're dump bunnies, raised on rotting food, full of worms.

I cruise into the night-scent of wet eucalyptus, roll through a funnel of bugs humming under a floodlight, and I stare straight on because I don't want to get to know the animals the way some people would. I don't name them or follow too closely their movements. Back on patrol, when I rolled past houses and through alleys, I never looked in those windows or wondered if the sons were in their beds, because if you let up out there, if you let your thoughts start to wander, there wasn't one house you couldn't picture without chalk lines in the drive or yellow tape across the door. This isn't nostalgia, here, not the voice of an ex-cop with a wife and a boy and nine years on the force. My goals these days are less ambitious. I am a security guard now, lucky to get this job, and tonight, as the rising moon blues the asphalt before me, I am hunting only rabbits.

I've got a little Remington .22 semiauto, but it's unwise to shoot at any distance in a zoo, so I'm driving around to check a set of heavy-mesh raccoon traps I put out on my first rounds. The zoo is nestled in Papago foothills that slope into the shallow pan of south Phoenix, which is where I used to patrol. Occasionally, through breaks in the trees, I can see the bright city grid expand below, and every streetcorner, every alleyway, comes back to me in the orange glow. I know these spots in my nightly rounds where my old life appears suddenly and all too bright, and so I have trained myself to look at my coffee in its little holder on the dash, at my hands on the plastic wheel, because it has happened before that I have seen silent red and blues out there, and it let myself wonder *is that Ted or Jose or Woco* out there running something down. Then it's all too easy to start wondering about the runner, *how old is he, what's he running from?*

No, I try to keep focused on the task at hand. Sometimes high school kids try to jump the gates and occasionally there's a problem in the main lot because of the adult bookstore down the road, but other than that, it's best to stick to rounds. Mr. Bern, the zoo director, is still a little leery of me, so we talk through Post-it notes. I come to work, peel my note off the guard shack, and do what it says without thought. Speculation won't change the animals on the list. Dwelling won't bring my son in from the parking lots and canal roads below.

I wheel the cart around in the soft mulch of the Petting Zoo and head uphill to an exhibit called Your Own Backyard, which contains species of lesser interest like donkeys and javelinas, animals most people forego because of the hike. At the top, it happens like it always does: the zoo gives way to a wash of Phoenix light, wavering unsteady in the heat. It makes you look, look away, then look again. At the highest point in the park, the zoo also is reduced; it is now only the tops of trees, a rising breath from the green, and for a moment I feel for these rams and sheep, to whom this dangerous city appears brilliant and alluring. From below, there is a faint call of lemurs, and the thought crosses my mind to turn the cart around, to check the trap in the morning, because honestly, I can stare out into that city for hours. But then I near the trap, and the sight makes me stop and set the brake. I turn the headlights on and grab the semiauto.

There is a full-sized dog in the raccoon trap, its bony haunches pressed against the gate, and this, too, is part of my job. It is wedged in so tight it can neither sit nor stand, and it is frozen there, silent, as if in midleap. Its gray fur juts through the mesh on every side, and the bridge of its nose and forehead are pressed flat against the far end of the cage so that it appears to be in deep contemplation of its paws below. I bend to look for a collar but there is none, only the slightest of quivering on its breath. I walk around the cage to view it from all sides, and the dog knows this is not good, that things have gone forever astray, but it is wedged in so tight its eyes can follow nothing but my shoes.

That this dog cannot fully see me is a small relief, though it is not enough to stop me from wondering if, when it happens, his body will have room to go limp, or whether it will behave as if nothing happened, and be just as hard to pull out afterward. The thought is neither sentimental nor cold. My snake was a Post-it note. So was my bird. But I already have a dog, and eventually you have to decide how much you can afford to care. A couple years on Traffic will teach you that. They put you on Traffic first, so you got used to such things. On Traffic, you'll see pelvic wings unfold against steering columns. There'll be breast plates you can see light through, dentures imbedded in dashboards. Stuff you need the kitty litter for. Kitty litter was standard procedure. The older cops said you could even get used to the sight of kids getting hurt, though I pretty much quit before that. Regardless, I lift my gun. The dog will be easier to get out after, I decide, and turn my back to the city lights as it stares at the old police shoes I have quit polishing.

This bothers me though, this dog staring at my shoes, so I swing around to the back of the cage and figure I'll do it from there. But right away I know this is a mistake because I see its haunches and wonder how hungry a dog has to be to worm into a cage for rabbit feed. I see its tail jammed in the trap spring and start to think about my own dog for a moment, am bending down to loosen its tail even before I consider if this is best. I release the spring catch with my thumb, and the only reaction from the dog is a light trickle of urine. Standing, things only get worse for I am suddenly faced with that great bank of city lights.

Before I can realize what a minute of wandering thoughts will cost me, I am held fixed for a moment, mesmerized, because nearly all the people I care about in the world are out there tonight, including my son, Mac. I stand, mouth open, held, until I come to my senses, until I remember the dog and my finger feels for the semiauto's safety. The way you shoot a tiger is the way you stick your head into the smoking cab of a Traffic rollover. It's the way you kick down a tenement door or pull the covers to shine your Maglight on the sheets of a rape scene. You just take that breath and go. It's how you drive your son home from school after he's broken another boy's fingers, three of them, for no reason, he says. It's how you keep from thinking what it means to have this dog's piddle on your worn-out cop shoes. You just take that breath. You go.

The next day, Woco and his new girlfriend, Tina, show up in the late afternoon to barbecue. I have already hosed down the patio furniture and stoked up the grill, and it is still hot enough out that the smoke doesn't want to rise. Sue is silent as she chops vegetables. She has been in the library all day and still has that fluorescent glow on her skin. The neighbor has informed her that Mac's eye is the result of his "arresting" and "detaining" two of the younger boys down the street, and coming home to the news we're having company is yet another ambush in her eyes. She could care less about my plan, she says as she goes at the carrots, whacking them down. She hasn't shaved her legs in a week, she adds. In the midst of all this is Mac, standing on a kitchen chair repeating mumbled words over and over to the African gray parrot. About his hair, Sue won't even speak.

So it is with caution that I answer the door when they arrive. Woco does a finger quick draw as he comes through the threshold and Mac spins and drops to the kitchen floor. Sue shoots Woco a wicked glance over the salad spinner as I watch my son jump up and smile after his near-death experience.

"Look at that hair," Woco says, his voice booming through the kitchen. "No wonder the kid's got a shiner with a haircut like that. What's next, you gonna make him wear a dress?" But even this gesture seems forced, and Mac doesn't quite buy it.

In the backyard, I put on hot dogs and pass out beers. We sit around a picnic table in the shocking heat, Sue leaning against a post with her feet in my lap and Tina massaging Woco's shoulder. It could be pleasant, this scene, but after the initial greetings are over, uneasiness settles. Sue takes soft pulls off her beer. Tina feigns interest in the empty yard behind me.

Woco opens his mouth a few times, but always pauses and thinks better of it. He is unsure these days of what's safe to talk about, and without news of holdups or hit-and-runs, there is little to say and we are silent. These are the dangerous moments in my life lately. As the hot dogs sizzle and our eyes float around the yard it seems we're all wondering how many more of these fumbling evenings we have left in us, how long before we're all at a loss. On the force, there were two levels of response to things: one and ten. It was either a polite *are you aware this is a school zone?* or you were reaching for the thumb break on your holster. On the force there were no in-betweens. What I have learned in the past year, since the time my son first felt a finger break in his hand, is that life on one is the harder of the two.

Sue finally breaks the silence. "Are you going to tell him?"

Woco smiles and looks from her to me and back. "What?"

"Go get the paper plates," she says to Mac.

He just rubs the shaved back of his head. "What for?"

"Kitchen. Counter," she says and glares at him until he's inside and the door is shut. She leans back again and speaks to the porch roof, not quite bitter, but more or less resigned. "He's got a plan. He thinks if he gives you all his old uniforms in front of Mac, it will solve everything. He's got them dry-cleaned, in the hall closet, ready to go. His big plan. Uniforms."

Woco looks to me for confirmation. Listening to Sue describe the scene I can see it for the foolish notion it is. *The grand symbolic act,* she'll be calling it, *his solution to the bomb.* I shake my head at Woco.

"What can hurt at this point?" I ask him. "I mean, it's worth a shot."

"Worth a shot," Sue mutters to the roof.

Tina speaks. She hooks her hand around Woco's neck and takes a drink off his beer. "What's this all about?"

Woco pats her leg under the table. "Kid's got growing pains."

"It's more than growing pains," I say as Mac comes out the door eating a carrot. He walks with the other hand on his belt buckle like it's a light he's shining in your eyes, a habit picked up from me. Orange mouthed, he's grinning, so I know something's up. I watch him all the way to the bench, where he tosses the paper plates, face down.

Inside we hear the parrot screech twice. Then it says, "Code—nine." What was Mac's silly phrase yesterday now has me by the collarbones, a sudden anxiety that stuns me until I realize the parrot has the perfect scratchiness of a radio dispatcher. *Code nine,* the parrot repeats and a knowing smile comes across Mac's face so obscene it scares the shit out of me. I watch him silently mouth *fuck yeah.*

I feel myself moving toward ten. "Did you teach that bird to say that?"

Mac blankly chews his carrot.

"It's going to say that forever. Do you know that?" All of us are watching now, and suddenly it's not so easy for him to smile. His face is bunching up, getting flustered, and I want this. I want to get through to him. I want him to stand in the hot glow of ten. "Forever. Did you think about that?"

"Okay," Sue says, "enough."

"Answer me," I say. "Answer."

But then something strange happens. There is a splash in the dog pool, a sharp plunk. Something bounces off the barbecue, sending sparks out the dome. Then I see it, a short hail of rocks sailing in from the alley. There is the crunching of feet in the alleyway and the stones bounce off the roof and skitter onto the porch as a group of kids yells and taunts Mac.

Mac is moving across the yard before I know it. With one high step and a leap, he's over a six-foot fence and all I have of him are streaks of pumping arms through fence slats as he begins his pursuit. Sue shakes her head like I should get up to follow, but I don't. I will not chase my son like a fugitive down our alley.

"So much for the grand solution," she says.

We sit there in the quiet, looking at each other through the smoke of burned hot dogs, listening to the sounds of disappearing feet. On the force things would be easy. On the force I would know what to do. But now, there is no procedure, and I can only close my eyes and try not to think.

After a while he appears, breathless through the side gate. His ribs are heaving, his feet a throbbing mess. "I need my shoes," he declares and then puts his hands on his knees, breathing deep. "I need shoes." Sue glares at me.

At the zoo a yellow Post-it waits on the guard shack. I don't look forward to these notes, to the extra duties Mr. Bern has waiting, but it's best to just plow onward and get it over. Though tonight I pull up short. Mac is in my thoughts, has been since he pedaled down the drive at sunset, and as I picture him weaving off into the dark neighborhood, I can't help feeling a connection between my son and a distant note I can't quite read, though I know what news it will bring.

It's foolish, I know, standing here in the parking lot, afraid of a note. For the first time I think I'd rather Mr. Bern told me in person the animals I was to cull, that one night he'd follow me around to see what it takes to make these notes good. But, like I said, he's weary of me, and it was only because Sue's veterinary professors put in a good word that I was hired at all. When people find out you used to be a cop, you can see the options run in their eyes: couldn't hack it, not good enough, crooked. Or worse, they imagine some tragic life-and-death scene that makes you quit, that changes a guy forever. The stray bullet that hits a tourist. The kid with a toy pistol. People never pause to think that such scenes can stop being tragedies after a while.

I tell you, the only thing I ever shot on the force was a cow, which was one of the reasons Mr. Bern hired me. Still, I don't think he ever shot anything. I'd like to tour him around Traffic for a while, show him how to take that breath before you crawl underneath the axles of a tractor-trailer underride. If everyone did a year on Traffic, we'd all speak another language. My wife and I wouldn't end up silent in the kitchen, at a full loss. There would be no need for yellow notes.

In the distance, a caribou ruts his horns against a fence and calls in the heat. It is a lonely sound and I decide I will set no traps tonight. I pull myself together, tell myself such speculation is foolish, will only make things worse. But before I take two steps toward the guard shack, I again reconsider things. Into my head comes the notion that maybe I was wrong, that nobody should have to go on Traffic, that my son shouldn't feel he has to face the world, head on, before he's even ten. And, of course, he's learned what's out there from me.

The note, though, is not what I'd expected. It simply reads: Mind The Wolves. I examine it closely in the sulfurous flood-lights. It's the first time I've been asked to look after an animal rather than put it down, and as I aim the cart around toward the lower zoo, I can't help feeling a little high. I drive faster than usual and flip on the headlights to get a glimpse of animals that swivel their long necks to watch me pass. Rolling through Down Under, a wallaby bounds to pace me inside its fence. I sink into the light mist of Flamingo Island. Coming out of Sonoran Predators I see them, ruby bright eyes fixing me from a temporary enclosure near the Papago boulders that mark the end of the zoo.

There are three of them, Mexican Reds, and I watch them all night, forgetting all else. I have never seen a wolf before, but I know these are fresh off the range. The enclosure is only a fifty-foot square of chain link, yet the females manage to show little of themselves. But the male, he is magnificent, a coat of deep am-ber, slimmer, smaller than you might think. Soon I find myself running the outside of the fence with him as he lopes, bandy-legged, circling his pen in a rocking-horse motion that pulls up and freezes at the slight sounds of distant rabbits, now a little less sure about descending into the zoo. He is used to being pursued. I am used to pursuing, and we fall naturally into this motion.

His ears prick, he pauses. At these moments I stop with him. Earlier in the day he has sprayed these new fence posts to mark them as his, as if to say *the world can come no closer than this,* and in such a pause there is only the mutual huff of our breath, the musk of wolf-spray rising like spilled fuel, and the absolute si-lence of rabbits. I kneel down at the fence, and the wolf does not know what to make of me. He stands, wide and low, ready to be knocked down, but for a moment we speak the same language and he is unafraid. We seem to recognize we are both in from the range, to agree the chase can end.

At home, the house is quiet, unlit, and I look forward to a half hour in bed with my wife before she rises to go to school. I lock my gun above the refrigerator and slip out of my clothes in the kitchen. Naked, I make my way down the hallway. There is the slightest wolf smell on my skin and I am glad for it. In the bedroom, open books are spread along the foot of the bed and Sue, in her deepest sleep, is beyond peaceful. My dream about Mac will not come tonight, I know that now, looking at her. It is a simple dream, short as a school play, yet can come sudden, lung-punching, like high-speed chrome.

I slide my leg under the covers and am drawn to the warmth of her back, the slightly sour smell of her hair. She is curled away from me but her head rolls back, craned to her shoulder. One eye opens. Wide and unfocused, the pupil slowly floats across the ceiling, moving through her puffy lids as if in sea water. "Baba," she murmurs. "Cum sle wis me." I wrap my arm around until my fingers fit the slots of her ribs. She hums a single, short note. At the scent of her shoulders and the sound of her sleepy talk, I know her so fully it loosens my jaw, makes me exhale deep.

Her foot drifts over to scratch an itch against the hair on my legs, and near sleep, I hear *Mind* The Wolves. I say it to myself, now wondering if instead of *take care of* the wolves, it means *watch out for* the wolves. *Stay clear. Beware.* Suddenly, I wonder what Mac is dreaming under his Bart Simpson bedsheets. We gave him the street-side room when he was little and I picture him fitful and turning now as late-night cars drive by and headlights steal in his windows.

My eyes are drawn to the wall, to an unseen boy not twenty feet away, and I want him to be restless, to dream about his black eye, about bent fingers, but I know what is really true: he is dead-to-the-world asleep, eyes rolled back, sheets on the floor, sunk so deep in his unconscious he is lucky to be breathing. He was as easy with a fist as I was with a wolf, and I want us both troubled by this in our sleep. My hand pulls against the flex of Sue's ribs. "Gon a sle," she says as her hand finds mine, squeezes, goes limp.

I decide Mac's hair is best fixed by professionals, but a trip to the mall, it turns out, is a bad idea. Even at noon, on a weekday, we are forced to park a quarter mile away. Daytime is generally more difficult for me, and entire days, one-on-one with my son, have recently given me reason to be leery. Any lightness I felt last night is reduced to the uneasiness of walking on heat-weakened asphalt and the feeling of dark potential that can come from a sea of fuming cars. I have decided to be "up" today, a carefree father despite the fact that Mac now refuses to wear his shoes, which he woke me up by announcing were for "pussies."

This is how we move through the parking lot: I, holding his sneakers, walk down the middle of the lane, while he zigzags back and forth before me from the relative cool of one car shadow to the next, saying *ow, ow,* and this motion, it seems to me, in the oven-breath of the mall, is the essence of our relationship.

Mac has never before had a store-bought haircut, and it is the tools of the trade that interest him. He leans over to pump himself up in the chair. He uses the vacuum hose to suck red circles in his arm. He smells the blue fluid the combs are in. The young woman cutting his hair says something to him and he laughs. He closes his eyes, rolls his head to grin toward her shoulder, and I can see in his reflection a boy who's forgotten his sullenness, forgotten his father the ex-cop is waiting with his sneakers.

But with a razor nick at the back of his neck I see his fists lift on instinct and I feel a pang in my gut that makes me want to curl. He sits stark, straight up, his head whipped around to glare at the girl with the comb. What you need to understand about this, what I need to make clear to you is that regardless of what Sue or anybody says, I've lost this kid, I've lost him. I can get him back, I know that. What hurts, here, on this bench, amid waves of passing families, is that I have no idea how.

At work, there are three yellow notes waiting for me on the guard shack, and I walk right past them to the front power panel, where I shut down every light in the zoo. I step into my golf cart, and for a long time, just stare through the windshield into a night I have blackened. A light wind, unusual for this place, floats down from the Papagos, bringing a taste of wolf-scent like warmed ammonia, and I can feel those notes hanging on the guard shack behind me. Then I hear him bay. The wolf's voice rises and turns in the bowl of the zoo, curls down around me and resonates in my bones. The two females join in and their wail rings from the rocks like dished metal, a clear, sonorous sound that hangs in the air and moves me long after they stop, and I hope the call rolls far into the city below, makes people sit straight up from their sleep.

I drop the parking brake and wheel the cart around, drawn to the lesser animals, the mule deer, the desert burros, to the spot where I shot the dog. A wave runs through me as I remember the swooshing thud he made as I grabbed his paws and swung him into the Dumpster. I feel the urge to stand on the spot where I first found him trapped, to look at it again. But I don't do that. What I do when I reach the top of the hill is sit and stare for hours into the brazier of city lights below, looking and looking.

Eventually I hear the short whoop of a police siren in the main lot and I cruise down the cart path until I can see Woco far below, leaning on his patrol car, thumping his Maglight against the front tire and watching the light short on and off. I hold up and observe from a distance as he approaches the chain link with a cardboard box from the crime lab, and I know they have finally cleaned out my locker at the station. He just stands down there, holding all my old gear, waiting longer than I am comfortable with, and it is like the barbecue last evening, the awkwardness, the distance, the desire to jump shotgun into his cruiser and race off with him, the silent waiting for him to leave.

Later, after I have read Mr. Bern's notes and done my work, I leave the zoo early and patrol old neighborhoods with my cruising lights on. I turn the Ford down low-lit streets and roll past residence after residence where homeowners raise their juveniles. I put down four kit fox pups before I left. The zoo listed them for three weeks on the National Animal Bank, but no one wanted foxes, so Mr. Bern must have decided today was the day. His note suggested I use Ambutol on them but I didn't. It is a slow drug, painful to watch, and they deserved better. The fifth one is on the seat next to me, in the empty crime lab box, wide eyed and unsure. Already his piddle has soaked through to the fabric. In a few months he'll begin marking the house with fox spray, which is some of the worst, and I'll have to get rid of him. But for now the world outside the car windows does not concern him; he just sits amid the passing darkness with his legs spread, trying not to fall down in the turns.

I find myself near home, two blocks from my street, when I see a figure dash from the road in the murk of streetlamps, a blur of a boy, it seems to me, diving for the cover of bushes. I give chase. I pull down the alley and reach for the spotlight lever that is no longer there. I prowl the backstreets of my neighborhood, figuring, following, until the fox is asleep, until it is my own house I patrol past.

At home, Mac is in the kitchen eating cereal by himself. I enter and stare at him, at his hands and ribs and feet, as if some element of what I felt out there might still linger on him.

"What's wrong with you?" he asks and stretches, rubbing the sleep from his eyes, and I can't tell if this move is genuine, if he's a sleepy five-year-old or a devious fifteen.

"I almost had you," I say.

He squints at me. He lifts the bowl of sugary milk and downs it before rising and silently returning to his bedroom. "Here I am," he says from down the hallway.

It's when I go to put my gun away that I notice a chair pulled up against the cabinet, the footprints on the counter below the locking doors. The clasp and hinges have not been jimmied, are untouched, but I can feel his presence here, feel that he's been meditating long on what's inside, cheek to wood, and I decide here, in the kitchen, that he will shoot a gun.

I stride down the hall, and in his room, grab his wrist. Two more hours of dark, I think, looking into his seditious eyes, and his shoulder socket knocks as I tow him down the hall and out toward the car, still idling in the alley.

Past the zoo gates, he lags far behind as we cross the footbridge that will land us in the park. That is how I see him nearing me, a black outline against the bank of city lights behind, and as I grab the .22 rifle and two boxes of shells from the guard shack, I want him to look into the leukemia-yellow eyes of a tiger. But rabbits are all I have left to scare my son back to me.

Mac is sitting in the driver seat of the cart when I come out, and without speaking we are off, rolling past the Arizona Collection, in what seems an underwhelming first driving experience. He's driving one-handed, eyes wide and unfocused, a style he's learned from me. I give him no directions because the zoo is circular, though he doesn't know that, and he heads best speed through unknown turns, clacking the pedal up and down on the floor, upset the cart will go no faster.

We pass through the main exhibits, and I kill the lights as we near the rear of the zoo and reach over to turn off the key as we pass the makeshift wolf pen, leaving Mac to coast us past the last reaches of the fences. Standing in the fields that foot the Papagos, the stars brilliant despite the glow of the city below, I show him how to lever the little bullets, the features of the safety and sights. He inspects the rifle like he is viewing it through the wonder of another boy's glasses. I make Mac click the safety off and on to make sure he can finger the operation in the dark, but this does little to reassure me.

I bring the cart about and set him up in front of it, Indian legged on the ground with the barrel benched on the grill. He points it off into the black landscape.

"The lights will come on and you'll see the rabbits," I tell him. "They'll stand on their hind legs and then the eyes will light up." He looks from me to the darkness and back. "Aim only that way or the bullets may come back to the wolves or burros." I point toward the dark field but he doesn't follow.

"Where's the wolves?"

"Over there." He turns to look but there is only the hood of the golf cart. "Are you sure you're ready?"

He's still straining to see the wolf pen. Then he looks up, his face blank, and the safety clicks off. "Affirmative," he says.

I walk to the power pole unsure if I've made a big mistake. *Grand symbolic act number two*, I hear Sue say. I take a breath, for both of us, and throw the toggle switch to the floodlights above. They glow a dull sodium orange before flashing to show an empty field, and slowly the rabbits begin to stand up and stare toward the light. The semiauto snaps to life as Mac levers eleven rounds with amazing speed, just the way I taught him: pump sight breathe squeeze, pump sight breathe squeeze.

Little patches of dust stand frozen in the distance as we walk together, our shadows long before us. Mac opens and closes the breech to smell the smoke. I try to read the expression on his face, and as the moment I've been banking on nears, the moment he sees what a gun is capable of, what he's capable of, I begin to change my mind and hope he has missed.

I am wrong. We find a rabbit sprawled beside a small outcropping and I realize the worst has happened: Mac is neither scared nor disgusted, only indifferent. He picks it up by its long ears like he were handling a milk jug. It slowly rotates by its stretched skin. With his finger he inspects the little hole in its chest. With his finger he opens its mouth and looks inside.

"Maybe we could feed it to Sam," he says.

"Negative."

"Ten-four," he says, mocking me, and spots another a few yards away. It is larger than the last one and Mac picks it up and shakes it. "What about this one," he asks, holding it up, as if weighing it in the light. I watch its front legs circle in the air.

Jesus, I think. "Put it down."

"No. It's still good," he says and shakes it hard. Its body rocks some and then its back legs slowly rear up, as if charging, and suddenly tear down his arm. Mac drops it and moves to kick it but I stop him. I grab his shoulder and pull him, squeeze him to my stomach until I can feel my pulse in his back. The jackrabbit skitters away and overbounds into the dark and I am left pressing my boy to me while trying to think of a way to explain the difference between killing an animal and beating it.

I turn him around, but I can't deal with his sullen, angry face. Mac's arm is scratched pretty good. But I can't even deal with him. I take the gun, hand him the flashlight, and walk away for the first aid kit. I should bring him to the cart, to where the light is better, though honestly, I don't want to see him any closer tonight.

Anger has settled to a kind of emptiness by the time I reach the cart. I find the first aid kit and begin the slow walk back to Mac, my son, whom I will patch up with gauze and Bactine. I make my way along the edge of the open desert and I know in a little while I will have to call Sue to come pick him up because even here, in a simple field under the stars, I am ill-suited for any of this.

I reach the spot where Mac should be, and it takes a moment to bring my head back down to earth and realize he is gone. I do a slow turn before I see him standing down by the wolf pen, shirtless, with a rabbit in his hand. He is rattling it temptingly against the chain link while his flashlight follows in its beam the dim image of a wolf in the dark, more eyes than anything as it sidles, circling, on loping legs. Mac is saying things I can't quite hear. His free fingers hold the mesh, and he is bent some, talking in hushed tones.

I call to him but he does not respond. He seems to finish what he is saying and his awkward body stands up straight. The light turns off. Then his arm lifts to lob the rabbit over the fence and I am moving. I see the rabbit do two slow turns in the air and I am almost running. It lands on the other side, not four feet from where he stands transfixed, fingers wrapped in the fence. *Mac,* I call.

He rolls his head to look at me blankly and I slow some. Soon, I am stopped, breathing heavy and watching from behind. It becomes quiet, and as I notice the shh of late-night cars on Van Buren, I wonder what had me running a moment ago. Then it appears from the dark, cautiously, legs wide, watching Mac as it comes close enough to shovel the rabbit into its mouth before it is gone. Mac is glued to the scene, and the thought that he feels connected to this animal brings him closer to me in the one way I do not want.

And then the wolf is back. It is only a gray glow in the moon-light, but belly low it nears the fence again. It pauses and sniffs, then nears more, and I have never seen anything like it, this wolf and my son. Through the fence its nose runs up and down his jeans, and Mac seems almost to press himself against the fence as it sniffs, neck stretched to Mac's shiny legs. Then it turns away from him, as if to leave, yet pauses. At first I think it is smelling the spot where the rabbit had lain, but the wolf lowers its head, and with a quivering of its hindlegs, sends three great blasts of spray and foamy urine trolloping down Mac.

He turns, mouth open, a mist coming off him beyond smell, and his is the kind of terror I was getting used to on the force. I move to embrace him with everything I've got, but when he sees me run at him, he is gone; his legs shudder then burst, a flash of a boy racing down dark paths.

I chase him. I take a breath and run, my keys jangling, my nametag flying off to scramble in the green-black grass. We are running for all we are worth, and soon he is losing me, soon he is only the glint of working shoulder blades and the white arcs of elbows in the moon, and I run. I run until the saliva puddles in my mouth and I am only following his scent. I feel my gun belt take on its familiar cantering rhythm, and I picture him hop-ping the zoo gate to blur down Van Buren Avenue under dim streetlamps, chasing the traffic, running shirtless past the adult bookstore. I ditch the Maglight and revolver and belt and pull my shirt off until there are only the sounds of my breathing off the as-phalt. I round into the wide open of Your Own Backyard, and I know he has gotten away from me, suddenly I've chased this kid a thousand times, in an instant I am heading again down old alleys and yards, over hedgerows, across empty causeways, and as a stitch starts in my side all I can do is follow that awful smell on my son and hope it will never leave him because there's no other way I'll find him in the dark.

THE DEATH-DEALING
CASSINI SATELLITE

Tonight the bus is unusually responsive—brakes crisp, tires gripping—jockeying lane to lane so smoothly your passengers forget they're moving as they turn to talk over the seats, high heels dangling out into the aisle, teeth bright with vodka and the lemon rinds they pull from clear plastic bags in their purses. Some stand, hanging loosely from overhead handles, wrists looped in white plastic straps, smiling as their bodies lean unnaturally far with the curves. Off-balance, half-falling, this position has its advantages: hips flare and sway behind you, ribs thumb their way through fabric, and this it seems is the view you've grown used to, daring you to touch, poised to knock you down.

You don't even know where you're driving yet, but through breaks in the trees, you can see red and blues on the Parkway and know traffic cops are working the outflow of an I-High baseball game. The school is not a place you want to be near tonight, especially bumper-to-bumper with old teammates, especially as a nineteen-year-old go-nowhere who drives a charter bus for a cancer victim support group on Thursday nights. So you're banking a turn onto the Cascade Expressway instead—not an easy feat in a fifty-six-foot BlueLiner—when you catch a glimpse of Mrs. Cassini walking down the long aisle toward you, her figure vibrating in the overhead mirror, and you know you're in trouble. Her husband built the Cassini Satellite, the one powered by seventy-two pounds of plutonium, so you know what you're dealing with.

Your eyes double back from carloads of teenagers behind victory-soaped windows to the sight of Mrs. Cassini growing in the mirror: she's running the tips of her fingers across the green-black vinyl seat backs, and she's closing on you in a black Lycra cocktail dress that's Olympic time-trial tight. The streetlights through the bus windows are flashing across her torso, her arms and neck taking on the cobalt blue of barium dye, and even from here you can make out the bubble-gum ridges of her mastectomy scars. All the other women seem to lean in her wake, as if she is their talisman, this woman who's walked through the flames, who's beat cancer three times. The old BlueLiner wants to wander in the fast lane.

Only when Mrs. Cassini reaches the front of the bus do you notice the flask in her hand. At the sight of your SAT study guides on the dash, she says, "Relax, Ben," and sloshes back some scotch. Amber traces down her chin, pauses at the base of her neck. She slips a tape into the deck and *Blue Danube* starts over the loudspeakers.

As she leans the backs of her legs against the dash, the door lever forces her closer to you, and the black wing of her pelvis glows an edgy green from the dash gauges. She stares at you hard—eyes rimmed a renal yellow, the color of canary diamonds—then lifts and places a heel in the pocket of seat between your legs. This move hitches her skirt high enough that you can see the white-clamped tip of her catheter dangling before you, and you're trying not to stare, but man . . .

Then Mrs. Cassini leans over, her hand like it's going for your belt loops, and you go limp, drop a hand from the wheel and *give her room*. "That's better, Benny," she says, and soon her strong chest is in your face—you're in the fast lane!—as she fumbles around on the far side of your captain's chair. She comes up with the microphone handset, the loopy cord bouncing in your face. When she's composed herself a little, you give the BlueLiner a quick burst of gas and watch the tip of that catheter circle into a tight orbit below her hem. Cassini smiles sideways at you.

You two've done this routine before.

Blue Danube kicks into gear, and across the women's faces in the mirror comes a certain serenity, like they're all picturing the slow-tumbling spaceships from *2001: A Space Odyssey*, a movie you thought was pretty sexual—all that docking and pod work—and which your dad said was a coded history of existentialism.

She lifts her flask high. "For my husband," she says into the mike, addressing the bus like a lounge singer. "Scholar. Diplomat. NASA scientist of the year." Here she *whoops* loud, and the women are swaying to the music just enough to make the bus woozy between lanes.

"He has a permit to buy weapons-grade plutonium, reserved parking at JPL. He wrote his name in the wet cement of Cape Canaveral's launch pad, but it's Thursday night, and he can't come within five hundred feet of his wife for four more hours."

The bus explodes, the women are in the aisles, some with their arms in the air, dancing and pirouetting homages to both the famous Cassini satellite and the weekly, six-hour Cassini restraining order.

Mrs. Cassini tosses the mike into your lap and from her glowing abandon, you're trying to guess the destination this week: Shocking the tourists at the Idanha Hotel? Maybe scar-strutting with the black ties at the Capitol Club or lobbying complimentary cocktails from the Westin convention staff.

Cassini moves closer, her lips just brushing your ear, and you want to close your eyes. "To the Cove, young captain," she mouths and you know there's both a difficult U-turn and some slumming ahead. But your shoulders start to loll to the music and soon you have the old BlueLiner waltzing through the backroads of Boise, a little too fast perhaps, though none of your passengers are very worried about crashing because they've all had cancer, and the motion of their bodies tonight seems to confirm both *Space Odyssey* theories.

At the Cove, you wheel the bus around in a crush of white gypsum and bottle caps, coming to rest under the yellow buzz of bug lights and a single beer sign humming blue enough that cars look stripped of their paint. The Cove through the windscreen is a square slump-block hut set off by its brighter parking lot, dark-bordering pine, and backdrop of lake that's snowmelt still.

The women descend beside you, heels sinking in gravel, and make for the only door there is. They move past, winking, patting your shoulders, letting the sheen of their nylons run staticky along your forearm as you hold the door lever. There are some new faces in the Cancer Survivor's Club this week, but you don't have the energy to meet their eyes. You look to familiar faces instead, the veterans. It's pathetic, for sure, but they ladle love on you and you take it, these Thursday-night women who flirt with you, rub your shoulders, teach you to foxtrot. Judge Helen—the one who granted the restraining order—is the last to leave, and she already has her weekly Winston in her lips. She is a bigger woman with short, spiked hair who is not afraid to wear black spandex, and you like her for that.

They all cross the blue-yellow parking lot with a motion only cancer survivors can muster, a sexy, patient gait that comes with the knowledge bosses can't fire dying women, that cops won't cart them off, that bartenders don't tell bald women they've had too much. Through a door padded with red vinyl and brass studs, they disappear, and you are alone again.

Out stumble two men who turn back to stare at the red door in disbelief. One is wearing fishing gaiters. They look at each other, at the bus, strain a glance at the sky as if the weather might have something to do with the women they've seen and then backtrack, heads shaking, for an old Subaru by the Dumpster.

You shut the door, check your watch, and pull out a *Miller's Analogies* workbook. The college entrance test is Saturday, and you're more than a year behind on everything. You put your feet up on the console and flip through the pages, a stream of letters and numbers that don't even register.

"I'll scream rape," comes from the back of the bus, singed with mock-play and the smell of tobacco.

"You know the rules, Mrs. Cassini. No smoking on the Blue-Liner." You say this over your shoulder, feigning interest in antonyms in an effort not to encourage her. But you can feel her nearing, hear her slapping the overhead straps on the way, leaving them to swing in the dark behind her.

"I could have Helen throw away the key," she says and pauses, smoking. "I'm willing to bargain on your punishment, though."

"Cat-o'-nine-tails? Thousand licks, Mrs. Cassini?" Your voice is flat, disinterested.

"Benny, your tongue. You're lacking a refining, feminine influence."

"And you're the best I've got?"

She's standing beside you now, taking one step down toward the door so that she is lower, but farther, so she has to lean. "Oh, Ben. If you only knew how much control it takes to be a role model for you." She runs a hand through your hair in a circular motion that leaves her holding your earlobe. It's a thing your mother used to do. "Seriously, though, how's things? Stan okay?"

"You know Dad, he's sawing wood. I got a test coming up."

"Good, good. You study hard and I'll throw you a party." She taps the cigarette ash into her hand. "In the meantime, are you gonna help me get off?"

"Mrs. Cassini?"

She nods her head at the lever, and you swivel the doors open for her. "Relax, Benny. Go with things, okay? Live for me." She turns to leave, but on the last step stops and lifts her skirt for a full bare-ass flash before jumping down and trotting off toward the red vinyl of home, and you're left shivering with a knob in your hand. You know these women well. You know a side of them no-body sees, and Mrs. Cassini's been playing the flirting "auntie" for a long time. Back then, though, you were seventeen and your mom was on this bus. Now you're nineteen, a lot of things have changed, and it's fifty-fifty at best whether you'll even show for that test.

You swing the doors shut and set the lock, more to keep your-self on the bus than anything, but the static is still in your arm, smoke hangs in the air. Your dad has a small State Farm branch—which is why Mom was insured to the teeth and you're covered to drive a fifty-six-foot bus—but one time he took you with him to underwrite a warehouse, a windowless cinder building that stored marine batteries. Everything was primer gray except for the stacks of yellow cells with their red and green posts, but there was a pulse to that place that twitched like copper windings and made your mouth taste of zinc. You remember thinking this must be what it's like inside a hydroelectric dam, with stands of vibrating water behind the walls. This is what you feel now from the Cove, this draw.

You pick up your books and set them down.

Your mom once said cancer was the best thing on earth, that as long as it didn't kill you, you were going to *live*. When she and

Cassini and the others started the club, they sat outside in your mom's cactus garden, drinking tea and sharing. It wasn't long before they started searching for stronger medicine and held rituals in the trees out back, events in the twilight where they buried their hopes and burned their fears in the group holes they'd dug. Except for a few veterans, the turnover rate in the club is pretty high, and you understand why green tea and empathy eventually yielded to Donna Karan dresses and a tang of vermouth.

The I-High school counselor, Mrs. Crowley, said writing an essay about struggling with your mom's death could open the doors of a lot of good colleges. You didn't jump at that idea. She said look at the big picture: it could help you get into medical school someday, where you could make a difference, where you could find a cure for what took your mother.

You told Mrs. Crowley she had something there, that working with radon and lab rats had always been a dream, but your real plans include asbestos. For some reason, you confessed to stealing your father's drill bits, to once lying about the reading on your mother's thermometer so you could go see *Forrest Gump* at the drive-in, admitted to sometimes eating her chemotherapy pills when she wasn't around. Mrs. Crowley said remember to turn in the combination for your locker and bring a photo of yourself to the SAT.

What you couldn't explain to Mrs. Crowley was that the real danger is in handling it too well. Managing loss is your father's business. He's pretty good at it. He got mom the best medical plan, the best doctors, the best palliative counselor. Dad knew the stages of grief and there were no surprises. Mom even died on schedule. Those doctors were amazing; they called it within a weekend.

Dad joined a support group and took up woodworking. He bought you a brass trumpet and a punching bag. Now he comes

home from work, checks the Weather Channel—he's crazy about
the weather—puts on a shop apron, and goes into the garage to
build the look-alikes of colonial furniture that fill your house.

Sometimes he gets nostalgic on Sundays or has a few too many
beers over dinner and tells you things about Mom when she was
young. You've heard most of them many times, but once in a while
he says something new, and you feel close to him for that. Your
mom had a pony named Applejack when she was girl. In college,
her favorite movie was *The Andromeda Strain*. That, pregnant
with you, she was in Albertson's supermarket when her water
broke, and she calmly took a jar of pickles from the shelf, dropped
it over the fluid on the floor, and moved on.

But even these moments of disclosure from your father seem
expected in a way, and his power tools never seem to rattle him
the way you'd think they might, the way the BlueLiner's big diesel
can vibrate something loose in you that makes you forget where it
is you are driving, makes you check and check the overhead mirror for her in row six. You think if Dad could have seen her on this
bus one time, bright-eyed and destination bound, all those pieces
from his replica projects wouldn't fit together so well.

You hear the thump of the red door and look out the windscreen to see a kid your age cross the lot with a white bucket of
beer caps. He cuts around to the back dock, where he starts
dumping them in the lake. It's dark and a long way off, but you
think you know him from the baseball team, from before you quit.
He leans against the rail and he pours slowly, watching the caps
go down like all those green innings in a near-championship stadium. His name might be Tony. Finished, he spits on what is
probably his own reflection and goes inside. When the door
closes, though, there is a woman standing beneath the blue beer
sign.

She crosses the lot, circling wide to avoid the floodlight. With calm, measured steps she walks around the far side of the bus, where she grabs a sapling with both hands and stares at her feet.

She's in trouble, about to be sick, but there's something about her shoulders, the way her ribs flare and trim toward her waist. She's younger, new to the club, and caught your eye in the mirror on the way over. You could tell she was drawn to the mood on the bus, the abandon, the acceptance of being out without her wig. For everyone on the BlueLiner, the worst has already happened, and this is how they can laugh and talk to one another across newly emptied seats. This is what your mother wanted: for everything to race on without her.

Now, she retches, the thin branches shaking above her. When her shoes and ankles get wet, you know you should look away, but there is something necessary in the sight. It makes you wish your mother could have shown this side, the alone-and-sick, slipping-outside part of the deal, because all her strength, like your father's adaptability, did nothing to brace you for after.

Her heels shift in the gravel again, heading for the bus, where she shakes the locked doors. You find her seat, her purse, and at the cab, strip the towel off your captain's chair before levering open the door. With the bright lights behind, she is more than alluring. She is here and real.

She takes her bag from your hand. "Jesus," she says. "This stuff I'm taking."

"I'm Ben," you tell her. Inside you're feeling that pulse, and don't know what to say because somehow you're already beyond small talk. And even just talking means you're making an investment of some kind. It's like standing before a brass trumpet or boxer's bag: they promise to show you a lot more of yourself than a red face or sore hands, and you're unsure if you want to touch them for that.

You climb down to the last step and sit, so she's taller. "Here," you say, holding the towel in the air before her, and there's this thing between you so clear that she grabs the door molding for balance and places a foot in your hand. You begin with her calf, stroking down to the heel.

"Do you feel better?"

"Sue. I'm sorry, Sue."

"Do you feel better, Sue?"

"No, not really."

She has a Hickman port in her chest, a sort of gray button connected to a white tube that disappears into the skin below the collarbone. You know your cancers pretty well, and the Hickman's a bad sign. It's made so they can inject really strong drugs like vinblastine, chemicals that will burn out the veins unless they're pumped straight into the superior vena cava, straight into the heart. You can feel the slim bones of her foot through the towel. Vinblastine is made from the purple blossoms of the periwinkle plant. You want to push that button.

"I mean you're nice for this, but this medicine . . ."

"Ben."

"This medicine, Ben." She shakes her head.

You take her other foot when she offers, wanting to make her legs dry and clean. You want to tell her you understand, that you've tasted Cytoxan, that it made your fingernails loose and teeth hurt. The feeling like your molars have been pulled returns: platinum spark plugs have been screwed into your jaw, and for a moment, it's like when they'd crackle to life in the middle of the night, making you see blue on the inside of your eyelids. "It's okay," you tell Sue.

"What's okay?"

"Everything. It feels pretty bad now, I know, but it'll all work out."

She pulls her foot back.

Your voice is thinner even than Mrs. Crowley's, but still you say, "Things'll be fine."

"I'm pretty fucked, thank you. I'm screwed."

She says this and hops once, slipping a shoe strap over her heel before walking away.

From your wallet you pull your entrance ticket to the SAT. The picture you glued to it doesn't look anything like you. You cut it out of your sophomore yearbook, a dull-faced goofy kid who has no idea what's coming, who doesn't suspect that no one in his family will take a photo for the next three years.

You follow the route Sue took through the cars, into the Cove.

Inside, things are about what you'd thought. Several women have corralled two wrecker drivers into a group jitterbug that has them spinning off balance from woman to woman, their eyes unsure where to land—avoiding chests and hairlines—while their hands clutch at waists as if for emergency brakes. Oblivious to the fast rhythm, Mrs. Boyden dances with a small, older gentleman in a brown jumpsuit. They move like strangers on liberty, her fingers hooked in his collar, his hands gathering the fabric of her emerald dress like parachute cord, a move that smoothes where his head lay sideways on her sternum, listening, as if to the source of the softer music they seem to move to. There is no sign of Sue.

Nothing seems to involve you. You sit at the bar wanting ice water while the bartender watches the *Tonight Show* on a soundless set. The music and laughing seem to sweep past, and it is as still on this stool as afternoons when you pull one of your father's pine Louis XIV chairs into your mother's cactus garden and contemplate in the half-light where she might've dug her holes. Lately, though, this is a riskier proposition because after only a year, you're no longer so sure of what she hoped for and feared. If you wrote it, this is what your college essay would be about: Feeling for divots in a dark lawn with your toes. Renting movies like

The Fighting Seabees with your father. Living in a house filled with cactus all winter, sleeping in a room made small by jade-green ribs and spines while the smell of hot saw blades from the garage blows in through the heat vent.

Sue takes the stool next to you, and she also is ignored by the bartender. You ignore her too. In front of you is a wall-length mirror littered with business cards, snapshots in cheap plastic frames, and several yards of dollar bills signed with red marker. There is a crisp five-dollar bill that says *Work-Battle-Battle-Win* in beautiful script; it was the motto of your I-High baseball team, a stupid ritual you chanted before every game.

At the end of the bar, like sisters, Judge Helen smokes and chats with a woman who has rad-therapy lines tattooed on her neck. If you catch her from the other side, where they took the lung, Judge Helen's smoking can be spooky. But from here, her ribs expand as she drags and exhales, her laugh comes with a rise in her chest.

If you were sick, you and Sue would be laughing like this. You're pretty sure you might even have her in the back of the bus right now. But if you were sick, there'd be a hell of an essay in it, and you'd probably be at Harvard. As your mind hovers over cancer and college and Sue on hot vinyl, your eyes wander the mirror, and there, framed by shoulder-length black hair, are the brown eyes of your mother.

This snapshot—taken by who, the bartender?—depicts your mother about to limbo under a pool cue held by her best friend, Mrs. Cassini, and another woman who's no longer in the club. The colors are washed out, the eyes red, and Mom's just starting to descend, her eyes reckoning the height of that bar. There is confetti in her hair and for now her breasts are whole, so you know this must be her thirty-eighth birthday, and that despite the sheer dresses, the snow outside the Cove is deep. Her friends have set the bar at a ridiculous height, a point from which no one could be expected to rise, and you're wondering where you were when this picture was taken. Everyone smiles. She is about to fall, yet there is a thrill in this, too. They all lean forward, breath held, and for this moment, it looks like she is going to make it.

You turn to Sue. "What do you want for your birthday?"

She doesn't miss a beat. "A fishing pole. Maybe a pass to the zoo."

"That's my mom," you say, nodding at the bank of pictures.

"Where?"

"Doing the limbo."

Sue doesn't know what to say. "She's pretty."

"You think so?"

"She was in the club?"

"She started it. That shot's from later, though, from her birthday. I was trying to remember if I got her anything that year. I might have forgot."

"And you're thinking, what are you supposed to get for the woman who'll lose everything?"

You shrug. "Judge Helen was telling a story one time on the bus, about how when it didn't look like she was going to make it, her sister sent away to one of those mail-order companies that specializes in this. It names stars after people. God, they were howling over that one, I mean, laughing up their drinks. An eternal dot in the sky named Helen. Actually, it was Helen B-63, that's how good business was."

Sue pauses. "Your mother, is she?"

"No."

"Good. That makes me feel a little better."

"I'm sorry, I meant she died last year."

"You mean, less than a year after that picture?"

"Ten months."

"Fuck," she says. "What am I doing around you people?"

Sue stares at the dull brass of the bar rail, and you feel for her, but can't get past that picture. The bartender is shaking glasses in soapy water. You tell him you want to take a look at something on his wall, and he looks at you like you've just asked for a key to the Ladies'.

"Give him the damn picture, Bill," Mrs. Cassini says and she's right behind you once again this evening. "In fact, give him anything he wants. We'll start with the picture, six shots, and an order for five taxis at midnight."

"Mrs. Cassini, I got to drive that bus."

"Oh, be quiet, Ben. Listen to your Auntie Cassini for once," she says and slides onto the barstool next to you. It feels like being between the posts of a marine battery, as if you touched both these women at the same time, you'd see that blue light again.

You're handed a framed photo of your mother that's been wiped with a bar towel. Tequila appears, lime and salt. Cassini licks the back of her hand. Sue bumps you as she hooks a heel in a rung of your barstool to better brace herself. The salt and alcohol burn in your fingernails. Three rims touch in front of you, and as usual, life seems to be moving just beyond your control, but for the moment, the place you're headed feels good.

"To cancer," Cassini says. "A growth industry." And you all nearly spray your drinks with laughter. In the mirror, Sue's smooth head rolls back, a nautilus-curve. Her throat lifts and relaxes, and you drink too. A sharp, patient burn, like cactus, winters in your throat.

Sue is fine until the lime. She lifts it to her mouth but the smell of it triggers something in her that makes her stand up. She puts her hands on the bar. "Not again," she says, turning, pushing away the hand you offer.

"Let her go," Cassini says, anticipating your urge to follow. "She asked about you, you know. She'll be back."

"When?"

She passes you the salt. "Just a bit ago. Out back by the lake. I told her you were dead in the water."

"Great. Thanks."

"Stuck in a rut. Afraid to move on. Staring at your feet."

"Okay, I get it."

"It's true," she says and fumbles for a cigarette in her cocktail purse.

The bartender has the Weather Channel on now, and you glance at the bottle-necked shape of Idaho, seen from space. You are some-where on that screen, you think. Idaho is blue, and Mrs. Cassini is in that blue next to you. So is your mother, somewhere. Your dad is watching this, you're sure, but what he sees is clear skies.

Mrs. Cassini lights a smoke, and you do another shot together.

"I also told her you were looking to get laid."

You lick the tequila off your teeth and shake your head. It's all you can do. "You're killing me, Mrs. Cassini."

"Who gets the pretty one's other shot?"

"Go ahead," you say.

"See, that's what I'm talking about. A rut. No zest. Your mom and I were pretty close. You know what she asked me? I mean at the end. She didn't say *look out for my baby* or any crap like that. She said, 'keep things interesting for Ben.' "

"Life doesn't seem that thrilling right now."

"Trust me. The excitement never stops," she says, with a touch of bitterness.

Your mom's picture is surrounded by shot glasses. "That's easy for you to say."

"Oh, you can be a little bastard."

"I didn't mean it that way."

Mrs. Cassini puffs on her cigarette and looks at you. "You want a thrill?"

You meet her eyes.

"I'm serious. I'll give you a grade-A thrill, right here."

It's like you're standing in your backyard, and you can feel that spot where that hole is, feel all those fears and desires hot through your feet.

"Okay," you tell her.

Mrs. Cassini stamps out her cigarette on the bar. Then she takes your hand, wet with lime and alcohol, and places it under her dress. For a moment, nothing registers. The old man in the brown jumpsuit stands at the end of the bar, talking into a telephone. The Weather Channel now shows the whole northern hemisphere, all of Idaho lost under its curve, and then your fingers start to feel the inside of her hipbone, the moist heat from below. She guides your hand to the edge of a vinyl-smooth scar and traces it with your fingers downward to the edge of her pubic hair. You can't help it, you close your eyes.

It's not a dance your hands are in, but a mechanical tracing. You are guided to the other side of her navel, where there, soft and flat, is skin you feel as blue.

"It's on the other side now," she says and you open your eyes to meet a face without anger or sadness, and that holds you all the more for it. The strong bones of her fingers push yours hard against her skin, deep into the wall of her abdomen until you know it must hurt. "There," she says, rolling the tips of your fingers. "Do you feel it?"

There's nothing there you can make out, nothing but heat and resistance, a yellow, oily pressure. You pull your hand away.

"That's the new baby."

Your fingers are red and you rub them under the bar, wanting another taste of lime for the brass in your mouth.

"That sounded pretty bitter, didn't it? I don't know why I called it that."

There is nothing you can say to her.

You do the shot on the bar and order two more.

"That's my Benny."

The bartender pours the tequila without limes or salt and when he changes the TV to the late news, Mrs. Cassini yells, "What time is it?" She turns to you, excited, and runs her hand though your hair, shaking your head with your earlobe at the end. "Come on, young captain. It's time."

Waving her hand to the bar, she yells, "To the satellite!"

With that great pull of Mrs. Cassini, you let yourself be swept. Reaching for the bar, you barely manage to grab a portrait of your mother and down that shot.

Outside, the patrons empty onto an oil-planked T-pier, and drinks in hand, stroll above black water lightly pushed from a breeze farther out. The clatter and footsteps of those moving ahead seem to echo from landings across the lake a pitch higher, like the tin of old wire or metal that's been spun, and it feels good to be part of a group moving together to see a sight.

Mrs. Cassini is only a strong voice over the others, Sue, a glimpse through the shoulders ahead, and you follow at the edge, skeptical about what you'll find ahead, even though you get that feeling like you're safe behind the BlueLiner's wheel, like nothing bad can come within fifty-six feet.

At the end of the pier everybody looks up. You hear the soft thunk of a wrecker driver's Zippo, his eyes scanning the night above the hands that cup his smoke. Mrs. Boyden and the older man are together again, each with a hand to the brow as if the stars were too bright to consider straight on. Even the boy who might be Tony squints into the night, and the way he absently wipes his hands on his apron makes you see him as of an earlier version of your father, thinking of policies and premiums as he looks to the future, though covered each way for whatever comes.

"I told my husband I wanted to see the new satellite. Then this morning, *over breakfast,* he changes the sweep of its orbit with his laptop," Mrs. Cassini says, and guides us across the sky with her hand. "It'll be coming from Seattle and heading toward Vegas, with enough plutonium to make a glass ashtray of Texas."

Judge Helen coughs.

You look at everyone's faces and you know this is stupid. You can't put a restraining order on a satellite the same way you can't change the path of a tumor. It's stupid to think you can just wave your hand and summons up something that doesn't care about any of us.

"There," Judge Helen says and points back and away from where everyone was looking. They all turn in unison but you.

"Yes," says Sue.

"Of course," says the kid in the apron, with all the battle-battle-win optimism of a near-champion, and you look just to prove him wrong, because deep down you want to believe.

Twenty fingers guide you to it. At first it's too much to take in, all those stars. You wish your mother had thrown herself into something the last year of her life, like writing a cookbook or sketching cloudscapes, so that you could make some of those recipes and see how they tasted to her, so you could look up and see what she saw. Overhead, though, is a sky splattered as laughed-up milk, about as shaped as the mass in Mrs. Cassini's belly. Until suddenly you say *of course.* It's that simple. You see it: the green light of the Cassini satellite ticking its chronometer path toward Vegas. You remember the earth-shot on the Weather Channel and the thought that a satellite couldn't see you but you can see it feels pretty damn good. It makes you want to write *of course* on a ten-dollar bill in red ink.

Mrs. Cassini dives into the ice-cold lake and begins backstroking.

At the end of the pier, you hear Judge Helen whistling the *Blue Danube* and look up to see her balanced on a tall shoring post. She launches, extending, and executes a thunderous jackknife, the crowd throwing up whoops as people begin diving in.

The kid in the apron stands in disbelief, and you walk to him. It's not your father he looks too much like, but yourself. In his hands you place the picture.

"Hold this for me," you tell him. "It's important."

He angles the glass against the light off the lake to see. "Okay," he says.

You slip off your shoes, and barefoot, hop up to balance atop a post. From here you can see no more of the lake, but the women below are clear as they stroke and stretch as if doing rehab exercises. There will always be a reason not to jump in a cold lake, thousands of them, and a certain sense emerges from this. It's like the logic of getting a court order against a husband who spends his evenings watching TV in the basement. It's the desire to control anything you can.

Mrs. Cassini floats on her back in the cold water, facing the sky. She looks at you, then closes her eyes, floating. "I'm twice as alive as you are," she says softly, her voice so vital she almost sounds angry. Some women clap water in the air while others backstroke into deeper water, their arms lifting in graceful salute to a satellite that cannot see us, that for tonight at least, just passes on by.

You jump. One slow tumble in the air that unfolds into a sailor's dive, and you enter with your arms at your sides, chin out, barreling toward the beer caps awaiting below. You hadn't planned on hitting the bottom, but it's somehow not a surprise. The muted rustling of tin, when you make contact, is the exact sound of the BlueLiner's air brakes—the shh of compressed air releasing—and the flash of pain in your eyes is bright enough to fire your irises white.

Surfacing, you can feel the flap on your jaw and the warmth on your throat. You swim to Sue and kiss her, awkwardly, half on the nose.

"Easy there, bus driver," she says and has to smile, just her slick face showing.

"You shouldn't swim with a Hickman port," you say. "You could get an infection and die."

"And that kiss was any safer?"

"I suppose it wasn't much of a kiss."

"I think you gave me a fat lip."

"I can do better."

"Another one like that and I won't need the zoo pass."

"The fishing pole, then."

"Maybe it was the satellite," she says. "All that pressure to perform."

"They're watching us on the Weather Channel right now."

Sue gets a conspiratorial look on her face. "I saw at least three satellites up there. How many did you count?"

You're both treading water, breathing hard between phrases.

"They were fucking *everywhere*," you tell her.

"That Mrs. Cassini. I think the satellite she's talking about is halfway to Saturn."

Sue's treading water with you, and that's a good sign. You know you're going to kiss her again. You have a photo of your mother safe with a friend and a mild case of shock. You're immersed in ice water, losing blood fast, and still you feel an erection coming on, the kind you'd get when you were sixteen, appearing out of nowhere, surprising you with its awkward insistence on the terrifying prospect of joy ahead.

TRAUMA PLATE

1

The Body Armor Emporium opened down the street a few months back, and I tell you, it's killing mom-and-pop bulletproof vest rental shops like ours. We've tried all the gimmicks: two-for-one rentals, the VIP card, a night drop. But the end is near, and lately we have taken to bringing the VCR with us to the shop, where we sit around watching old movies.

Lakeview was supposed to expand our way, but receded toward the interstate, and here we are, in an abandoned strip mall, next to the closed-down Double Drive In where Jane and I spent our youth. After Kmart moved out, most of the stores followed, leaving only us, a Godfather's Pizza, and a store, I swear, that sells nothing but purified water and ice. It is afternoon, near the time when Ruthie gets out of school, and behind the counter, Jane and I face forty acres of empty parking spaces while watching *Blue Hawaii*.

I am inspecting the vests—again—for wear and tear, a real time killer, and the way Jane sighs when Elvis scoops the orphan kid into the Jeep tells me this movie may make her cry. "When's he going to dive off that cliff?" I ask.

"That's *Fun in Acapulco*," Jane says. "We used to have it on Beta." She sets down her design pad. "God, remember Beta?"

"Jesus, we were kids," I say, though I feel it, the failed rightness of Betamax smiling at us from the past.

"I loved Betamax," she says.

I only rented one vest yesterday, and doubtful I'll rent another today, await its safe return. There aren't many customers like Mrs. Espers anymore. She's a widow and only rents vests to attend a support group that meets near the airport. The airpark's only a medium on threat potential, but I always send her out armed with my best: thirty-six-layer Kevlar, German made, with lace side panels and a removable titanium trauma plate that slides into a Velcro pocket over the heart the size of a love letter. The Kevlar will field a .45 hit, but it's the trauma plate that will knock down a twelve-gauge slug and leave it sizzling in your pant cuff. I wear a lighter, two-panel model, while Jane goes for the Cadillac—a fourteen-hundred-dollar field vest with over-shoulders and a combat collar. *It's like a daylong bear hug,* she says. *It feels that safe.* She hasn't worn a bra in three years.

The State Fair is two weeks away, which is usually our busiest season, so Jane's working on a new designer line we think may turn things around. Everyone's heard the reports of trouble the State Fair has caused other places: clown killings in Omaha, that Midway shootout in Columbus, 4-H snipers in Fargo.

Her custom work started with the training vest she made for Ruthie, our fourteen-year-old. It was my idea, really, but Jane's the artist. The frame's actually a small men's, with the bottom ring of Kevlar removed, so it's like a bulletproof bolero, an extra set of ribs really. The whole lower GI tract is exposed, but fashion, comfort, anything to get the kids to wear their vests these days. Last week I had Jane line a backpack with Kevlar, which I think will rent because it not only saves important gear, but protects the upper spine in a quick exit. Next I want to toy with a Kevlar baby carrier, but the problem as I see it will be making a rig that's stiff enough to support the kid, yet loose enough to move full-speed in. We'll see.

Through the windows, there's a Volvo crossing the huge lot, and I can tell by the way it ignores the lane markings that it's not the kind of person who cares about the dangers of tainted water and stray bullets. The car veers toward Godfather's Pizza, almost aiming for the potholes, and Jane sniffles as Elvis hulas with the wide-eyed orphan at the beach party. "Remember Ruthie at that age?" I ask.

"You bet," Jane says.

"Let's have another baby."

"Sure," she answers, but she's only half listening. She really gets into these movies.

After Elvis is over, Jane makes iced teas while I drag two chairs out into the parking lot so we can enjoy some of the coming evening's cool. We bring the cordless phone, lean back in the chairs, and point our feet toward sunset. This time of day brings a certain relief because even in September, a good vest is like an oven.

There is a freedom that comes with doom, and lately we use our large lot to play Frisbee in the evening or football in the near-dark, with Ruthie always outrunning one of us for the long bomb. Some nights the Filipinos who own the water store drift out under the awnings to watch us. They wipe their brows with apron ends and seem to wonder what kind of place this America is.

Honestly, I've lost most of my spirit in the fight against the Emporium. When we opened, we were cutting edge, we were thinking franchise. Our customers were middle class, people like us; they still wanted to believe but understood that, hey, once in a while you needed a little insurance. Their lives were normal, but nobody went out on New Years without a vest. To buy a vest ten years ago was to admit defeat, to say *what's out there* isn't just knocking at the door—it's upstairs, using your toothbrush, saying good morning to your wife.

As the sun sinks lower, we watch the first pizza delivery boys of the evening zoom off in their compact cars, and it's a sight that hurts to see. These are high-school kids, most of them too poor to afford or too young to appreciate the value of a vest. I mean, they're going out there every night *as is,* which makes them all the more alluring to Ruth.

People used to make excuses when they came in to rent a vest—*vacationing in Mexico, weekend in the city, reception at a Ramada Inn, flying Delta.* Now they're haggling over expired rent-nine-get-one-free coupons. Now they're going to the Emporium to buy sixteen-layer Taiwanese knockoffs for three hundred bucks. The Emporium is 24-hours, something I'm philosophically against: you should see the tattoos on some of those guys coming out of there at 3:00 A.M. These days people are making the investment. They're admitting the world's a dangerous place.

Across the parking lot, we see Ruth pedaling toward us. She's wearing a one-piece red Speedo, her training vest, and the Kevlar backpack. Her hair is still wet from freshmen swim practice. She meanders over, awkward on a Schwinn she is now too big for, and pedaling big, easy loops around us, announces that she's an outcast. "Only dorks wear their vests to school," she says. "You're killing my scene."

It feels good though, the open-endedness of the day, the last light on my feet, being the center of my daughter's universe for a few minutes. Ruth pedals then coasts, pedals then coasts, the buzz of her wheel bearings filling the gaps in our afternoon, and I almost forget about the Emporium.

Later, after Jane leaves to find Ruthie and take her home for the evening, I'm sitting in the shop when Mrs. Espers comes in. She looks a little down, is holding the vest like it's made of burlap and I know the feeling: it's been one of those days for me too.

"How was the support group?" I ask as I fill out her receipt.

"I've crossed the line," she says.

"How's that?"

"I'm not afraid of flying anymore."

I'm not sure what this means in terms of her group, of whether she'll no longer be needing my services, but you know, I say, "Great, congratulations."

"I'm not afraid of anything," she says with a certain formality.

"Wow, good, good."

She pauses at the sight of her held-out receipt and shakes her head no. "I'm sorry, Bill, but I've made the decision."

She says this and leaves, and I'm left thinking she's decided to go to the Emporium to make the purchase. I figure some flying counselor talked her into the idea of permenant protection, but it is when I go to throw her vest atop the "in" stack, when I remove the titanium trauma plate, that I know she will never wear a vest again. The shiny titanium is lead-streaked, and as I rub my thumb in the indention some bullet has made, I can still feel her body heat on it.

I float out into the parking lot and watch her red taillights disappear into the night, and know that she's right, she's free, that nobody gets shot in the heart twice. I stand in a handicapped parking spot, rubbing the titanium, and I lean against the old shopping cart bin. The faint laughter of distant gunfire comes from the direction of the rail yard, and I look at the lighted windows of the few shops left in the mall, but can only see the darkened stores between them. In my hands, the bright titanium reflects the stars my fourteen-year-old already knows by heart, but I no longer have it in me to look up, to lift my head to the place of our dreams, Jane's and mine, when we were eighteen.

I wander the mall, waiting for my wife to return, something that takes longer and longer these days. She gets a little melancholy now and then, needs a little space to herself, and I understand; these are hard times we're living in. Leaving the shop wide open, I head for Godfather's. But when I get there, I'm confused because I see my daughter through the window, the girl my wife said she was taking home.

Ruth is leaned up against an ancient Donkey Kong machine, talking to a delivery boy on a backward chair. She is wearing her training vest with nothing on under, you can tell, and this boy stares at the exposed plane of her stomach. She has her cheek against the side of the video game, chatting about something, while the boy subtly marvels at how the fine hairs around her navel hum pink in the neon beer light, and I am roaring through the door. I walk right up to my daughter and thump her trauma plate to hear the squish of a cigarette pack and the crack of a CD case. Out of the pocket that should cover her heart forever, I pull Aerosmith and menthols.

I grab her by the wrist. "Where's your protection?"

"Jesus, Dad," she says and starts to dig in the backpack at her feet.

The pizza boy looks like he's about to pipe in, and I wheel on him, "Your parents don't love you."

"Dad, nobody wears their vests to school. I'm a total outcast."

This is my daughter. This is the age she is at.

Jane eventually returns, finds me watching *Cool Hand Luke* in the dark store, and neither of us says anything. She puts her hands on the counter when she comes in and I ask no questions about where she's been. I place my hands on hers, stroke the backs of her fingers, and then turn out the lights, closing up shop a little early.

Lately we have taken to cruising late at night under the guise of R&D. We'll pull the tarp off the '72 Monte Carlo her mom left us, the car Jane used to run wild in. It has the optional swivel passenger seat, black leather, that can turn 180 degrees. We grab the foam cooler and Jane swivels the seat all the way around so her feet are on the backseat and her head reclines to the dash, so she can watch me drive her wherever she wants to go. We'll glide by the boarded-up Ice Plant where we once drank on summer nights, feet dangling off the loading ramps. We prowl past by the Roadhouse with our lights off and count the Ninja motorcycles lined up out front. The cemetery these days is fenced and locked and a security guard cruises the old stadium in a golf cart, but we circle nonetheless.

Midnight finds us rolling through the waves of the old Double Drive In, the gravel crunching under our tires, the Monte Carlo's trunk bottoming out like it used to, and all the broken glass, beer caps, and bullet casings now sparkle like stars.

We park and sit on the warm, ticking car hood and look off at the Emporium across the street. We have his-and-hers binoculars, 7X40s from her father on our tenth anniversary, and we sit here, side by side in the dark, as we check out their customers. We train our lenses at the bright displays. Jane rolls her focus in and out.

"Is that Fred Sayles?" she asks. "By the baby armor."

I focus in on him fondling the competition's goods. "That son of a bitch."

"Remember the night he streaked through the second feature?"

"We all turned on our headlights. *The Day the Earth Stood Still*, right?"

"*Plan Nine From Outer Space*," she says. "Remember window speakers?"

"Remember high-point beer."

"Nash seats."

"Trunkloads."

"Keys left in the ignition."

"*Mars Invades*."

We both look up.

11

It is a moment near the end of things, a point at which, seated in a lawn chair amid the vast emptiness of a Kmart parking lot, Jane is forced to reflect. Her husband is giving driving lessons to her daughter, who loops circles around Jane in the old Caprice they are now reduced to driving. The circles are big and slow, impending as Jane's thoughts, which come to focus on the notion that Ruthie's sixteen, and Bill should have taught her this a year ago.

The Caprice stops, backs up, parallel parks between a pair of worn yellow lines somehow chosen from the thousands in front of the closed-down discounter. It's just like Bill, she thinks, to worry about lines when there's not another car for miles. Jane lifts her hand and the sun disappears. In this brief shade she notices the moon, too, is up there.

Check your mirrors, she can hear Bill say, even from here, as he trains her daughter to always, always be on the lookout. But Jane knows Ruthie's come to be on intimate terms with her blind spot. It's one of the few things they share these days.

Behind her their small rental store is empty. These days, the final ones, he has a VCR running all day in the shop. Over her shoulder she can hear the melancholic coo of *Jailhouse Rock*— Bill's choice today—and it feels like it is their whole history looming behind them: the mom-and-pop store, those liberal-arts dreams, their own *let's put on a barn dance* notion of being their own bosses, here, in a strip mall. She has the cordless phone with her, but it doesn't ring, has not in *we don't talk about how long,* and Jane reclines some in the heat, points her feet toward the horizon.

Look out, Bill yells, *you just hit a Volvo,* and slaps the dash for effect, leaving Ruthie momentarily breathless: she swivels her head to see the chrome and glass she must have missed, but there is only forty acres of empty parking.

The sun swoops low, Ruthie pedals off to junior-varsity swim practice, and *no,* Jane says, not *The Treasure of Sierra Madre* again. On the counter before them are two dozen bulletproof vests frayed to the point that they wouldn't stop slingshots and sixty or seventy videos Bill got cheap when the Video-Utopia store closed three stores down. *And here's where we are,* Jane thinks, between a Chapter 11 pizza joint and a store that has made the switch from water to spirits. *This is the place we are at,* around the corner from the drive-in theater where she and Bill spent their youth, a place she won't even look at because these days, even worse than hope, nostalgia is her enemy.

Bill shrugs his shoulders, lights a menthol, and pops in *Viva Las Vegas,* as if Elvis can soothe her anymore, as if Elvis wasn't 187,000 miles away.

Jane begins to toy with the register, hitting *no sale, no sale,* a sound she knows can wound him. But Bill's busy doing "R&D," as he calls it. First he thought bulletproof teen wear would save the business, and he made Ruthie wear a "training" vest to school for two years to drum up business. Now she won't take the vest off for her life.

His ongoing obsession is a bulletproof baby carrier, something he's reworked twenty times, and if there's anything that offends Jane more than the grandeur of his optimism, it's the notion of wanting to make infants bulletproof, of fusing the two ideas into the same breath. The whole idea is fatally flawed, she knows as she teases the few remaining twenties in the register. It's not what's out there you need to look out for, but what's closer, what's making your cereal crackle, what's tinkering in the garage, or crashing all around like unseen cars.

Bill tugs the straps of his Kevlar carrier, trying to simulate every force that could come between a mother and child. Then he begins stuffing the carrier with videotapes—Clint Eastwood, Annette Funicello, Benji—until, he seems to decide, the carrier takes on the mass and weight of a small person, and he is off on tonight's R&D, running laps around the abandoned drive-in to gauge the carrier's give and take, its ability to cradle a baby at full speed.

Now that he is gone, Jane unfastens the chest-crushing vest, and it smolders off her with all that body heat. She pinches the sticky shirt from her side, runs her hand underneath, over creases in the skin she knows are red. She wakes up some nights, thinking the oven has been left on. She can feel the coils glowing downstairs, but she won't go check, she won't give it that. Now she pulls the twenties, tens, and fives from the till, *for safety's sake,* she thinks, so she can feel the lightweight cash in her pocket.

Wandering, she strolls along the grit-worn sidewalk, stares at stars through holes in the Kmart awning. This way it all looks black up there, the occasional star the rarity. There are bullet holes in the masonry between her and the old Godfather's, and she stops to twist her pinkie in the lead-traced pocks. Mr. Ortiz, the Filipino who owns the liquor store, has started keeping a gun in his register, she's sure. She hasn't seen it, but there's a weight in the cash drawer that nearly pulls the register off the counter when he makes a sale.

There was a day when she was scared of guns, when the vest store seemed like the right idea, a public service even. *Jesus,* they had really said that to each other. Though she has never touched a gun, she's confident now she could heft one pretty handily, squeeze off a few rounds, rest it warm against her cheek and smell the breech.

Where the masonry meets glass, she thinks she gets a glimpse of him reflected out there, an aberration in the dark lot. Behind her, she's sure it's his arms glinting, racing nearly invisible in a sheen of black Kevlar. But she does not turn to be sure.

At the pizza joint, she sees through the window her daughter stretched across the empty bartop, drafting two beers into Styrofoam cups. Ruthie's hair is still wet from JV swim, and she wears loose-hanging jeans over her red Speedo. Now she's got her trauma plate pulled out and is using it as a lipstick mirror, drinking between applications. This is something Jane has never before seen, Ruthie so loose with her trauma plate, and this makes Jane stop outside and stare.

There is a boy, one of those big Ortiz kids it looks like, and he and Ruthie are drinking hard and fast together. Jane looks at them for some time through the soap paint on the window, an interstellar pizza scene. Ruthie laughs, they drink, something is said to her, and she punches him hard. He thumps her back, *there,* in the chest, and then she's holding him again, cupping his chin in the open throat of her palms, the Vulcan oven glowing behind them. She holds him, they dance three slow steps, he spins her. They drink, they laugh, they box each other's ears, they drink again, laughing till fine mists of beer shoot pink from their mouths in the neon light.

This is a careless spirit Jane has forgotten. As she sees them whisper, she remembers a time before Bill, and tries to read her daughter's lips. Ruthie rubs her forehead against the jut of this boy's cheekbone, whispering, and Jane almost thinks she can make it out—*let's make a break for Texas,* her daughter might be saying, and *I want my Monte Carlo back,* Jane thinks. She imagines a car she will never see again, enters it under maroon T-tops, feels the rocking slosh of dual fuel tanks, smells the leather, hears the spark plugs crackle to life, and swivels in custom seats to see it all disappear behind her.

Later, after she has dropped Ruthie off at home, Jane steers the Caprice the long way back to the shop, where she will wait out the last hour with Bill before closing. He will want to make love tonight, she knows—Westerns always do that to him, especially *The Treasure of Sierra Madre*—and that's okay with her. But there's one stop she needs to make.

She slowly eases past the Body Armor Emporium, and just getting caught in its gallery lights is enough to draw her in. She's been here before, enough times it would kill Bill to know. Inside, the lights are of the brightest variety, the walls white, expansive, always that smell like aspirin coming off the rows and rows of black nylon vests. Jane could care less about every vest in the world, but she runs her fingers down whole groves of them because unlike her husband, she feels safe in the arms of the enemy.

There is a tall man, older, with close-cropped gray hair and no-fooling shoulders he seems almost embarrassed of—a by-product of the joy of exertion—and he beckons her into the fitting mirrors where she sees herself in satellite view, from three different angles. For a moment, there are no blind spots and she is at ease. This man takes her measurements quietly, as he has done many times before—humming and storing numbers in his head—the little green tape zipping under his thumbnail as he circles the wings of her pelvis and cliff dives down to her pant cuffs. He is calm, confident, placing his hand warm on her sternum to demonstrate where the trama plate will be. She closes her eyes, remembering a time when she still believed, feels his fingers measuring over, under the cups of her breasts—Jane inhaling—for the purchase she will never make.

111

Let's say you're seventeen. Your mom checked out a while ago. Some nights she just disappears, the Caprice peeling out in front of the family rental store, and maybe you'll see her near morning, standing out there in the parking lot, buzzed, taking potshots at the giant drive-in screens two miles away.

Your old man's a little whacked-out too. Let's say you're crashed out with Hector, both of you sleeping in the Home Improvement section of Kmart, his hand over the nylon vest he again tried to remove tonight, and even though you quit the team, you're dreaming you're swimming the butterfly. *Stroke stroke, dig dig,* Mr. Halverson is yelling in the dream but you can go no faster. Hector is swimming under you, upside-down, telling you *use your back, your chest, put your shoulders into it,* but it is useless because these are the parts of you that are always, always off limits.

So you're sleeping, 3:00 A.M. say, when your dad rents a vest to some punk who uses it to rob the Filipino drug store two doors down, and after, Mr. Ortiz, Hector's dad, stands waving his Colt .45 and saying he's going to put a hole in your old man big as a mantel clock. And there is your father, facing him in a vast black parking lot, wearing an Israeli *alz-hesjhad* forty-eight-layer combat field vest and he's shouting *come on, come on and get some.* You watch this scene with Hector from the bankrupt pizza place, both of you curious if his dad will shoot your dad, and Hector tells you he's heard there's a smell when the hot bullet melts the nylon on its way toward Kevlar. *Like a cross between Tanqueray gin and burning hair,* he says, *a green-black gum.* You remember that Canis Major was wheeling overhead that night.

Let's say that Pluto's gone, that the little planet swings wide one day and never comes back. Your varsity swim coach is also your Advanced Placement Astronomy teacher, and in AP Astronomy, the boys never stop because yours are the only breasts that are a mystery to them. It's a game they play, rapping on your titanium trauma plate when they pass in the hall, though you know the spirit of their fingers goes deeper, and you learn to put your arms up in anticipation. In class, the sun and earth are two white dots, while Pluto's historical orbit, as Mr. Halverson calls it, races away with his running chalk line across four blackboards. Sometimes he lectures directly to the Kevlar outline of your chest. These boys have never seen Pluto, have never reached for it across a black sky, but they moan and wring their hands, as if they can feel its loss, just out of reach, as Mr. Halverson's orbit line comes to a halt at the end of the black slate.

There's nothing out there but starlight and locomotion, Halverson tells you at night swim practice. You think about this for five thousand yards, back-stroking through the blue lanes, the steam rising off your arms to the batter-black sky.

And this is what you come home wet to, the place where you grew up: a hole in the wall behind a Dumpster that opens into the dust-flashing cavern of a closed-down Kmart. Here is where you learn to drive at thirteen, racing rusty carts full tilt through Automotive. Among the smashed racks of Entertainment is where Hector always waits for you. You first kiss in the room above, with mirrors that are really windows, lookouts over a discount wasteland. Through the ductwork, you can hear the nonstop static of your old man's stupid movies. You hear him joking through the vent, endlessly joking. *Always take a bomb with you when you fly on an airplane,* he says to a rare customer, *it's safer, because the odds of there being two bombs on board are astronomical.*

You've slept with seven boys in here, *making love,* they call it, for your sake, but you know better. Through the hole, into the dark Kmart, they come, and you are waiting for them. But none ever fingers your ribs, strokes your shoulders, handles that hollow under your heart because every time one starts to tug on those Velcro straps you are in terror. That is your event horizon, Mr. Halverson calls it at swim practice, the speed beyond which you can no longer safely swim without changing your form, the point at which you must let yourself be taken by your own current. *Safety is your enemy,* he likes to say, and you know he's right. In your own Kmart you're safe, vested, with thirty-six layers of Kevlar to help you take a boy's weight on top of you. But in a Speedo, wet, leaning over the starting block, dripping on the springboard, it's like being naked under floodlights, unshouldered and alone. That's what made you break the school record in the 400 Individual Medly last month—the arm-throwing terror of being vestless before the shouts of those who want the most from you. You took your little trophy—a golden girl, hands up, chest out—and quit the team.

Karen Coles, whose locker is above yours, is seeing Mr. Halverson. Everybody knows since she crashed his Volvo last week. But only you've seen the notes that have floated through the cracks into your locker, only you know that she veered on purpose, that she was testing what was between them when she crossed the centerline, that she was saying I love you even as the airbags blew in their faces.

Your father is different since Mr. Ortiz fired those warning shots in the parking lot that night. He tries to be even more happy-go-lucky, but there is a nervous edge to it, and you know that he is the one on the lookout now. He has bought a gun, a little silver number, your mom calls it, and she stores it under her end of the counter. You remember the excuse he gave, leaning down to you at fourteen: *it's for that one bullet, that one well-intended bullet, and after that the odds say you're good.* This is the line that made you cinch your Velcro straps and wonder if you'd hear the bullet coming. But now you wonder if deep down, your old man isn't disappointed Mr. Ortiz didn't shoot for the heart. At home, you turn the oven on before climbing into bed.

It is the last of the warm days, the end of the semester nearing, one more till you graduate, and Mr. Halverson has saved the best for last: black holes. For now, the black and the hole do not seem to concern him. It is a thing called the event horizon he describes, the line beyond which light is forever drawn in, and you know this is going to be his *big metaphor for life,* his contribution toward bettering your future, a lecture, you can tell, he has made before. He draws a big, easy circle on the board and asks everyone to reflect a moment on the point of no return. But you know it is a mistake to call it that because nothing ever returns, really. Orbits are only historical. You like the swim-team explanation better: call it a line beyond which you can expect only a change in form and high rates of speed, a point of sudden inevitability. You lean back in your desk, your foot looping big, easily drawing his attention, and with a rift in his breathing, he returns his lecture to an institutional mode, comparing the point of no return to drugs and dropouts, to the joys of college learning and beyond. *And we all know what happens in the black hole,* he concludes, but his heart is no longer in it. You know those airbags were his event horizon.

In bed, at night, you sweat. You dream in shades of pink and green of gin and burning hair. In the morning, you, your mom, your dad, all eat breakfast in boxer shorts and bulletproof vests. Dad has a VCR set up on the table and watches *Clambake!* while your mom stares at her cereal.

You had been thinking about it this way: there's a ring around the thing that draws you near—the palms of Hector's hands, say, or your reflection in Halverson's glasses—and to cross that line is to be taken, swept, changed. But today you see it different. Today, standing in the empty AP classroom, not wanting to believe the rumors that Halverson's fired, packed up in his rental car and gone, you wonder where is your event horizon, where is the line beyond which something will forever be drawn to you. His handwriting is still on the blackboard. *Binary star homework due Tuesday*, is all it says, and he can't be gone, he can't be. Stupidly waiting under the Styrofoam–coat hanger model of the solar system you reach up and set it in motion. But the hand-colored planets swing too smoothly it seems to you, too safely Halverson would say, and plucking Pluto from the mix sets the model wildly spinning.

So it's not just anybody waiting for you in the Kmart after school, not just some boy grabbing you by the vest straps and pulling you to him, but Hector. It's Hector's drugstore heart thumping next to yours, Hector's letterman chest against yours, Hector's dive team hips gaining on yours and you want to believe, you want.

Hector has his father's gun, you your mother's, and you will ask the boy you love to break the plate guarding your heart. Hector has a Monte Carlo and you've seen the movie *Bullitt* enough times in your dad's shop that there's a California road map in your head as clear as the grooves around Steve McQueen's eyes, deep as the veins in Hector's arms, but it is not enough. The line must be crossed. He's ten feet from you, a parking space away. You hand him your mother's silver little number. It will knock you down, you know, there will be that smell, but soon there will be no more vests, no more fears, only Hector's fingers on the bruise he's made, on your sternum, and the line will be crossed, the event set in motion, at the highest of speeds.

CLIFF GODS
OF ACAPULCO

My father is dying in Zaire, though I don't necessarily know that yet as I drive to Vegas with Jimbo. I do know my dad is a Rover driver for Mobil geologists and, instead of seismic surveys, he carries two ammo clips and a military discharge that's semiautomatic. This is 1985, and I'm going to Vegas because I'm still in those hazy couple years after high school when I read a lot of racing magazines, drink with secretaries at Bennigan's every night, and take things at face value. I'm failing mythology, my lone course at Riverside Community College, and Jimbo and I test diodes all day for Futron, an electronics firm that makes black-market cable boxes and will shortly be shut down by the FCC. Between us, we have 244 TV channels.

My favorite viewing is always the live coverage on the Canadian Motorsports Network. Jimbo prefers the Playboy Channel, whose only movie I remember liking is *The Black Box*, a soft-core in which, following an emergency landing on a desert island, naughty stewardesses screw survivors on inflatable rafts, yellow escape slides, galley carts, and even a thirty-thousand-horse pulse-injector tail engine. What the crew doesn't know is that the sex is being transmitted by the flight data recorders, which leads to hilarity when the Coast Guard comes to "rescue" them. Getting the Playboy Channel free for yourself is simple; just connect two parallax converters in tandem with a P-9 capacitor, then bridge the diode with an alligator clip.

Jimbo's from Vegas, and we make the hop every couple weeks, though our thing is usually to get a United flight that leaves us about eighteen hours of solid bingo-bingo before we sleep on a flight home to six hundred transistors waiting for the green light. On United, I fly free. For Jimbo, the best I can do is drink coupons. Today we drive instead of fly because of FAA rules: you can't take poisonous animals (scorpions) on commercial airliners. Jimbo has a whole box of them, a ridiculously large cardboard box for the dozen red scorpions the label says are within. They're a special gift for a friend who has a "death thing," Jimbo says. The box doesn't have airholes, and is so light I don't believe there's anything in there—there can't be. Jimbo's excited to see what's inside, keeps talking about opening it, though he wants me to do it. But the trick to life, it seems to me so far, is learning to tolerate the not knowing. I can take that box or leave it.

Jimbo's big into thrills, and our hotfoot to Nevada is all him describing this new indoor skydiving attraction we're going to try when we get there. I don't tell him my mythology teacher says thrill rides are a mix of sky worship and disaster simulation, both primitive kinds of foreplay. I can't explain it the way my teacher does, so outside the state line, I just tell Jimbo, "Let's piss already."

Detouring over Hoover Dam, Jimbo leans hard into the canyon curves, chuting the two-lane fast enough that the scorpion box slides back and forth in the hatch, cornering tight enough that we flirt with guardrails and great heights. Such driving does not appeal to me. The thrills I go for are more predictable—a pistol kick, a sudden loss of cabin pressure, the way a secretary or nurse at Houlihan's will try to lay you by chewing ice from her drink and saying things like, "Grrr." Thrilling driving takes place on oval tracks, especially thousand-lap endurance races that stretch late into night—tight, boxy circuits—spinning long after you turn off the TV and go to bed, races in which the victor is a mystery until the last lap, when you're crashed already and dreaming.

Entering the shadows of great saguaros and graffiti-covered rock faces, we pull over to take a leak in the bluffs above Lake Mead. The outcrops are like lava, and we walk through the shoulder's gravel and ground glass to stand among barrel-chested Joshua trees. "My old man used to take me up here when I was a kid, to see the bomb tests," Jimbo says, unzipping. Jimbo keeps his dope in his Jockeys, so he holds the Baggie in his teeth as he points. I look up through outstretched cactus limbs to the bluffs, which are low and could not offer much of a view, then scan the distant scrub plains and tawny hills below.

"You'd need some L-5 optics for that," I say, using a testing term from Futron.

"We're talking about nukes," Jimbo says, "which tend to be large events, and our binoculars were Bushnells, the best." Speaking through the plastic bag, he goes on to describe how the military would build a little dummy city for every explosion, complete with town halls and fire stations. "My old man would flip. Some of the houses were two stories, with yards and barns. He'd look through those Bushnells and ask, 'Is that a Cadillac in that driveway? Tell me that's not a Caddy they're gonna cook.' But the white flash always shut him up."

Talk of the white flash, which I imagine too clearly, shuts me up as well. We do not go on to discuss either bombs or fathers here among the Joshua trees; we just piss into their hairy arms and leave.

What would I have to say anyway?

Actually, I will never know if my father is pulled from his Rover and shot in a sorghum field in West Africa. My only confirmation comes from a man who arrives out of nowhere one day and claims to be my father's best friend, who begins seeing my mother, and finally convinces her to move from Michigan to Acapulco with him. His name is Ted, and all I know about the whole deal is the sketchy portrait he paints of guarding Mobil interests from tribal warlords, and the general fact that Acapulco is a place where, in long streaks of flashing skin, people throw themselves from cliff tops into the frothy abyss.

Before Ted takes my mom to Mexico, the only time we see her is in LAX on Sunday mornings. Ted and I both find ourselves at the SkyLounge cocktail rail, eating prepopped popcorn and watching people go by until my mother's red-eye comes through, a point at which we have thirty-five minutes with her before she stows tray tables and passes out pillows all the way back to her base in Detroit. The first time we meet, Ted tells me he and my father really took some heat from the local screws in Africa. "Things are different on the continent," he says, and I watch his teeth. Ted has knuckles for teeth. "Those screws were coming at us from all sides. There was no dealing with them."

I have yet to watch enough cable movies to know "screw" is prison talk.

Ted is going to become a saga, but that's not a concern right now. It has no bearing as Jimbo and I drive to Vegas. This story is about amputation.

For these couple of years I am unshakable, so the back roads through Vegas speak nothing to me. I do not think about the people who wander the edges of sidewalkless causeways, the cars that shift and float as if unused to daylight, or the particular strains of Vegas trash that string wire-lined gullies. The power lines simply sink and rise above us, the sky is only October blue, and it seems perfectly natural that people hitchhike in the dips, where freshly blacked streets wash over with sugar sand.

The plan is to get stoned and ride a new attraction called Fly Away, which basically consists of indoor skydiving in a room shaped like a padded tube. There's a wire net at the bottom that keeps you from falling into the DC-3 engine below. Actually, it's Jimbo's plan. I don't smoke dope, and I'm a big guy. I don't believe I will fly.

Key to the plan is going to see Jimbo's old friend Marty. He's the one the scorpions are for. The whole ride out is Marty this and Marty that, an old-school parade of Marty memories, but what's important is this: Marty's girlfriend, Tasha, is the preflight girl at Fly Away, the one who suits you up, so we're headed to Marty's to get some good dope and the VIP from his girlfriend.

"Wait'll you get a load of Tasha," Jimbo says as we crest the foothills outside Vegas. He's pretty stoned, and from his description of Tasha, I know she's the kind of thank-God-it's-Friday secretary I'd work at Bennigan's.

"Tasha's seen the other side," he says.

"The other side of what?"

Jimbo just raises his eyebrows, and we drive for a while.

"Maybe I'll show her the white flash," I tell him.

Jimbo doesn't quite know what I mean by this, but he likes the sound of it. He smiles and steps on the gas, sending us full tilt through the newly paved scrub desert leading to the suburbs. "White flash," he repeats.

Closing my eyes, I let the road's G-force take me. I feel this Tasha woman cinch me into a billowy nylon flight suit, her hands folding Velcro, running zippers, jerking my straps tight. I hear her knock my helmet twice, meaning A-okay, thumbs up, as I follow her into Fly Away's engine room. It is a more modern version of this engine, the DC-9, that kills my mother's best friend, Tammy, climbing out of Dulles International. You've seen the footage, the one that goes into the icy river. I say this because Tammy is a fox, too, a woman I stare at endlessly as she and my mother sit by our condo's swimming pool in white bikinis.

Marty's house is on a pie-shaped lot at the end of a cul-de-sac in west Vegas. It's long and low, hard-lined and brown, the kind of house John Wayne would've lived in, if he'd never been famous. Beyond the sprawling roof rise two jagged outcrops of stone, one with a five-story radio tower that flashes red strobes bright enough to make us wince a bit, even at noon. The light's glow pattern is two fast and one slow, which warns overhead airplanes that this particular hazard's in the approach lane.

On the front steps, we stare into twin, rough-hewn doors and Jimbo rings the bell again. "Like I said, Marty's a soap-opera case," he whispers. "Don't say anything about his face. He's sensitive about his face."

I'll tell you this. Jimbo's not a good friend. He's shallow and deceptive, and there's a hole in him that will make him say anything. I'm not a good friend either. I am asleep in an essential way, and I will not begin to wake up for several years, not until I learn the meaning of the word *loss,* until I am in Acapulco and Ted hands me his favorite pistol, a chrome Super-25.

A woman finally answers the door in a UNLV Runnin' Rebels T-shirt she's adorned with glitter and spangles. She is clearly not happy to see us. I'm six foot four. Jimbo has no neck, and he's holding a box labeled LIVE ANIMALS POISONOUS.

It takes her three full seconds to place Jimbo, then she turns and walks away.

We let ourselves into a room carpeted in cream wall-to-wall, with a black pumice fireplace and a ranch-style bar made from dark wood and warbled green glass. There is an elaborate

seventies intercom system, with talk stations on every wall. Jimbo
heads straight for a Wurlitzer and works its silent keys. "We used
to play Ozzy on this," he says. The walls are covered with photos
of Marty, blond-haired, blue-eyed: Marty in a football uniform,
Marty in a powder-blue prom cravat, Marty midair in front of
a white '66 Mustang, which it turns out is the crash vehicle in
question.

The Marty that rounds the corner, though, is hard to look at.
He is tall, slightly stooped, with long jet hair that curtains his
face. One eye points down and in a bit, making him seem half interested in something just beyond the tip of his nose. He looks almost sad, which is not what I expected after all of Jimbo's
descriptions of the crash scene on our drive up—"They found
the steering wheel in the tree, a fucking tree, man"—the amne-
sia's peculiar effects—"He doesn't even know his dad's name but
he walks right to his locker and wheels out the combo"—horrific
surgeries—"The third time they sewed it on it stuck"—and high
school dramas—"Tasha and I stood by him at the pep rallies; we
were the only ones."

Jimbo and Marty do an elaborate handshake that ends with a
knuckle punch and slips into a last toke off an imaginary joint;
"fff," they inhale. There are a lot of "wow"s and "dude"s in their re-
union, and after neither notices that I am standing right next to
them, I imagine as sort of a joke that they walk off without speaking to me, which they do.

I follow clear carpet runners down the hall, where there are
two white doors. I open the wrong one. Inside sits a boy of about
fourteen. His swingarm desk lamp is on, and he leans back in a
blue director's chair, his feet up on the white laminated desk,
reading a racing magazine. He looks at me, looks back at the page.
But I know this chair, the way canvas webbing gathers under your
shoulder blades after a certain amount of nothing. I know how

long it takes your ankles to go numb from propping them on a desk like that. I see years of airplane models and electric cars, a thousand magazines read atop tiger print sheets, all the things anyone would see, if they'd just open the door.

The kid sets down his issue of *PitCrew*. It's the one featuring Rick Kreiger's 500 win. Then he does a strange thing. He takes his desk lamp and swivels its armature so the hard bulb shines in my face.

This is where one story could become another.

This other story I could tell would be about the following years when your father doesn't open the door. It would have to do with the after-school jobs you pick up to kill time, about the GM family sedan proving ground behind Futron's industrial park, how you can spend whole lunch breaks without taking your eyes off circling cars that stop only to change the drivers who will run them into the ground. This different story would have to do with a mythology class in which you discover the gods are all-petty and their names are hard to remember, or the endless chain of nature shows about Africa a skilled TV viewer can find from midnight on, or the place your mind goes while waiting for a diode to finally light reject-red.

A *woo-hoo* high-five sounds in the next room, and this boy and I look toward the source, our eyes landing on a poster of the space shuttle. There is a white plastic intercom next to my shoulder that surprises me when it comes to life. "What's your 10–20, copy?" a man asks over a hail of barking—the kid's dad, I assume. When there is no answer, the father says, "Roger this: the griddle is firing up. The Runnin' Rebs won the toss, and they're taking the field."

The boy returns the light to his magazine. "Please," he says, with an air of boredom and indifference aimed at me, his father, and life in general. I have nothing deep to add, so I go.

When I open Marty's door, there is a giant snake, but I try to act cool. The room's darker than I expect, though I can clearly see the snake cage takes up a third of it, framed floor to ceiling with studs and chicken wire, and there is a faint smell of cat piss. Marty is shaking the box of scorpions. He holds it to his ear, his eyes roaming the room, looking right past me as he listens. He squints some, smiles. Satisfied, he sets it on a junk-strewn desk without opening it. Marty doesn't need to look in that box just yet, either.

Jimbo reloads the bong and holds it out to me. It hovers between us, and I do not take it. In less than a year, after I fail mythology and the doors of Futron are chained shut, Jimbo will kiss me, awkwardly, on the neck, in a secretary stable named Fuddrucker's. Even now, I look at him suspiciously. He knows I don't smoke, and this stoner's etiquette is only for Marty's benefit. The snake hangs from a ceiling beam at the edge of my vision, its skin the felt green of a Vegas gaming table.

"Go for it," Marty says. "Bong up."

Again, one eye points down, and the way he has to look out of the top of it humbles him in a way I don't expect.

Over the intercom, the dad says, "The Rebs are kicking off." Marty ignores him, even though the barking in the background makes it sound like his father is being eaten by wolves or something. With the static on the intercom, I imagine a man on a radio in Africa. Or a pilot with hydraulic trouble, cutting up with the tower.

There is a Polaroid taped to the wall, and I know this must be Tasha. She's everything I hoped she'd be: posed in a skydiving dragsuit, her chi-chis are perfect, even through billowy orange nylon, as she stands above a dark and sleeping DC-3.

I nod toward the photo. "Who's the fox?"

"That's Tasha, the love of my life. We almost died together."

"That when you messed up your face?"

Jimbo looks at me like, *You fuck, we had ground rules.*

"Car crash," Marty says.

"Rough deal," I tell him. "Jimbo says you can't remember most stuff."

"Some stuff."

"At least you had Tasha." We glance at the wall. "You couldn't forget her."

Marty's not sure if I'm dicking with him or not. "She says we were just dating before the crash, but I know it was more than that. On the outside she was a stranger, and I couldn't say much about her life, but I knew her, you know?"

Marty says this, and my head wanders across eight time zones, a continent away. I find myself looking through the snake cage to the wall beyond, thinking about the boy in the next room.

"It doesn't bite," Marty says.

"What?"

"Its mouth is open to check you out. It has glands that can see your heat."

Sure enough, the snake's mouth is open. It has three loops around a pine ceiling beam, and it screws itself down some, tail sucking up into the coil of its square trunk, head unreeling to arc closer to my heat.

"What's with the snake?" I ask.

"It's hard to explain."

"Let's feed it," Jimbo says.

"No, it ate last week."

Jimbo lifts his eyebrows. "Meow," he says.

"Meow," Marty says.

"What about the caiman—you still got the caiman?" Jimbo asks Marty, then looks at me. "Wait till you see the fucking caiman."

I think of the Cayman Islands, which my mom says is the worst route there is. After Tammy dies, my mother covers her schedule there for a while, but she won't even speak of the layovers. *They don't have any laws down there,* she says. *You will never know,* is all she tells me. But after a couple years with Ted my mother changes her tune, and they even pop over to beach bum a time or two. Tammy is never pulled from under the D.C. river ice, and Mom likes to say Tammy's really just laying low in the Caymans, high on piña coladas and that special light they have down there, playing baccarat with the boys at the Royale.

Marty sees the confusion on my face. "A caiman's a kind of crocodile," he says, "from Central America."

"You have a crocodile?"

"It's a kind of crocodile."

"Bullshit."

Jimbo smiles.

We go out back to see the caiman. There is a blue pool with green patio furniture, all surrounded by silver fencing that leads to the base of the bluff above. Everything looks cool, my hands are in my pockets, and the sun is bright in my eyes. Then the wolves come at us, sprinting across a triangular yard of close-cropped yellow grass with their long necks down, their rolling haunches kicking out behind them. The chain-link fence between us isn't even chest high—four, four and a half feet at best. When they reach the fence, they are coming over, I know it, and the assault at hand is something I feel first as a rattle in my breath and then as a loosening in my veins. Instead, they plunge to the base of the fence, legs splayed, and snap at us out of the sides of their mouths as if they are chewing the metal sprinkler heads.

"Shut those damn wolves up," Marty's father says from the patio. He is shirtless, in swim trunks, basting a mounded platter of meat with a sauce-stiffened brush, the kind you use to paint a house.

"They're only half wolf, Dad. Half Mackenzie, half malamute."

"I'll kill them, Marty. I swear," his father says in a soft way, speaking to meat he dabs with care.

For now though, the wolves are barking machines, vicious and ceaseless, noxious as tire fires. Marty walks, arms crossed, past the pool, until he stands looking down over the short fence in admiration at their snarling faces, as if big, mean animals were a rarity in this world.

Jimbo follows suit. He kneels before the fence and touches their wet noses whenever snapping teeth catch in the chain link. In a sweet, childlike voice, he insults them. "Come to Daddy, you iddle widdle teethy fucks," he says, and pinches a nose, prompting one wolf to reel back and pop the other's folded ear.

"Christ," Marty's father yells. "Leave the damn things be. It's Saturday. The Rebs are playing." The woman who first answered the door slides a blue-screened TV out the kitchen pass-through, and Marty's father turns all the knobs on the intercom, shouting "Game time" into every room.

Because of all the *Wild Kingdom* episodes I talk about, my mom tells Ted I'm a big nature fan. One Sunday morning at the SkyLounge, he brings me the gift of a "Safariland" snow globe he says is from Africa, though there's something like Safariland in Florida, too. The globe features plastic cheetahs, giraffes, and gazelles in brown grasslands, racing full hilt into a surprise blizzard. It is *Hecho en Mexico*.

So I'm suspicious of the wolves, which are at once completely unreal in this Vegas backyard, yet so obviously dangerous I feel it in my toes. To a lesser degree, I feel the same way about a family barbecue, which is something I've never been to.

Somehow satisfied with the wolves at hand, Marty stares up at the imposing rock formations above. Out in the bright light of day, the scars on Marty's face pronounce themselves with the clear slickness of sexual skin. I follow his gaze up to the communications tower, and the hard throb of the red light on top hypnotizes me. It's the red light I look for with my current meter all day at Futron, and this red seems right, the way, after looking into a million circuits, you can just feel when one's going to go reject on you.

Above the tower, a jet splits the October sky, wavering and adjusting on approach to LAS. Its nose floats much lower than a DC-9. This is a Lockheed L-1011.

I know the outlines of airplanes because, at sixteen, I spend a weekend making marker drawings of jetliners and quizzing my mother as we sit on a gold-comforted hotel bed in Michigan. When she gets all the flash cards right, I know she will pass her United test in the morning and move to Detroit the following week. The L-1011 is an easy one: its wingtips curve up at the ends, so from below they look cut off.

Ted tells me he can fly a jet, if push comes to shove, if that's what it comes down to. I don't have much to say to that. The statement somehow implies my father doesn't have what it takes, when it comes down to it, which is why he may or may not be dead. I tell Ted there's a god of flying. Rickimus maybe. Rick something or other. Something-something-rus, for sure.

Marty's father tries a softer tone. He is standing at the grill with a long fork, and the heat from the coals is enough to distort the edges of things, to make the brown of the roof and the blue of the sky trade places for an instant. "Come on, Marty," he says, "bring your friends over for some grub. The Runnin' Rebs are playing. They're your favorite. They're playing Arizona. Remember that big game against Arizona a few years back? You loved that game."

"We're just going to look at the caiman, Dad."

"Why can't you leave that gator alone?"

"It's called a caiman, Dad."

With a fork in one hand and the platter in other, Marty's father lifts his arms in a shrug of indifference. "Whatever. I don't see the attraction. You tell me the appeal."

He throws the meat on a grill so hot the steaks bounce; they squeak and whine. The wolves go crazy over this. They too let out short, high moans, like children.

The sounds remind me of a nature program I see one night that sticks in my head for reasons that will remain unclear until I eventually meet Ted. On the show, a man walks into brown savanna chewgrass to reconstruct a takedown. From the dirt, he collects whitened ribs and hocks and knuckles. He examines them, noting teeth and claw marks. A horn, he decides, is an important clue. A soundtrack of feasting hyenas plays as he points at trees and hills, deciding how many predators, direction of attack, strategy, and carcass distribution. Then this man looks into the camera. *There's no rest for the hungry,* he says. *So come, let's see what the lions are up to,* and we watch his Jeep drive off into the plain, the bumper folding down tall grass that springs up behind him, and he is gone.

Ted tells me he has my father's binoculars, which are all that's left. He's been meaning to give them to me.

Marty nods a forget-him look toward his father and leads us to the caiman. Jimbo's eyes light up at the prospect, and we walk, hands in pockets, in our natural order—indifferent, disruptive, and doubtful—along pool decking bordered by chain link and wolves that cut their faces trying to take our ankles.

In the other corner of the yard is the most ridiculous thing I have seen. Another chain-link fence, complete with posts and gate, stands a foot and a half tall. I mean, it doesn't even come to your knees.

"You're kidding me with this," I say.

"It's all you need," Marty says. "Caimans can't climb."

"This is such bullshit," I tell him and make a show of stepping over the fence, rather than through the tiny gate. Jimbo follows my lead. We cross tan gravel that crunches under our boots, stop in front of a lone blue kiddie pool. There is no shade, just brown and blue.

"There it is," Marty says.

"Did I fuckin' tell you, or what," Jimbo says.

Inside the pool floats a four-foot reptile, motionless, with a thin, tooth-rimmed snout. It can't weigh thirty-five pounds. Its eyes are cataract-black, and it doesn't even seem to breathe.

In life, some things will come clear to you. There are the knowns—the exact video-feed frequency that unscrambles pornography, for instance, the foot-pounds of lift inside the hot, distorted edge of air cutting over a 737 wing, the speed at which your mother endlessly circles the city in her gold Cadillac after your father leaves, or the way young dictators are known to buy stewardesses drinks in the lounge of the Cayman Royale.

And then there are the others, the things that aren't so easy. There's the boxy loop of youth, a decade that leaves your ears ringing with television and loneliness. There is the way Tammy's body becomes one of the "urecoverables" beneath the D.C. ice. Then there's an overbright morning at the SkyLounge when Ted mentions that, technically, I might have a younger brother in Africa. Eventually comes a moment you accept the not knowing, like a first step into the blue, when you must trust the shifty cliff gods to see you down.

I stand and stare at the reptile. Reflected in the water is the tower above, the deep ruby strobe seeming to beat from the caiman itself. "That's totally fake," I say.

"Come on, look at it," Jimbo says. "There it is."

"Fumble," Marty's father calls out to us. "Check it out. Rebs're first and goal." He is sitting in a folding chair strung with nylon webbing, beer and fork in the same hand, but he's watching more of us than the game.

The wolves still sprint along the perimeter of their run, frothing and clipping, their legs tripping them into balls that tumble, roll, and emerge as charging blurs.

"The Rebs are going to reverse. Hundred bucks says it. Remember when I taught you the reverse? You weren't even ten."

"Sure, Dad."

"The Rebs are gonna go for it. Bring your friends over and check out the game," he says, and when we don't respond, he stands up. "I'm telling you to leave that stupid thing alone."

Marty and his father have a moment when they eye each other across the pool. Jimbo leans in close to me, his mouth hovering by my ear. "I dare you to touch it," he whispers. Signals I don't understand pass between father and son. Marty's father then heads for us, walking barefoot and stiff-legged around the pool with his beer, throwing dirty looks at the ceaseless wolves. He, too, steps right over the fence and walks gingerly, arms out, over the rocks. He comes to stand beside me at the edge of the kiddie pool, so that he has to yell past me and Jimbo at his son. "What's the fucking deal with this thing," he says. "Show me the appeal. It doesn't do anything. It just sits there."

"I think it's fake."

Drinking his beer, he glares at me like I'm an idiot. "What's the point? What's the big deal? You got a car and a girl and a family. Your favorite game's on. There's steaks and beer. You do fucking remember what steak tastes like, don't you?" He stops and turns toward the wolves. "Shut up," he yells.

"Dad, I'm not hearing you now, not when you're like this."

I stare at the caiman that hovers in the water, unblinking, legs out, heartbeat red.

"I'm with him," I say. "What's the point?"

"There is no point," Marty's father says and kicks the side of the kiddie pool. The sides yaw and wow with the waves, and the caiman, frozen, rides up and down. "See?" he says. "It doesn't do anything."

There is no motion from the caiman, nothing.

We look from the pool to Marty's father as he knocks back the last of his beer. "Watch this," he says and leans out to drop the can on the caiman's back. There is only a hollow sound when it bounces off. "Boy, what a barrel of fun this thing is. I'm glad it takes up a third of our yard. I'm glad I can't sleep for those fucking wolves, too."

"That's it. We're leaving," Marty says, as if this isn't really our plan.

I look at Jimbo, who shrugs. "It's fake anyway," I tell him.

Without taking his eyes off us, Marty's father shouts "shut up" over his shoulder. "Where do you think *you're* going?"

"To Fly Away."

"You're going to Fly Away?"

"Yeah."

"Well, the rest of the family will just pal around with the gator then." He leans out, dips his toes in the pool, and splashes water on it. "I *know*, 'It's a caiman.' "

"You don't know anything about me," Marty says.

Marty's father puts a hand on my shoulder for balance. With this touch, things suddenly become real for me, and my eyes shift from the hand that grips me to the bare leg below it, swinging back into the blue of the kiddie pool.

This is how a toe comes off. When it happens, it is simple: a sound seems to come before the water even moves, the cracking of a wet sheet maybe, and the caiman rises in motion, turning, too

fast to take in. The light changes on the water, there is the popping sound of a hock joint, and I feel fingers grip deep into my
shoulder. Then Marty's father turns from us.

We all just stand there as he hobbles across the gravel, and we
watch what is to be one, slow lap around the pool, alone. As he
moves past the pool's shallow steps, the blood starts in earnest,
and when he rounds the deep end, we can see his big toe is hanging by a flap.

He moves slowly, foot and heel, foot and heel, looking up at the
sun. We have never seen so much blood, and as he passes the
wolves, they go crazy with it, heads pressed against the chain link,
eyes rolled back, rear legs digging in place.

He says something through his teeth, something we can't make
out, and looks back at us. He comes to the diving board, but instead of going around, he labors over, arms out, in hard-placed
steps. Up, off balance, he stares down his yard, the charring meat,
the Saturday this is. He looks back at us again.

"Who are you?" he asks. "What are you doing here?"

He comes down hard, half stumbling, and this is when Marty
and Jimbo rush to him. But I don't rush. I look at that caiman, the
red strobe warping across its back and the curve of the blue bottom. It sits motionless, rocking in its own wake, and it looks more
fake than ever. I get the urge to kick it, too, but I don't have the
guts.

When I catch up, they are in the garage, lowering Marty's father into the Chrysler. The goal is to elevate his pumping foot on
the dash, but they are forced to settle for the open throat of the
glove box. Jimbo turns to me. We are standing by the trunk, giving
room, and I really think I will be invited along with the family to
pace and fret in the emergency room. Instead, Jimbo unzips his
pants and spreads the ears of his fly to reveal the white of his
Jockeys. When I realize he doesn't want to take his dope to the

hospital, I just shake my head and unbuckle my pants, looping a thumb in the elastic of my underwear in anticipation. Jimbo reaches deep into his groin and fishes out the sweaty bag of weed just as Marty's mother rounds the fender. Her shirt reads: RUN, REBELS, RUN!

They all load up and drive away, leaving me looking from the dark garage out into the overbright harrows of sharp-cornered tract homes, and I am alone in a stranger's garage. On the wall are spray-painted silhouettes of missing tools—wrench, hammer, plane—just the empty hooks, and I become aware of the cool air on my legs, pouring from an open door, past me through the garage and out into the world.

"They gone?" a voice asks. I'd forgotten about the boy.

There is a white plastic intercom near the garage door, and I push the button. "Yeah," I tell him, "everyone left."

Out back, I find him balancing a plate of burned meat as he drags a patio chair around the pool, where he parks it in front of the wolves. Except for deeper pockets in the pool-decking, the blood is turning dark and colorless, the dull metallic of high photography or the platinum-black of some fish—a bullhead or drum, maybe—that you see on *Freshwater Sportsman*.

I pull up a chair and join him, our feet outstretched to the edge of the fence, a move that leaves the wolves insane with rage, slathering each other's necks, roaring at our faces. The boy throws a piece of meat over the fence, and it just disappears. I, too, grab a fillet and loft it over the short fence. All you see is the sudden white of upstretched necks and the falling punch of the throat that gets it.

We lean back in our chairs then, staring straight at those wolves with our heads cocked in a lazy, curious way.

"What'd you do yesterday?" I ask him.

"I don't know," he says.

There are gods who are raised by wolves, but I don't recall the details. It was one of the seventy-three questions I missed on the midterm.

"You'd think they'd get tired of this."

"I think it's the waves from that thing." The boy nods toward the tower. "That's what drives them crazy."

Above, I hear another bird on approach. Wobbling in, it seems to nearly clip the tower.

Bird is a term my mother first picks up from Tammy when they're flying the Cancun-Kingston-Cayman triangle eight times a week. It is outbound from Jamaica that my mother's bird, an MD-80 wide-body with bad fuel lines, drops seventeen thousand feet over Cuba. Tammy, with her overtan skin and tired blue eyes, tells my mother that drops happen, that you can learn to love the thrill.

I look up at the flashing tower, and this boy's radio-wave theory makes a certain kind of sense, but the mystery I'm trying to solve is what in the world keeps these wolves from coming over the fence.

The stupid part of this story is that the next day we all still go to Fly Away, Jimbo, Marty, and me. It is late afternoon when we arrive, the sun setting over the Vegas strip as we wait before a big muraled door out back by the Dumpsters. Its painting depicts a free-falling woman, limbs out, hair rushing up like fire, and, knowing this must be her, I study the tight body and thin scowl until the door opens to reveal its model, Tasha in the flesh, looking bored and irritable in yellow goggles and a signal-orange jumpsuit. I see the artist captured nearly perfectly the sullen indifference in Tasha's eyes, which can't be easy when you're painting in big jugs and winking lashes.

She eyeballs Marty and shakes her head. "You owe me."

We follow her in the back way, where we sit in preflight until the last paying customers of the day leave and Fly Away is ours. Between rows of echoing lockers, we strip to our underwear in front of her. Marty still has a quarterback's body and Jimbo's an ottoman of a man, but at the sight of me Tasha shakes her head, hands on hips, and decides I'll need a red drag suit, extralarge.

"Where'd you get the scar?" she asks, eyeing my sternum.

"I was a kid," I tell her. "I took a tumble."

Jimbo and Marty bake the last of their dope through a toilet-paper tube while suiting up slowly and without conversation. Tasha sits on a metal stool, watching as I strap into that red suit. She fixes her earplugs, removing then replacing them.

"You don't talk much," she says, licking the tips of the plugs before screwing them back in. "Not that that's bad."

"What's there to say?"

She leans forward, points at her ear. "What?" she asks.

Finally she leads us to the control room above the flight chamber, where she presets the engine with a bank of digital switches and relays. With little fanfare, we follow her downstairs to a round chamber, where, in a two-hundred-mile-per-hour wind, I fly. The padding on the walls is red vinyl, rolled and tucked, like the choice upholstery of an old Cadillac. Hovering over the wire mesh that separates me from the motor, I don't try any flips or fancy moves. I just float eye-level with those who hug the sides, waiting their turns while I take too long, as I am held transfixed, staring straight down the maw of a DC-3.

For the others, there are stunts and bloopers, amazing vaults and gymnastics from Tasha, but I don't really see any of it. After thirty minutes, the engine winds itself down, and we wiggle off our helmets to reveal sweaty, matted hair. Marty and Jimbo compare flight stories, gesturing with their hands like fins, their voices echoing with the strange sound in there, and I don't feel so hot.

Tasha comes over and places two fingers on my neck, clocking my pulse on her watch. The move surprises me at first, but there is purpose in her fingers, and I sense she knows what she's feeling for. She leans in close for her reading, and at this height I can watch how her ribs finger her suit when she exhales.

"You take everyone's pulse?"

"Only ones that look like you. They gave us a course on it." She nods at the motor below. "You know, heart attacks."

"Nothing's wrong with my heart," I say. "How do I look?"

"I've got that same scar on my chest, so save the story."

"From the crash?"

Marty just hears the edge of this but pipes in, "Don't get her started on that crash."

"Shut up," she says to him, and then turns back to me. "You're okay. You look good." She adjusts her fingers on my neck, pushes harder.

"We're going on a smoke run," Marty says, stripping his flight suit clean off, right in the chamber.

"Sure," she says. "Whatever."

Jimbo comes up to me. "Right back," he says and tries to do the complicated shake with me, leaving my hands fumbling to keep up. Jimbo punches the air and tokes an imaginary joint before the two of them cruise, half-naked, out the padded door.

Tasha slides her fingers from my neck to my helmet, which she pats. "Your pulse is strong, rising some, but fine."

"That scar—really, I was a kid. I fell on a rake."

Tasha sits next to me, throwing a leg across the padding. "Mine was heart massage. You know what that is?"

"That must have been some crash."

"I used to be a cheerleader. Can you believe that? What was I cheering for? I don't even see the point now."

" 'Cause you saw the other side?"

"The other side of what?"

"Jimbo says, you know, you saw the light."

" 'The light?' What an asshole."

We hear Jimbo and Marty bang a locker closed in preflight, and Tasha and I stare at each other. In our minds, we are both mentally following the dopey boys through the corridor, down the stairs until they pass a painting of Tasha that will wink them through a self-locking door, and we almost hold our breath listening for the sound of the exit's electric deadbolt.

"You wanna see the light? I'll show you light," she says.

Using a time delay, Tasha programs the motor for topspeed, 240 miles per hour, to get us off the ground together. On the wire mat, she lies face down, arms and legs out, and tells me to lay on top of her, so that we are stacked and spread-eagled, both with a view down into the DC-3. I immediately begin to swell in my dragsuit, and I know she can feel me harden. The pneumatic starter motor whines into life, and as the radial cylinders choke and sputter before firing up with authority, the lights turn out, leaving us in absolute blackness, something she must have programmed, too. With the sudden dark, Tasha says yes, and, given the earplugs and air pressure, it is more a vibration through our ribs than a sound.

There is no noise or light as the propellers clap up to a fast throttle. The ground simply falls away, and we rise, riding a column of air like a life raft on roiling, black breakers. Tasha does the balancing with her arms and I just hold on, wrapping around her, letting my fingers interlock her ribs, run the raised line of her breastplate scar. Mostly, I just hold on, but as my eyes start to adjust, I begin to see a faint light. From the dark engine below comes a coppery fire, the green-black glow of its hot cowls, and into this I look for a first glimpse of the future. In air hot and black as jet, this minor light speaks loud to me, winks at me as I feel Tasha reach back through the dark to unsnap the crotch flaps in our suits. She yells something I cannot hear.

I enter her without ceremony, and we screw spread-eagled, through wind-whipped nylon, the rattle making Tasha's flesh feel hard and fibrous inside, like the slick white, gumlike meat of coconut. In the wind tunnel below, the motor's buttery fire is the only light we have to guide us, and we fall endlessly toward it, like the path-dangling shimmer of a tree viper's heat pits, the golden Isis beetle burrowing beneath the Valley of Kings. I am a cliff diver, held midleap. I am between engine and ice, green felt and craps, hovering between the untrue city and the coming flash. Close by is my father, night falling, high on endorphins, somewhere after the bullet but before the hyenas, the constellations overhead forming themselves not into giant bears or crabs, but silver Jeeps, celestial banana clips, a great gavel. Of the hard, wheeling lights above, my father's eyes make out Ladder, Lariat, Fleece, and Sickle. From the stars of Serpens, Scorpio, Leo Major, and Lupus, he sees the Burning Chariot, the Lesser Wing, the False Book.

Tasha has her feet looped around my ankles, and she's elbowing me in the ribs, to fuck harder, I figure, so I jostle my hips as I am supposed to, yet I feel nothing. Losing my senses, I drift closer to my essential state: coupled and bound with someone I cannot see, hear, or feel. It is in this state—floating, hungry, tethered—that I have a moment of clarity, a vision: I see a resort permanently frozen in glass, like a "Wish you were here" diorama in a snow globe, with plastic figurines of those who people my life, while around them whips a constant category-three storm. If there is a heaven or hell for Tammy, it is the same place—this hot tub she reclines in, with enough chlorine to burn her hair blond again, while above tumbles a sky of yellow masks, complimentary Tanquereys, and wheeling black boxes. On a white towel, my mother sleeps under this sun, margarita gone warm. Of Ted, there is only the red tip of his snorkel as he examines bright fish trapped in clear blue plastic. And driving blind through a storm of seismic charges, MP badges, and Togo masks is my father, one hand on the wheel, the other holding binoculars focused so that everything near him is overblown and blurry, so that all beyond is bathed in tempting, miraculous light.

The storm around me, however, begins to subside, and our column of air becomes unsteady as the engine tires down. While I'm still inside Tasha, we slowly settle on the wire mat, lightly bouncing from its spring as we begin to gain weight. I don't know if I came in her or not. I thought there'd be that white flash, the divine light, so to speak, but I may have missed it.

Finished, we strip out of our sweaty suits, and, naked, skin red-streaked, we lie facedown together on the mesh, letting our forearms dangle through the squares of wire. We let it go quiet, and above the smoldering engine, the aluminum sounds of our breathing echo from its turbines, mingling together, so that it whispers back.

Tasha shifts so her breasts swing through, and above the pale ticking blue of hot manifolds, we both let our bladders go, our ears following the urine as it dribbles to crackle and hiss in the blades below. The glowing steam that lifts, a fog of pissy vinegar, drowsily mumbles to us with our own breath, and it is the first true ghost I have seen, though there will be others.

"There it is," she says. "There's your light."

This is the point of the story where I'm supposed to tell you how everything works out and then hit you with the big picture. I'll give it a shot.

It turns out that, after three operations, Marty's father loses half the foot to infection and later he sways when he stands. Jimbo shakes his head as he tells me this on the last night I see him, when I go to his house to watch *Speedweek*'s coverage of LeMans. *Speedweek* puts me in a bad mood because there are too many commercials. There are no breaks or second halves in the real world. You can't call time-out at two hundred miles an hour. Around lap four hundred, Jimbo returns from the kitchen shirtless, holding two Millers. Smiling, he asks me if I'd like a beer with head.

The Runnin' Rebels go on to win the conference title.

Mythology isn't for me. Right before I fail, though, as an aside, the teacher says something I remember. *Of course there are no gods, really,* he tells us, which surprises me, because I'd gotten used to the idea. But it makes sense. I know there's no great hand that shuttles jets safely down or suggests to scavengers that they find other meals.

Ted says he hears from somebody who hears from somebody that my dad is caught bartering military radios for low-grade emeralds in Tanganyika and is deported by the British. They say he makes it out of Africa A-okay, but the more I get used to Ted, the less I trust him. Back when we first meet, when I am nobody in his eyes, the truths come hard and fast. Now I see Ted often, and he no longer says things like *Tough break* and *Face it.* Assuming he's ever even met my father, which is still in question, Ted's little stories suggest a bigger truth: he's begun to care enough to lie.

Some days, sure as the sun, I know my father is dead. Others, I hear his Rover circling the oil-field perimeter wire full throttle. I see him on a drilling platform set in a sea of chewgrass, scanning heat waves for signs of motion between the drilling towers, his fingers running in and out the focus of his brass-bound marine binoculars. Maybe he studies the sky, impossibly blue, or eyes distant villages, rising phoenixlike from the tawny-rose savanna clay. Of course he sees women, bronze from this distance, hair dyed like inky wine in the evening sun, as they move their burdens silently along the horizon.

The best version of things I won't be able to imagine till later, when I am alone in a way I didn't know people could be. I move to Acapulco, where cliff diving at night is all the rage, and on Friday evenings, Ted and I sit with tourists in silence as we follow bodies that drop through darkness into a pumice-colored sea. On some Sundays, Ted teaches me target-match shooting on the brown plains just beyond the brochure-beautiful mountains of coastal Mexico. Ted's pistols are of tournament quality, quiet and firm in your hand as they snap and ring the distant silhouettes. On these mornings we leave the church bells and take his Jeep up the winding mountain roads, past Chidiaz and El Agujero, to the high, grassy plains that extend into the heart of mid-Guerrero. The fields whip in the wind, and we shoot into the brown waves whenever the red targets flash through the grass. Ted never produces my father's binoculars, but it doesn't matter. We walk into the scrub to see what we hit. We examine the targets, decide angles, hit-and-miss ratios, and then walk out of the brush together to the Jeep, parked on a ridge that divides our view of the world in three: a khaki run of grass, a thin strip of indigo ocean, and the sky, palest of blues.

Ted thumbs the indentations our bullets make in silhouettes of pronghorns and lions and boar. He looks at me hard, in a way he has never done before. He squints. In Africa, Ted tells me, gods live in animals and trees, even in things like tables and radios. There is a big problem over there of gods taking human form and sleeping with women. The god then changes back, and the woman is alone, but for the boy that is born things are worse: he's a semigod, with small powers he doesn't understand, and like his father, he's a roamer, with one wing in heaven, one foot on earth, doomed to wander toward every distant mud city that appears golden in his half-divine sight. His real father might be a bird or storm, sea-beast or lion, so this typical young man, Ted says, must learn to find his fathers where he can.

This story Ted tells me is a good one, though I'm sure he's probably making it up. I don't remember my mythology teacher lecturing on this topic. Ted does have a point, though. You can't go around talking to trees and radios. You must learn to live with the unknown, never taking your eyes off it, but not growing used to it, either. For instance, from this vantage, it looks like these cliffs deadfall straight into the ocean's abyss. But there's a strip of land between the ledge and the surf that you can't quite see from here. You'd have to listen for the church bells or smell for the meat smokers in the market to know this stretch of shore is below. You'd have to use all your powers, because in life you can count on the most important things being beyond your knowing, like a decade you can't remember, a lost younger brother, or this hidden beach where your mother's villa is, where she sleeps late after flying all night through turbulence.

THE JUGHEAD OF BERLIN

The doors to my heart get kicked down in the middle of the night, and I wake still dreaming of muscly ATF agents with black cargo pants, lean haircuts, and tough-luck smiles, so that when my father comes down into the game room, I am sitting up in bed, hot. He flips a bank of light switches at the foot of the stairs, making the darkness buzz as the fluorescent tubes hum-up. I begin to make out my father, crash helmet under arm, the Jughead of Berlin.

He can't sleep some nights since he quit drinking, and he doesn't seem surprised to see his daughter awake, either. Judging by his spent eyes and wild hair, he has had the same dream about Bureau of Alcohol, Tobacco, and Firearms commandos, though for different reasons.

"So you're home," he says, as if he's surprised to see me in my bed.

I roll my eyes in the stuttering light and reach for my flight goggles. "Like I'm some alley cat slut or something," I tell him. "I wasn't even dreaming about sex."

"Maybe we should ask Randy what he's dreaming of."

"I'm a complete virgin, Dad."

He grunts once, which is military for *likely*.

Germany is where my father and his friends were stationed during the Cold War—where he learned "importing and exporting," as he puts it on his tax forms—and though I never learned what he did to become the Jughead of Berlin, the name stuck, and Berlin is all I've ever heard him called, even by Mom. When people phone our house and ask for Charles Primeaux, I hang up—it can only be a bill collector, a lawyer, or even the ATF themselves, who sometimes ring up impersonating lawyers and collectors. Everybody in Coubillion Parish knows Berlin.

I've taken to sleeping in the game room, and I do so in a shimmery emerald chemise. I swing my legs out of bed, and over green silk, I pull on a thick jersey and jeans, then start to lace my duck boots.

Berlin takes in what remains of his game room. There's been no gambling down here in the year since they made the riverboat casinos legal, and though he's pretty much accepted that his past life is over, he still calls it his game room. Here he was once the top pit boss in all south Louisiana, but tonight he just shakes his head at the red-foil wallpaper and boot-blacked windows of a room that now reeks of *Petit-Chou*, the stupid perfume I've armed myself with in an effort to snare Randy.

Sobriety and poverty have made my father newly interested in my affairs. From nowhere, he says, "For God's sake, Auddie, put on a bra."

"What? I'm wearing a sweatshirt."

"We're going flying. There's a lot of G forces involved, stuff you don't even know about." Berlin acts all pissed, but his voice is closer to a whisper. He'd be better off crashing another plane than waking up Mom, who's been preparing the house nonstop since we got a tip that we might finally be served a warrant this week.

"I think they mentioned gravity to us in school, Dad."

"And don't go rolling your dang eyes."

I silently mouth *yes sir.*

He walks away at this and starts fumbling with one of the slot machines we have to ditch before the raid. He grabs a silver dollar off the bar and takes a pull. Seven Bar Seven.

He taps another silver dollar on the bar, then looks at me. "So, am I going to meet this boy before he points a gun at me on Sunday?"

I come up beside Berlin, lean against the poker pit railing. I take a dollar and spin, pulling Bell Cherry Cherry. The slot machines are old, from Cuba, with burnished silver casings and hand-painted tumblers—green stars, black bars, crackled gold bells. Berlin's probably going to bury them tomorrow, and I don't know how I'm going to sleep without them in quiet formation around me.

"First of all," I tell him, pulling again, "the ATF won't even let Randy touch a gun yet, and second, I invited him to our fish fry tonight. You'll like him."

Berlin looks away, then meets my eyes, meaning maybe he'll like Randy and maybe he won't, meaning he's not going to speak to the possibility yet.

As the tumblers stop, three silver horseshoes align, sending a brief stream of Kennedy dollars into the pewter hopper below. But this is not luck. Our family has gotten where it is in this world by knowing the future. In back of each machine, below the scroll-work, is a little screw that adjusts how much it pays out.

"Couldn't we keep one of them?"

He grunts. "Hell," he says, turning. "Let's just fly."

We make our way through the abandoned blackjack and booray tables toward the garage, half-shielding our eyes from what is an all-too-bright past. Except for my bed, it still feels like a bayou

version of Vegas in here: fleur-de-lis carpet, wet bar, twin ice machines, a row of banker's lamps, and a brass smoker's companion
that now holds the keys to the '69 Super Sport I'll drive with abandon after Randy agrees to escort me to the Sadie Hawkins dance
Saturday night.

"I figure they'll come in through there," Berlin says, nodding
as we pass the double side doors that lead out to the back parking lot.

I picture a wave of ATF agents and Gaming Commissioners
busting through my bedroom door with bright lights and loudspeakers in a raid no one's supposed to know about. And of course,
bringing up the rear, in black body armor, will be Randy. He's the
captain of his JROTC unit at school, but he's really into the ATF.
They have a program called Future ATF that lets you do tons of
ride alongs until you pass your entrance exams.

I come up and screw with Dad's hair, which pisses him off,
though he's kind of a sucker for it. "You're still the king," I tell him.
"You're the Jughead of Berlin."

"Yeah, yeah," he says.

In the garage, I peel back the car cover to check out the Super
Sport while Berlin hunts for his aviator glasses through engine
parts strewn across oily workbenches. Though he's sold his cargo
planes, it's hard to imagine they'll run without all these pieces left
behind. He's been rounding up his tools because he starts as a
mechanic for Grumman at Chenault Airfield next week, going to
work for the first time since he left the air force ten years ago.

The Super Sport's paint job, under the droplights, is beyond
black. It's like you spread black jelly across the Chevy's curves. I
crouch to stare into the fenders, and they are almost teary with it.
When you reach to touch, you don't even know where the car will
begin, the paint's that deep, and this girl reflected in the black
enamel looks a little older, a solid seventeen, with force and direc-

tion. This is the girl Randy's after, and I imagine him riding shot-gun as they race down parish back roads, his surplus Airborne boots on the Super Sport's dash, her wrist brushing his thigh as she shifts for fourth.

It's like cayenne in Lycra pants, this thought, and I have to look away from the dark mirror of the quarter panel. Daydreaming like this is what screwed up my spirit drill last night at the wrestling meet. Just the sight of Randy warming up in his blue-and-silver Fighting Catfish tanksuit. Beyond sexy. Those leather mat booties, and that headgear they wear? He had me. I mean, he was practic-ing hammerlocks.

I come up and lean against the workbench. Mixed with jet en-gine bearings and platinum spark plugs are superblue feathers, left from when our garage was filled with blue hyacinth macaws, the rarest birds on earth. Berlin's old air force crash pack is piled among the junk. I run my hands over its black nylon, picture my father's cargo jet cutting out over Bulgaria or something. Inside are bandages, fishhooks, a crusty bottle of iodine. The pack smells like old mosquito repellent, which somehow makes me think of Randy.

"So, did they give you suicide pills in case the Russians shot you down?"

"Suicide pills?" He shakes his head. "Who would put suicide pills in a survival kit?"

"Just asking," I say.

"Look," he says. "The closest I came to the enemy was shooting white russians at thirty thousand feet while airlifting New Year's vodka to all the boonie NATO outposts."

I strap the crash pack over my shoulder, and it feels pretty tough.

Berlin finds his flying glasses. He rubs the yellow lenses with a shop towel, then holds them up to the work lights, okays them.

"So this raid," I say. "It's like a sure thing, right?"

"We'll go stay at Aunt Clara's a while."

"What's a while, a week?"

"You just worry about school," he tells me. "Worry about learning your Spirit Squad routines, about not letting the other girls down."

"Those girls? They're so fake. Those are the girls who wrote 'stay the same, never change' on my cast when my arm got broke. What's that supposed to mean? All they care about is *Juniors Rule!* And crap like that."

Berlin walks to the sink to wash his oily hands. Talk of my arm usually shuts him up, but not today. "Seems to me that if you cared a little more about juniors ruling, your precious Randy wouldn't have lost his wrestling match last night," he says and reaches for some *Fosforpuro*, a Mexican soap that's illegal here because it's bad for the environment. Totally ignoring me, he starts lathering his hands.

On the shelves above the laundry sink are packages of Chiapan fireworks and bottles of sea turtle oil from Belize, leftovers from thousands of transports Berlin's made down south. Mostly, the cargoes were unexciting—charter down archaeological supplies or missionary Bibles, then bring back frozen Argentinean crawfish and tins of fish eggs. But sometimes there were raw emeralds, vials of curare, or nearly extinct birds.

The well pump is slow tonight, and he looks at me like it's my fault.

"The Spirit Squad's stupid," I say. "So I can pom-pom and do the splits. What good's that going to do me in the real world?"

He turns the trickle of water off, though his hands are still sudsy blue. "You don't let your friends down. That's what the real world's about."

Berlin looks for a clean rag to wipe the greasy soap off his hands, and I hand him my Spirit Squad sweater from the laundry pile. While he works his hands clean, I stare at taped-up photos of airplanes on runways hand-cut from exotic scenery, aerials of Toltecan waterfalls and Montserrat, afire.

Then he realizes he's oiling up my white Spirit Squad top. "What'd you do that for?" he asks. There's a flash of anger on his face, quick then gone, like when Randy hears the word *Waco*.

I shrug.

"Look," he says and hits the garage opener. "Next week this will all be over." The garage door hinges screech in a way that used to drive the macaws crazy.

"Next week, I'll have a regular job, and we'll be normal, like everybody else."

The governor used to duck hunt with my father. Exxon sent us Christmas cards. On Sundays, the sheriff would drive the parish prisoners out to mow our lawn. But since Berlin crashed our sea-plane last year, we've entered a world where it's hard to say what will happen next. According to Randy, the ATF doesn't worry about things like planning: they give you Level IV body armor, Mylar riot gear, a pouch of shock grenades, and then they point you toward the unknown.

Walking out the door, I grab my Spirit Squad minimegaphone off the dryer. During sports games, I'm supposed to point it at the crowds and convince them that we're going to win, though we usually don't. Today, I decide, I will become an ex-Spirit Squad leader.

It's full dark outside, with a slight breeze, so that wandering mist from our lake is pushed into the orderly rows of our small pecan grove. The driveway is really a levee that divides the marsh grass from Mom's victory roses, and we walk along a lake-rim of cypress knees. I spin the minimegaphone by its wrist strap. Throwing things out of airplanes is cool for a while, but then it wears off. So this is not like some huge gesture or anything.

The pecans canopy the drive, so that when they sway, dew comes down in volleys. It is sweeter than water. It sticks to your eyelashes, tastes of tonic. Berlin goes through all his jumpsuit's zippers to see what he may have left in his pockets last time out— a habit from his gin days. He finds gum, and we chew together so we'll be able to clear our ears on ascent.

Someone crunches through the shale ahead, and out of the mist appears Doc Teeg with a bait bucket and a fishing rod you can telescope with the flick of a wrist. After Teeg's wife left him, he backed his four-door pickup to our lake and dumped all her belongings to the bottom in an effort to create the kind of artificial reef that trophy-size sportfish prefer. He figures a thirty-thousand-dollar donation of Limoges china and Rochefoucauld silver makes Berlin's fishing hole part his. My mother won't speak to him.

He hails us, and first thing, grabs my forearm, rotating my ulna while feeling deep with a thumb. Doc Teeg's not a doctor anymore, though he set my arm last spring and is tracking Berlin's stomach and liver. Now that they took his certificates, his work is free and you don't need to make appointments. His bedside manner is better since he became an ex-doctor, the same way Berlin became a better father after they took his pilot's licenses and he left the fame of his gin.

Doc Teeg finds the fracture line with his thumbnail, and tracing it under my skin almost makes me sing.

"Berlin, I hear your girl half-nelsoned herself quite a wrestler last night," Teeg says, like I'm not even there.

"Don't start on Randy," I tell him. "That little wrestler rappels out of Blackhawk helicopters."

Berlin ignores me. "We'll need that big-ass pickup of yours today."

Teeg squints, feels deep into my arm with his fingertips, as if he's imagining my fracture from the inside. He's chewing gum, too; he looks me in the face, jawing it. "Auddie," he says, "your arm isn't strong enough yet to go taking on any championship wrestlers. I suggest some daily wrist exercises to get you in shape for any big matches you've been planning."

Berlin lifts his hand to cut him off. "Stop it with the wrist talk."

"Rehab the problem area with an up-and-down, circular motion."

"Teeg," Berlin warns.

"I'm talking about fishing," Teeg says and snaps his rod to full length. He mock reels in a big one and smiles. "I'm prescribing fishing therapy for the girl's wrist."

Doc Teeg owes my father four hundred grand. Or it's the other way around. They don't talk about the money the same way they don't talk about the reason Teeg can't practice medicine anymore or how my father became the Jughead of Berlin.

"You just bring that truck by," Berlin says.

"Where's that dog of yours?" Teeg asks me, meaning the dog he lost to Berlin at cards two years ago, a blue-merle catahoula pighound named Beau. Beau's fast and wild, and my dog by default. The little advice I have to offer the world, at age sixteen, is to never name a dog Beau because it will never learn the word *no*.

Sometimes Teeg really misses that dog, and my dad's not against giving a man his dog back, especially if it might be in lieu of four hundred grand. It's that Berlin believes you should remember your screwups, so he tries to keep his past life within sight, but just out of reach. It is on this thinking that he gave me the keys to his Super Sport. This is also why, I believe, we strap on our gear and go stunting in his last airplane on these nights he can't sleep.

From behind his gum, Teeg whistles a call I could never do, one he says he learned during his triage field training in Stuttgart, and through the dark trees come the sounds of Beau thrashing in the distance, bounding our way. This means he'll probably chase us down the runway, snapping in the prop wash.

For a moment, we are held by the noisy rush of Beau, charging the underbrush for us. Berlin and Teeg seem to hear in this ruckus something I don't, as if the dog were fetching something they'd rather not see again. A couple years ago, these two'd still be drinking this time of night, bright-faced and loud in the poker room where I now sleep. This morning, though, they have little to say, and we part before Beau arrives. Doc Teeg rolls off alone toward his ex-wife's possessions and a dog that's no longer his, while Dad and I head down the levee because we fly only in the dark, under the radar.

The old Custer biplane sits at the end of our strip, acock under a musty tarp. We peel back the canvas, draining water pooled over the twin cockpit holes, and then check the fuselage for cottonmouths, even though you can smell a cottonmouth ten feet away. Berlin had the Custer painted the same black as the Super Sport, so on nights we're out over the Gulf, the underbelly of the wings take on a deepwater cast, like the unborn, sea-black of caviar.

Berlin hoists the tail around so the Custer points down the dark void between trees, while I wipe the windscreen and pull control cables. There is the squeak of ailerons, a high whine from the air starter, and soon blue smoke pours from the cowling as we jar down a strip I'm supposed to keep mowed. The grass is tall enough in some spots that the prop blasts us with a faint green mist, more the smell of itch than anything, and in one stroke, we lift and roll south over the dark pine stand, charging out of a shallow fog into a moonless sky that's star-chart clear.

I plug in my intercom. "Check."

"Check," Berlin says and points the nose due south, the stick in front of me leaning toward the Gulf of Mexico with my father's ghost hand.

We rise above a Louisiana lost beneath spring sheets of fog, and as long as we're under a four hundred-foot radar ceiling, the curve of the earth is ours. Being an ex-pilot has its beauty. There's no flight patterns, tower clearances, or radio commands. Forget inspections, insurance, manifests, and checkouts. Licensed pilots aren't allowed to buzz their friends, land on parish roads, or sleep at the controls, the reason we're up here in the middle of the night.

The Custer levels into perfect air, sharp and pressing, tinted from below by the husky smell of rice fields and a lingering mildew from the biplane's canvas seats, while ahead is the pristine scent of a high-friction, hardwood propeller, infusing salty air with the finest mist of motor oil. This was Berlin's first airplane, and though he at one time owned thirteen, it is his last. The license-revoking event is no secret. This time last year, he lifted his ten-seater Bonanza seaplane off our lake to take a group of oil executives fishing in the outbank islands. The men had driven late from Houston, were in our game room all night, so when they climbed in the Bonanza at dawn, they all beamed with drinky exhaustion and the kind of elation gamblers get after risking lots and coming out even.

I was eating breakfast on the dock when Berlin lifted off and banked over me. Water from the floats rained on my eggs. I never went on those fishing trips. At home fishing's easy—we *know* where they are—but on the Gulf, you can spend all day with no idea if you're in the right place. You're just casting out there, blind. Where's the fun in that?

All this is public record now. Flying over the Atchafalaya Basin, Berlin scanned for forecasts. Civil Air Radio called for midlevel clouds, thickening, with winds fifteen knots from the east, and the Coast Guard broadcast a muddy chop on an outbound tide. Berlin reevaluated his fishing strategy. In these conditions, the big tarpon fish would go for shiners and not the shrimp he'd brought. There was also a general call for more alcohol, so Berlin decided to put down and change bait.

Descending through a haze of gin, my father set the seaplane down on the number two runway of Thibodeaux Regional, causing a crash that seems filled with certainty, destiny even. Clear and beautiful, it was the last sure thing in our lives, and I see it often:

The Bonanza floats in from the west. White egrets lift from the runway ditches, and banking away, beat each other's wings. The hull, swan-dive smooth, hovers close to the asphalt, touches. Lacking landing gear, the plane's breast digs in, flipping the craft, so that everything assumes an unintended motion: Propellers knurl. Orange tackleboxes burst. Fits of ice magnify the light. Dried fish scales, glued to the bait coolers for years, are freed—they litter the air, stick to people's lips. Graphite rods flex, coils of monofilament unspooling. And then there are the lures, poised midair; jewel-eyed, cut from iridescent polymers and tensile steel, they teem like African insects. At last, belly skyward, the fuselage smokes with the near-ignition yellow of smoldering fiberglass. On the ground, shrimp flip and turn in puddles of hydraulic fluid and bourbon. For a while, there is only Johnny Cash, American hero, Berlin's favorite.

No one got off easy. The FAA entertained accounts of gambling and drinking. The Gaming Commission was called, and the ATF, whose year of subsequent investigation will culminate in a secret raid, forty-eight hours from now, give or take. The airport tower faces an action for clearing a marine aircraft to land, and there are rival lawsuits against Berlin, who surrendered his flying permits and hangar privileges, but not the bottle, which remained until my arm got broke.

Berlin puts the Custer through some brief drills—a slouching roll into a double barrel, a nose-up loggerhead—as we pass the twin trellises of the Intracoastal bridge that mark the edge of the Lacassine Wildlife Refuge. A brackish mist pushes over the lip of the ocean ahead. The stunts make my stomach drop, and the roll makes all of Randy's half-nelsons, cradles, and reverses suddenly come back from last night. I picture him working out in black body armor, teaching me arches, tucks, and bridges on a blue mat, his hands training my muscles to respond to a host of new moves. Randy's been a junior twice now, so technically he's a senior, which means he's past head games. He's way more mature than other guys, like the jerks on the squad who are always hiding your spirit basket. He's also a transfer from Oklahoma City, so he's not into all the high society and clubby-club stuff at school.

"About your friends," Berlin says, his voice sudden and crinkly over the intercom. "The girls in your squad. Promise me you'll make it up to them, because friends are what it's all about. You're a cripple without friends, a blind man."

He gets all soupy like this when we fly.

"You're right, Daddy. Friends are the best."

"We're about to find out who our friends really are. You'll see. In a couple days, you'll start to see."

"See what?" I ask. "What are you talking about?"

"Keep your grades up," is all he says.

Soon, we are over the ocean, flying under a sky the slick and grainy black of soaking charcoal, while beneath us the ocean is a milky, vinyl black, close to the Super Sport's upholstery, but undulating, like sweet crude oil. I raise the minimegaphone and imagine its long pink swirl to the rollers below, coming to rest under all that water like the possessions of Teeg's ex-wife or the booty of the pirate Jean Laffite. To the east, the horizon begins to faintly glow, which lends a sense of urgency to my officially becoming an ex-spirit leader. I'll still know all the cool girls, still get Randy, but not have to attend all those stupid rallies, and forget the Honor Code. It feels like I should shout something profound into the minimeg, but I can't think of anything. When my hand enters the sharp wind, it is simply taken from me, my hand left stinging.

Ahead are oil exploration platforms half lost in banks of fog that mark the edge of deeper, colder water. The blinking towers rise above the amber-glowing domes below, and I begin to make out Berlin's faint snoring, thrumming off and on in the headset. The engine, too, has settled into a perfect drone, more a changing pressure in your ears than anything. In this fluxing hum, I hear the cooing of the rarest birds on earth, sleeping in our garage until they are wholesaled out.

Taking the stick, I put the Custer into a slow-banking one-eighty. School starts in an hour, and though I'll have to wake my father to do the actual landing, he'll have his rest until then. The gin is gone now, and there's nothing to fear from sleep.

School is half day because of the Junior Crush Rally, so it's *parlez-vous*, hypotenuse, *The Red Badge of Verbiage*, and then Randy driving me home in his boss Jeep. We bark out of the senior's lot and lay flame past the cafeteria and gymnasium where the snare drum corps is psyching everyone up for the game and Sadie Hawkins dance. Suckers, I think, though I catch my lips moving with the distant Spirit Squad drill.

Rolling down Broad Street, we pass taxidermy shops, drive-through daiquiri huts, and Cajun J-Jon, the portable toilet storage lot that marks the edge of town. We shortcut across ML King Boulevard, our jerry cans sloshing with fuel on the train tracks, and I can tell Randy's in a bad mood. He's hunched up, steering with his elbows so he can crack his knuckles by bending each finger back.

"Listen to this shit," he says and glances at me. "The sixteen-inch barrel of an assault weapon is rifled at 1:32. What's the rotation of a bullet passing through at eighteen hundred feet per second?"

He's wearing a black tee with an open, brown JROTC uniform shirt over it, so that when his fingers pop, I can see the little wave of his pecs and a jump in that vein in his bicep. Brown polyester whips in the wind. I can smell his skin.

"What?" I ask. I'm in a pixie skirt, pleated to hide my thighs.

"Bootleggers cut sixty liters of eighty-proof rum with fifty liters of water. What proof results? Can you believe it? I'm sniper school material. My night vision is off the scale. I mean, I could have my ATF tactical badge today, but I got to learn this shit?"

Strewn across the backseat are coils of black rope.

"I'll tutor you," I tell him. "I'll be the answer to all your questions."

He glances up at the sky, smiles. "You gonna teach me Spanish, too?"

"You gotta learn Spanish?"

"Yeah, they say the whole future of the ATF is about Mexicans. They showed us this current events video. If you had seen this chart they had—by the year 2035, America is completely shaded yellow, with red zones in every major city."

"What's all the black rope for?" I run a loop through my fingers, feel the heat.

Randy trains his brown eyes on me, blinks back to the road. Past the fire station, we hit open road and pick up speed.

All his antennas start to sing. "Special ops," he says.

"Kinky," I tell him, and he kind of blushes. Behind him, the rice fields are a blur of gray-green water, and I wonder if he has any idea about the raid on my house or whether he's just not letting on to the fact that he'll be holding the flashlight when the advance team pulls me from my bed—in the semisheer emerald chemise I ordered special from Baton Rouge—only hours after he's kissed me goodnight from the dance.

This thought, combined with black rope, makes the cords in the back of my neck go electrical, and I know I should have joined the Future ATF instead of the stupid Spirit Squad. I want my ATF outfit—Gore-tex boots, black Kevlar, a Spectra assault suit with chemical-proof panels thick enough to stop sarin nerve gas, yet still elastic enough to let you kick for the throat.

"I got the Super Sport for tomorrow night," I tell him.

"About tomorrow."

"I know, I know. You haven't officially agreed to take me to the dance or anything, but my dress, forget about it. It's a black silk skirt over a skin-tight catsuit."

As we near the gates to my drive, we pass Jim Green, riding his bicycle at the edge of the road. Jim Green's the most powerful man in south Louisiana, and Randy's head turns as we pass him.

We park down the road a bit, and Randy leaves her running. I get out and lean against the Jeep's grill, which is papered with the wings of dragonflies. I can tell by the way he puts his hands in his back pockets when he gets out, how he places his feet just so in the shale gravel in front of me, that he'll try to give me another excuse.

"Look," he says, "I'm eighty-five percent sure I'll have tomorrow night off."

Randy works some nights as a watchman on an oil recovery vessel parked in the Black bayou.

"My dad can have that boat sunk by tomorrow," I say. "Towed to sea and burned. You don't believe me, but believe me."

Randy smirks. "Maybe it's more like ninety percent," he says. He casts a weary glance at the bicycle pedaling toward us. "That's James Green, isn't it? The former gravity drainage commissioner?"

The gravity drainage commissioner approves all building permits. He can rezone your house while you sleep, revoke water-table access, run a bayou through your land, or declare your property in a floodplain. Everyone must deal with him.

"Yeah, my dad and those guys all went to the Cold War together."

"They have a video on James Green in current events."

"Sobriety is their only current event. They flew high in Germany, that's for sure. Then they ran southwest Louisiana for a while. Now, they drink a lot of coffee."

"No offense, but your dad's had documented problems running boats, planes, and cars, let alone the eighteenth state of the union."

"You can't even manage taking me to a dance."

"I'm coming to your fish fry," he says, "and we're at ninety percent, okay?"

This is the point where he's supposed to kiss me. I'm assuming he wants to kiss me. I've got him loosened up, joking, but he glances away, wishing, I think, that I'd kiss him. This is half of why I'm sweet on him. But I won't let him off the hook.

"Bring a fishing pole," is all I tell him before he climbs in his Jeep and burns out, leaving zaggy trails in the shale.

Jim's brakes squeak him to a stop beside me. "I used to have a Jeep just like that," he says.

He dismounts, and we walk across the big grates that mark our property. The grates are made to break the ankles of cows that try to cross, but there's been no cows on our land for years.

"I presume that's the Future ATF boy Teeg told me about," Jim says. He wears a bubble-head helmet and Spandex cycling shorts tight enough that you can see his noodle, but he has dark, intense eyes and a silver tooth that will give you *les frisons* when he flashes it at you.

"He won't go to the Sadie Hawkins with me," I tell Jim.

"An obvious fool."

Ahead through the trees are the muffled sounds of an engine revving and the clipped barking of Beau.

"You sure that raid's this weekend? I mean, couldn't we get it moved back a week? You can make a call or something, right?"

Jim thinks a moment on this. A storm blew through last week, clearing all the dead wood from the pecans and live oaks, and the downed branches give like dry sponges under our feet.

"Wouldn't it be easier to get the dance moved back instead?" he asks me.

"Oh, I don't know," I say and stuff my hands in my pockets. He sounds pretty dang casual considering they raided his offices earlier this year. Though he knew they were coming, he didn't realize they were going to tear the place apart. All his fish died and his carpets still stink like pepper gas.

Around a bend in the drive, my father stands next to Doc Teeg's dually pickup, which has obviously just seen a rut. Brown water still drips from its panels, and there's about a thousand pounds of mud-splashed slot machine in back. They've been driving around our property unlocking all the old gates so that the ATF doesn't knock our fences down. My father's pants are wet, though Teeg's are clean.

"Shotgun," I call.

Berlin sits in the back seat with Jim as we drive down to throw the slots in our lake. I change all the radio presets while Teeg talks to my dad about Beau, the two of them eyeing each other in the rearview mirror.

"I'm just saying, maybe we should tie him up. I don't want him loose with all those people running around," Teeg says.

"Nothing's gonna happen to Beau," Berlin tells him.

"A man doesn't want his dog to get shot for no reason."

"He's not your dog anymore."

"Shot?" I ask.

"Whoa, whoa," Jim Green says. "Slow down now. From what I gather, there's a newer, friendlier ATF out there, one committed to nonlethal means—concussion canisters, caustic sprays, stun wands, and so on. They're not into bullets anymore."

Teeg opens his mouth to speak, but from above comes the drone of an airplane, and we all power down our windows to lean out for a look. The trees are thick though, so there's nothing to see.

At the water's edge, we back down the creosote planks of what was the seaplane dock. Our lake is really a long, open area where twenty miles of marshlands drain into the Coubillion River. The water is brackish, the color of chicory coffee, when it empties from the wetlands, but now, as the tide pushes seawater in from the Gulf, it is gray and cloudy with a shimmer to its surface, like hot fish broth.

Teeg drops the tailgate, and he and my father both hitch their pants before beginning the work that will erase the last traces of our past lives, that will be a final step on our year-long road to lame-o.

But before the first slot gets the heave, my mother appears in flower-print overalls, carrying a roll of duct tape and smelling of the heavy lemon wax she's been using to seal her cherry buffet, sidebar, and secretary. In the past two days, she's put down carpet runners, draped the antiques, and packed her grandmother's Rutherford crystal and Celine service for twenty-four.

She walks right by me, moving with deliberateness past the pylons. When she passes Jim Green, his awful bulge clearly outlined in those shorts, she lifts a hand in disgust and says "please."

She halts before Teeg and Berlin.

"It is enough," she says, "that my dining hall has suffered under green felt, fake gold trim, velvet wallpaper, and spangled flooring. It is sufficient that thirty men are to tromp through our house in short order. But that's my friend's china off the end of this pier, and you're not throwing your foolish gaming machines atop it."

Teeg closes his tailgate, carefully latches it. He tips his cap and nods to her.

"Don't you sheep me, Doctor," my mother says. "I know all about you. I was at those officers' parties, if you'll remember. I could read a German newspaper, too."

We hear another plane, faint and pitched, high in the bright haze above.

"Smile for the birdie," my mother says, but nobody looks.

I cross my arms and turn toward the water. The straight-on sun gives an illusion of great depth, and for the first time I wonder what else is at the bottom of that lake.

Six hours later, we are again on the end of the dock, this time in lawn chairs, fishing for dinner. The sun shines low at our backs, casting our outlines on the water. The lowering tide is draining the marshes, drawing currents rich with shrimp, bait crabs, and fingerlings into our lake. This is the time when gar and specs swim up the river to hunt in fast schools. But we're after redfish today, and Berlin has decided that light, temperature, and water-clarity all dictate the use of the simple gold spoon. Randy has joined us, and we cast flashing spoons in turn.

To keep from crossing lines, we have established zones: Berlin casts to the left of the dock, near shore, at ten o'clock; Teeg casts at eleven; my mother fishes over Mrs. Teeg's china at noon; I aim for one o'clock, while Randy must fish over the submerged slot machines we ended up dumping along his bank. The air holds the rotty smell of raw cane, and we drink Junior League tea, sweet enough to fur your teeth.

Randy and I have our shoes off, our pants cuffed, so when I swing my legs, our feet brush. Randy keeps snagging his lure. He tugs his line all different directions.

I'm afraid we'll pull up some strange article of Mrs. Teeg's, a brooch or brassiere she's been missing out in California.

"You say you're from Kansas City?" Berlin asks Randy.

"It's Oklahoma."

"Certainly, Oklahoma City," Berlin says. "Do much fishing in Oklahoma, son?"

"I can't say I got the opportunity."

Teeg asks, "So, what do they do for kicks in Oklahoma?"

"Terrorism, sir."

"Oh, boy," Teeg says and chuckles. "He's good. This boy's good."

"Don't mind him," I tell Randy. "He's pretending he's drunk for old times' sake."

"You know what the problem with the ATF is?" Teeg asks Randy.

Randy casts again, reels, pays great attention to the motion of his lure.

Teeg says, "The problem with the ATF is they eat too much mustard."

Berlin laughs.

"Boys," my mother says. She lifts a hand for silence, then squints as she feels the fishing line between her fingers. She cocks her head, eyeing the tip of the rod, before jerking it back to set a hook in the first redfish of the day. I dig through the tackle until I find the balloons and begin blowing up a medium-sized red one.

Berlin lands the fish and pays out six feet of line from his rod. Using the hole from the hook, he carefully feeds the line through the fish's lip and knots it, so that the fish has a stretch of monofiliment tied to its mouth. On the other end of the line, I tie the balloon and we let the fish go.

"What are you doing?" Randy asks.

I look at him funny. "Fishing," I tell him.

The balloon wanders haphazard into open water until it falls in with the rhythm of its school, and we watch it slowly backcircle around the lake.

There's no use casting until the school heads our way. Berlin rattles the ice in his tea. Teeg whistles long and loud for Beau, calling him for the feast of fish guts ahead. I put my hand on Randy's shoulder. He gives me this look, where, instead of shy, he looks older, like he's not sure he wants to get caught up in me because I'm only sixteen, like he thinks I'm going to be a lot of work.

When the balloon hunts its way around to the dock again, we know there are dozens of redfish, seventy or eighty, ghosting by under the surface. We all cast in volleys, the fish striking left and right.

Randy loses a lure on the submerged slot machines. He has to cut his line.

He's a little offended at the ease with which we land fish, I can tell. He keeps swiveling his head when someone's rod bends under a new weight. Every time a fish is netted and thumped with an oar, he shakes his head.

"What the heck does my line keep snagging on?" he asks.

"Don't be a sorry sport," I tell him.

In ten minutes, we have a dozen fish in a five-gallon bucket. Berlin starts cleaning, while Teeg skins, scales flying everywhere like lost contact lenses. I help my mother fold chairs because it's getting dark.

Randy still holds his pole. He nods toward the lake, where a balloon skirts through the current. "What about that fish?"

We all just look at him.

The next night, Saturday night, I stand in front of the mirror, upstairs, in my old bedroom. You can smell the old sheets, standing yellowy on the bed. On the walls hang my father's worn-out flight maps—Cuba, Cayman, the Dominican Republic—places that captivated me when I was younger. In the mirror, my lips are *Soft Chenille*, my nails, *Cosmopolitan-7*.

It's past seven thirty and still no Randy. I know he never promised *100 percent* to take me to the Sadie Hawkins', and for about a 5 percent chance, I have been to my mother's boutique in Lafayette, where homosexuals rubbed my scalp and conferred on how long my roots should burn. For maybe 10 percent, I let two Vietnamese women paint my toes, bought polka-dot stockings, and then doused myself—down my neck, along the backs of my arms—with *Petit-Chou*.

Who knows if there will be a raid tomorrow. Downstairs, I hear my mother loading china into the trunk of her Lincoln for the trip to Aunt Clara's, and from various rooms in the house come the sounds of Berlin opening all the old wood-frame windows and propping them up with dealers' canes. I lift the folds of my black skirt and let them fall, watching the sheer silk return to my legs in the mirror. The truth is the side slits point to my hips. I undress, folding everything into a garment bag, and put on a jersey and jeans before going down into the garage to pull the cover off the Super Sport.

Inside, the seats are soft as glycerin, the old leather smelling both sharp and sweet, like the limey mint of a julep. Clipped to the visor is a photo of my mother, young, in Germany, and next to that is the garage door remote, which makes me hear those birds again. I creep out of the garage on idle, and even though I'm just driving around to the front approach, you can feel the thumping pressure of the engine. The SS floats, hood raking, when I touch the gas.

At our front landing, I back up to my mother's Lincoln so the cars are parked trunk to trunk. She's loading watercolor paintings into the backseat when I climb out. All her potted flowers have been pulled out onto the porch.

"What am I going to do with these orchids?" she asks me, then realizes I'm in jeans. "Oh, honey, he's not going to show, is he?"

"Randy's busy," I say. "He's got an important job."

Mom lifts her eyebrows. "Looks like you've picked up the fine art of making excuses for the shortcomings of men. From me, no doubt."

"Oh, don't get heavy on me, Mom."

She throws up her hands, which is twice as bad as rolling your eyes, and we start loading up the Super Sport. As I stack cardboard boxes in the trunk, I realize they're not filled with china but ordinary junk like cleaning supplies and closet hangers. Then there's a whole crate of utensils from the kitchen, including a thing of ketchup and mustard.

"Mom, there'll probably be sauces at Clara's. I mean, do we really need to take this stuff? It's not like the ATF is coming here to grill burgers or anything."

"Would you just pack?" she asks. "Just trust me and pack?"

Berlin comes down and sits on the front steps. His shirt cuffs are unbuttoned, and his hair is dripping wet from the sink, something he does when he has a headache. "I opened all the doors and windows," he says, then runs his hands through his hair.

"You drive the Lincoln," she tells me. "Berlin will want to go in the SS, I'm sure."

There's a few more boxes standing on the porch, but I can tell Mom has lost her thirst for loading. Without any ceremony, they climb in the Super Sport, Dad sitting shotgun with a flower pot and a painting of a pink flock of roseate spoonbills.

I stick my head in the window, tell Dad to lean the seat back and get some rest.

"It's no use," he says. "I won't sleep again tonight."

My mother looks like she is going to say something comforting to me because of Randy, and though I know this is how she feels, she only says, "Drive safe. See you at Clara's." She puts the car in gear, but every time she even touches the gas pedal, the car leaps forward, tires spinning, sending a shower of gravel onto our porch.

"This car is simply inoperable," I hear her say, lurching down our shale drive.

When they're gone, I sit behind the wheel of the ivory Continental and clunk it into gear. Though the sky is clear, the air smells of oak pollen and storm, so that lumbering down the drive, I have the urge to turn on the wipers. Instead, I adjust the rearview mirror, aiming it back at our house, which is black, with a deeper black standing in the open doors and windows, waiting for something big that may or may not come.

I follow our weaving, tree-lined drive, and I know before I hit the parish road that I'm not going to aunt Clara's just yet. I'm headed to the Black Bayou, to Randy's oil-recovery vessel.

Flying south a couple miles, I turn onto the Bayou Works road, and across the levee, I can see the silver ship, with its orange rafts and black booms, looking from here like it is parked in a grassy field. A group of oil companies pitched in to buy it in hopes of preventing a Valdez-like spill on the Gulf, but they can't agree on a name or even a color to paint it. The ship sits silent under coats of galvanized primer, fixed to a mooring it has never left. Pulling up to the fence, I hit the high beams and honk.

Randy comes to the gate wearing boots, a black tee, and khaki pants with black stripes down the sides. There's a walkie-talkie in his back pocket. He pulls out a ring of keys and starts trying them, one-by-one, in the gate's padlock.

I hang my fingers in the chain link and look at him.

"They're serving a search warrant on my house tomorrow."

Randy pauses, a key about to enter the lock. "Who is?"

"Who? Who do you think? BATF."

"What for?" he asks.

"It's a long story. Did you know about it? I mean, are you going to be there?"

"Serving warrants is serious business—there's site containment, infra red, metal detection teams, void sweeps. They don't let me near that, and I don't really hear any news. Who the hell am I? I can't even pass my entrance test."

I hold his eyes. I get a feeling from him. I suppose I've always felt it, that he has no secrets, that I can believe him. "There went your one excuse for standing me up."

"Come on," he says, popping the lock. He shakes open the gate.

There's a huge concrete dock with a yellow-striped helipad.

At the edge of the deck, an anhinga dries its wings under the floodlights.

On the gangway, I stop him. "So tell me why you blew me off."

"I had to work. I told you I'd probably have to work."

"You're kidding me."

"You don't get it, do you? I have a job. What if there was a spill? Who'd open the gates? Who'd turn on the deck lights for the helicopters? Someone has to prime the tanks for the recovery crews."

"You should have called."

"What would I have said?" he asks. "You only hear what you want, anyway."

He turns and walks up the stairs. It takes me a moment, but I follow him, climbing behind, up four flights of grating. We enter the bridge, a dark, angled room filled with tall chairs that have shock absorbers and shoulder harnesses. Looking through the windscreen, you can't see anything. It's like being up in the Custer, flying out past the oil platforms, where there are no landmarks and the dark of the sky and the dark of the sea are one. This view has the same spookiness as flying in a dream, when you don't know what's keeping you afloat or how long it will last.

Randy flips all the equipment on and mans the console's island, where a Raytheon radar screen warms up and then ticks out a green-and-blue map, showing everything from the Intracoastal towers to the humped blips of the Sabine power station, thirty-five miles away.

Randy explains how radar works, and I listen, as if I didn't grow up around it.

There is a button-tipped joystick on the console, and Randy turns it on. Somewhere atop the boat a searchlight ignites, and it is like nothing I've seen. Through the windscreen, we suddenly see marshlands unfurl toward open water, while cloud banks drag their asses along glades of sawgrass and cane.

"This thing's made by Boeing," he says.

The light is bright enough to leave insects stunned and turn mist into steam, so that the beam is like a smoky tube extending to the horizon. Randy hands me a pair of pale yellow binoculars, and I follow as he trains the beam on a skiff, far in the distance. On the small boat, deep in the marsh grass, I make out a man with a police flashlight and a compound bow, poaching alligators in the dark.

"He's out there every night," Randy says. "I call Fish and Game, but by the time they get out here, he's gone. That's an endangered species, you know."

He aims the light west, pointing it toward Texas. "There's the city of Vidor, world Ku Klux Klan headquarters. And here's Toomey, dog fights, hate crimes, waterway piracy, and nine unsolved murders this year, a per-capita record, even for Louisiana."

Sitting on the edge of the panel, Randy works the joystick, and as he swivels the light to bear on another target, the beam flashes past a shotgun shack built on stilts along the banks of the Black Bayou. It's the kind of place Mom and I had to live in when I was a girl, during Berlin's first year in Germany. I don't remember that time really—we stayed there a while, then money started coming in the mail, and we moved.

Randy's free arm swings around my shoulders, so that he can better point by guiding my line of sight down his finger. Then he shifts the light toward an orange dome on the horizon. "That's Beaumont, rape capital of America. You ever want to get raped, just go to Beaumont."

"Thanks for the tip," I tell him, but my mind's on that shotgun shack, how my Mom and I lived out of boxes in a place just like it when my father went away, and it seemed like he was never coming back.

"It's a dangerous world out there," Randy tells me. "Did you know strange black airplanes fly around here at night? Then there's Port Arthur, home of Janis Joplin. Three tons of ammonium-phosphate fertilizer went missing there last week, and—"

I take the joystick from Randy, interrupting him, and I point the light back on the little shack. I'm not thinking about lawyers and lawsuits and warrants, but those bottles of ketchup and mustard. That's the kind of thing you pack when you're moving into a little house on stilts, when you'll never see your old house again.

"If you point the light that way," Randy says. "You'll see—"

"Shh," I tell him and study the house, its dangling clothesline, the rusty fish stringer on the rail. This is where normal people live, I think—vinyl siding, propane tanks. Then suddenly, a young couple stumbles out onto the porch. A man, wearing only sweatpants, stands sideways in the light, his hair sleep-wild and glowing, and the light's bright enough to show through the bedclothes of the young woman with him.

Randy flips a toggle, and the beam shuts down. In the dark, he lifts his hands.

"There you go," he says. "That's the kind of thing I'm talking about. You go and do something crazy like scare those people out of their bed, and you wonder why nobody asks you to the dance. They probably think we're aliens."

I can hear Randy, but the afterglow in my eyes only lets me see that girl, forearm braced against the light. That's when I lean over and flip the spotlight on again. I am an alien from outer space, and I've come to abduct her boyfriend, occupy her house, and if I feel like it, maybe even point my disappearing ray at her. It could be all three, and the only thing this earthling can do is wince in the light, hand high like a stop sign.

THE HISTORY OF CANCER

I t was the year we saw bathroom tile as a form of divination.
Sparkling, hard, it held all our answers. My friend Ralph's father came home in the early evenings, covered with white plaster,
and it was our job to haul the tile out of his truck and take it out
back. He never made it easy on us. The tile was hidden under
junk in five-gallon buckets or stuffed in all the drawers of his
toolbox. He had a huge lunch cooler with his name spelled on
the side—FORST—in black electrical tape, and you never knew
what to expect: it could weigh sixty pounds with stolen tile or be
light as orange peels. He pulled that cooler from the cab and
walked up the drive, swinging it, while Ralph and I took bets as to
whether or not it would drop us to the ground when he handed it
over, whether it would take both of us to drag it around back.

Forst had built a tile bin in the backyard out of old planking
and sagged plywood, though to us it was a tile palace, with its long
rows of shelves spilling with ceramics, great heaps of porcelain
so high you had to climb over on all fours. Here we separated
the tiles into mason's boxes and old grout buckets as we sat on

upturned caulking crates and discussed what a man could do with all that tile. It was clear this tile, smooth in our hands, was worth a great deal, and this was a lifetime's worth, enough to wall a gymnasium, though in a hundred different colors. The tile palace was also the place Forst kept his magazines.

Here's where the art came in. To separate tile by color—pink, tan, powder blue—was one thing, and separating by shape—rectangle, hexagram, star-and-diamond—was another, but we separated by kind as well: inner corners, coping edges, facing plates, running trim. No stack of tile was too small in our eyes, and on the back of a shelf alone might be set four, yellow, rectangular elbows. Once in a while, there would be a lone tile. I had a golden-speckled round tile that I carried in my back pocket all summer, and in its burnished finish I could nearly picture the family's house where this tile matched, could almost imagine a house in which there were no odd pieces left over at all.

I was a little jealous of Ralph, too. He had a certain condition that caused his skin to rise when you pressed on it. If you slapped his back, a few minutes later your hand would rise and appear. With your knuckle you could trace his bones underneath, and there they were. Or he would lie on the cool tile as we sorted, and we could both sit transfixed as triangles rose on his chest and stomach. Ralph couldn't wear a belt or tie his shoes, but I wanted that, to be able to react to things that touched me funny. Sometimes Forst beat Ralph with a rope. I'd come riding up to his house on my Huffy and there he'd be, covered with running welts. Ralph would explain that it was because of the magazines or some other reasonable sounding offense, though it was always difficult to tell just how hard he'd been hit. Ralph could welt up from a Hula Hoop. Then again, Forst was the largest man I'd ever imagined, and I'd seen the way he'd swung that cooler.

This was a time of great unknowns for me, and the absolute logic of Ralph's home had me hooked. There were simply no mysteries allowed, and I fell in with that. It's clear to me now that Forst's tile palace was really placed in the one spot it couldn't be seen from the road or the alley, and I can see the sadness and resentment of a man who built a monument to his daily, petty pilferings. I can see that there wasn't enough of any one kind of tile to even cover a dishpan. But inside that rickety bin those tiles held me in awe by their simple mass and order, by the vision of a man who would recognize their latent, unseen value, who would build a house to protect them.

I realize the women in those magazines were Filipino and not Mexican, as we'd thought. Once in a while one of their faces will come back to me, in their offset color and oversharp focus, and those forced smiles and folded bodies will erase where it was I was driving, make me overcook dinner. But in the sweltering heat of the tile palace it made sense that all Mexican women were ready to bend giggling over a bathtub, and we commented openly to that effect. On those hot Tucson summers it seemed only fitting that Ralph and I should both get beatings on a fairly regular basis, and we silently nodded that I'd just lucked out, not having a dad to give me mine. We often discussed in our scientific way the pros and cons of having a dad versus not having a dad, though we couldn't see how clear it was that Forst wasn't really Ralph's father.

What was a mystery was why some nights my mother would move me from the cool of my bed to the hot seats of her Monte Carlo, why we would drive and drive—the Oracle road, Baseline, Miracle Mile—without speaking, why it was the Mexican radio station, the one where we couldn't understand the words, that she listened to. The Monte Carlo didn't have air so you had to choose between wet vinyl and eye-cutting wind, and one night I woke suddenly, sweating, thinking of the pink heat lamp in our bathroom, something that always seemed ominous to me as it glowed and ticked above the toilet. There was dust crossing in our headlights. The road signs were in Spanish. I moaned in a way that always won response from her, but she only cracked my window with the power button on the console. "We're from Michigan," she told me. "We'll get used to the heat."

"Is my dad in Michigan?"

"No, honey."

"Is he in the navy?"

She turned to me, surprise on her face. "Of course not. What's gotten into you?"

"I never been to Michigan," I said.

"Sure you have, honey. We were Wolverines."

I didn't know what she was talking about.

"That's where things got all mixed up, remember?" she said.

"I never lived there."

She sighed. She lowered both our windows so the car roared inside, then powered them up tight. "I know what you mean," she said, after a while.

These were the conversations we had.

My mother was a phlebotemist at the hospital, but once she passed her pathology lab technician exam, the rust-colored iodine stains on her fingers changed to the purple and blue of the enhancer oils from the microscopes. She no longer simply pulled blood. Now she came home smelling like xylene, bright-eyed about sputum cultures and cervical cysts, though she wouldn't explain what words like *ovarian* meant.

The late cruising and trips to the Indian drive-in stopped with the new night shift. Now she woke late and slow, drinking coffee in a pink silk robe with a gold tiger embroidered on back. It read *TigerPak, 11th Sea Command* above the tiger, and below, around its outstretched paw, *Prowlin' the 17th Parallel*. When she'd turn away from me, that tiger could always catch my breath. The robe was something I couldn't get a fix on. I assumed my father had given it to her, though there'd never been any mention of its source. But the image of her—sleepy, drinking coffee, with that tiger always guarding what was behind her—was what I balanced in my head as I did wheelies in the neighborhood until it was noon and I could head to Ralph's.

I was told my father looked like Kris Kristofferson—still does, around the eyes, my cousin claims—and that summer my mother took me to watch the movie *Semi-Tough* five times. The theaters were ice-cold, matinee-empty, and all the soda I wanted was mine. One time a huge man came into the open theater with a tub of popcorn and sat directly behind my mother. It was just the three of us, and I watched him over my shoulder as he ate fistfuls of popcorn with his mouth open. Kris Kristofferson had a woman's neck cupped in his palm, and I could see how my mother's blue fingers twisted the fine hair that curled under her ear. When the man finished his popcorn, he tore a large U in the rim of the tub, so it looked like he'd taken an oversized bite of that too. He turned the tub upside-down in his lap and slid his hand into the slot he'd made. We all watched the movie for a while. Then the man leaned forward and smelled my mother's hair. His nose hovered right where my father's tiger would have been. It was the scene with Kris and that woman in the hot tub, so I knew my mother's eyes were closed.

Ralph had had a girlfriend but she'd died. My girlfriend had moved to International Falls, a site I'd chosen because it was always the coldest in the nation on the weather reports, which from

Arizona I imagined as a place where all you needed to know fell between the lines of a thermometer. By then, I'd also confused Michigan with Minnesota. The sole area of contention between Ralph and me was sex, and we fought like academics over the mechanics of how it worked. This was the reason we'd needed girlfriends: to back up our arguments with personal experience. It was the magazines that had sparked the debate, and it was in the magazines we looked for answers.

Forst had an old camper parked in the middle of the backyard. It was the glossy, aluminum kind meant to be towed behind a pickup and on summer nights we practically lived in there, passing the flashlight, turning the pages, making our arguments. Ralph's theory was this: the woman lay on her back and the man climbed on top of her, so they were face to face. That's how the screwing would occur, he was sure, and he pointed to the sleepy, dreamy looks on these women's faces. Why else would it happen in a bed? I was convinced it took the approach encouraged by the women on all fours. They had a way of swiveling their heads back to check on what was going on behind them that couldn't be denied. In these looks it was practical necessity that I saw, and that appealed to me in a way that dreaminess and mystery never would. Plus there was the way Ralph's German shepherd Hans would jump on your back if you were near the ground. Our views were irreconcilable on the entire matter, but Ralph had to give me that one.

Ralph had a little sister who'd just made the leap from diapers to panties, and we often looked to her for answers. In the yard, we'd strip her and crouch low, gesturing with our hands as we made our arguments. I'd seen my mother inspect cultures in her lab once, and I copied that long, squinting gaze of hers. Ralph was more animated. There was a blue car his sister loved, and when we could get her to crawl after it, we'd follow in a strange, balled-leg walk while he pointed and nodded like a scientist observing a test probe for Mars.

One day, we had her on her back, each holding a leg up in the air when Ralph's mom came out the back door. The first time I had ever met her, she hooked a thumb behind the elastic band of her velour shorts and pulled them down to the stubble of her pubic hair so she could show me her still-fresh hysterectomy scar. This was to demonstrate why I was to stay quiet in her house, make my own sandwiches, and not slam that damn ball against the carport. So I didn't know what to expect when she came out back to see her daughter wishboned by Ralph and the neighbor boy.

Ralph was pointing at the fleshy tuft of his sister's genitals when he wheeled on his mom. "Can't you see we're doing an experiment?"

She let out the kind of staged, knowing laugh you see only in old movies anymore, as if she somehow recognized herself in this scenario of me and Ralph pulling the backpedaling feet of a restless girl. Then she looked at me hard, as if to say it was behavior like this—male, probing, dangerous from birth—that got her where she was today: in sweltering Arizona with a backyard full of dirty tile and kids like us. "I'm through," she said. "Go see Forst if you want to know about babies."

"Babies?" Ralph said. "This is research." He looked at me and mouthed *babies?*

I shrugged. The baby thing I was still unsure of, but I knew it had to do with the glossy fist of a uterus I'd seen in one of my mother's pathology books.

We had no intention of talking to Forst about anything, but they were his magazines, and he became our next object of study. He was an ape of a man, the kind rarely seen these days: chest so large his ribs seemed barely to come round to meet, and even his belly—the *oiler*, he called it—paled underneath what his chest seemed to indicate was possible. But what bothered me was his belly button. It was an outie, and with all that weight behind it, it had swelled to a cone with a nub at the end that wiggled at you like bait.

On days when he came home early, it was *Bonanza* that he watched, a huge tumbler of iced tea resting on the grayed mat of his chest hair, his yellowed feet up on the ottoman. Forst identified with the character of Hoss, though it was a troubling figure to him. He would direct our attention to the screen, pointing out Hoss's deficiencies: his fat hands, the way his mouth always hung open, and of course, that stupid hat. "Why is he always smiling?" Forst asked us. "What the hell is he grinning about?"

It was a question I took seriously, and I agreed with Forst that there was something to that Hoss, that the big cowboy must have a hidden interior. I was considering Forst in this same light when he turned from his show to me. "What the hell are you gawking at?"

Forst was the kind of man to say *Houston, all systems go* before he farted, but I'd also once heard the fast slapping of his belt loops as went for leather in a hurry. Now he seemed serious.

He stared at me. It felt like he could look right inside me, and I took a chance. I asked him if he had been in the navy.

"Semper fidelis," he answered. "Marines."

"What are navy men like?"

"They screw each other."

I tried to model that in my head, avoiding Kris Kristofferson, whom I'd been picturing in a uniform for some time. "From the front or from the back?"

Forst paused on this question. "From the back."

"It really works like that?"

"Everybody gets screwed," Forst said.

About that time, I started watching my mother sleep.

Standing in the bedroom doorway, quietly eating my cereal, I would take her in: the skewed shape of her under fern-print sheets, the hair stuck to her face, the shine of her shoulders, rising and falling, an arm stretched across the empty space where my father would have been. At night I sometimes dreamed I could walk around and breathe underwater. I wondered what went through her mind as she slept off long nights at the lab, a place where she looked deep into people's blood and tissue, gazed into tumors, trying to trace the history of cancer. I envied her for that ability, but I didn't think she stopped to consider that people could miss a scoured lung or bad kidney, that in the hollow left behind, there was only emptiness, or worse, room for stranger things to grow. I didn't think she ever watched me sleep, from my doorway, wondering what I was dreaming.

Finally she caught me. I remember it was the week Ralph's dog died. She sat up in bed and I saw her lab coat was still on. Patting the covers, she signaled for me to sit with her, but I didn't want to. "Have it your way," she said. "But I talked to your father last night." She lit a cigarette, something else that had come with the shift change, while she paused to let that news sink in. "He wants to visit."

She'd used this one before. "When?"

"Soon, baby. Think of it, all of us together again."

"All the Wolverines," I said.

"Don't be like that. It will be good for you, having him around."

"For how long?"

"I don't know," she said. She was still unused to the smoke, and she fanned it from her face, leaning, trying to get away from it.

"You'll love him. He's handsome," she said and closed her eyes for a moment, like maybe she was picturing him.

For some reason, I thought of that man in the movie theater just then.

"What's the point?" I said and went to eat my breakfast.

That week I sorted a lot of tile. I wasn't supposed to be at Ralph's too early, and I remember Forst coming out in his bikini briefs, his hand shielding the bright morning light, to find me in his tile bin. I sat sorting on top of a stack of boxes, and it scared me to be near eye level with him. Once in a while one of the tiles would cut you, so I had a finger in my mouth as we looked at each other. I couldn't explain what I was doing there and I didn't try. Shuffling tiles into bins just made sense to me. They were something to hold. They had weight and purpose. I could see my reflection in some of them. Forst squinted at me for a long time, and then he seemed to understand something and went back inside. We didn't even speak.

Ralph was a little leery of my enthusiasm, but to us things had always been clear: the tiles needed sorting, and the solution was to dive in and get to work. The task was impossible on the surface, but you could picture a day when all the tiles had found their homes, and this knowledge carried us through long stretches of sorting where we didn't speak, where there were only the soft clicks and chinks of subtle progress. At home, there was no preparation for my father. No one vacuumed or cleaned the guest towels. No one whistled the Wolverine fight song. No one found the magazines I looked at, red under the hot bath lamp, as I sweated and stared into the eyes of women who seemed to know the primitive math I was working on their bodies. There was no hiding of a robe for a man who may or may not have prowled the seventeenth parallel.

When I rode up on Saturday morning, Ralph stood staring

at his dog Hans, dead of unknown causes in the mud behind the house. There was a water spigot on the side of the tile palace that dripped, and here was where the dog liked to dig and wallow. To keep him from burrowing under the tile bin, Forst always threw the cracked tiles in the hole, and this is where Hans was, sprawled on the broken shards, tongue in the mud. I approached and we stood silent for what seemed a great while.

"Dang," Ralph eventually said and marched off to get Forst.

Hans's coat was a little past charcoal, near black where his fur was soaked, and lying there, mouth open, gums graying, he looked lost and thirsty.

Ralph came back with Forst, who asked "what the hell?" of nobody in particular, and stood in shorts and socks sucking his fingers. I think he'd been eating barbecue potato chips. He licked the palm of his hand with several long strokes, and then nudged Hans with his toes. Next he kneeled down in the mud and used his thumb to open Hans's eye. "Shit," he said and hooked the dog's upper canine with his finger, swiveling its snout up, the throat falling open, so Forst could look inside. We leaned in close. He sniffed the dog's mouth but gave no reaction.

Forst then touched the dog's stomach delicately, tenderly almost, before putting his ear to Hans's belly, his other arm cautioning us to be still. I held my breath.

After a while he turned to us, and Forst, on his knees, stared straight in Ralph's eyes. "Did I teach you to care for that dog?" He pointed down but none of us looked.

Forst got up and shuffled through the yard in his socks, pausing to search here or there in the grass with his toes, and I was pretty sure he was looking for a piece of rope. Ralph crossed his arms and squeezed his shoulders while we watched, but Forst only kicked around the yard for a while before disappearing.

It gave me the creeps to see Forst like that, and I didn't know what to think. Ralph dropped his arms to his sides after Forst left, and the handprints on his shoulders made it look like he was being held, the way someone steadies you before they kiss you or punch you good. I felt held too, that day, that summer, but I had no such outward way to show it.

Forst returned with a short, hooked-blade linoleum knife and simply opened Hans up. The sawing motion jarred the dog in quick convulsions, briefly animating it. Suddenly, whole volumes of seething, blind worms poured milky pink from Hans's belly. We all stepped back and watched them writhe.

"Jesus," Forst said.

"Dang," Ralph said.

But I said nothing. It was a moment of swirling clarity for me, and I wished I could see the inner workings of all things so plainly, that someone would touch and listen, dig even, for all the strange things I felt growing inside me. I had to sit down. Through the sliding glass door I could make out Ralph's mother standing alone, observing us from the dark of the house. She looked on us as strangers, like she was already trying to find a way to put this behind her as she watched her husband wipe a knife on his sock. Looking at her, I considered the possibility it was a submarine my father was really on, and I hoped he wore a similar face every time he surfaced on the other side of the world.

Ralph's mother balanced a yellow plastic laundry basket on her hip, and through the greasy dog-paw prints on glass door, I could see the the lip of her hysterectomy scar peek out above her low-slung house-shorts. I wanted to go to her, just to touch her maybe, but what good would that do? From the grass, I stared at the scar and wondered if my mom had maybe worked on that uterus in her pathology lab, if she had held it up close in the light and peered inside, or just dry-froze it for cross-sectioning.

THE CANADANAUT

I was pouring liquid argon into a bowl of flatworms when Secretary Mulroney arrived at our lab. He'd flown through the perpetual dark and taken a Sno-Cat thirteen kilometers from a tiny icefield landing strip before snowshoeing blind along frozen lifelines. I was doing some side research on reanimation, and the worms had just begun to crackle and flip in the Pyrex when Mulroney pushed his way through our storm-proof doors, his war medals glowing amber in the light of the heaters.

Mulroney had never come out to our Tundra Lab before, so it was clear something big was up, something far too important to risk using the scramble phone. He stomped his boots and grabbed a pair of red UV goggles—we'd been having problems with gamma rays. Scotty lowered his L-7 analyzer and groaned. Vu killed the dyno-burner and spit on the floor. But I wasn't going to piss and moan. I believed in what we were doing. We hadn't bathed since Boxing Day—that's how serious we were. We all turned to Dr. Q for a reaction.

Dr. Q lifted his head slightly, bringing his eyes to bear on our surprise visitor, as if he knew right there that we were about to begin the greatest scientific odyssey in the history of Canadian weapons development. I looked at Q's eyes, red through the lenses, and then packed my worms into the deep freeze for a week's vacation, at which point I hoped to revive them.

"Gentlemen, I have an announcement," Mulroney said, but as his eyes adjusted to our lab's bright lights, he began to take in the deathray, something he'd never seen in person. He ran his eyes along the chrome transducer manifolds and walked agape down all seven meters of the glass charging tube, humming pink inside with energy. When he neared the radial accelerators, all the metal buttons flew off his jacket and raced for the field dampener, where they stuck in unison. That's living with giant magnets.

"My word," Mulroney said. "It's enormous. It's magnificent."

Even as secretary of the Canadian Intelligence Agency, he'd probably never seen more than a rough sketch from Dr. Q. That's how secret this was. Our supplies were dropped at night by multi-prop transports, and we had no contact with the outside world. I wouldn't even know Q's real name until after the nitrogen accident, until it was too late.

Mulroney stood at the control panel and admired all the switches and relays. It was clear this was the CIA's baby, and we were just building it. Mulroney could pull the plug anytime he felt like, and he didn't have to look far for reasons. First, we were way behind on the deathray—not to mention overbudget. This was 1963, and Canada was tightening its belt. Then we'd wasted a whole year on microwaves, like fools. Finally, we lost half the lab in the rabbit fire. Thank God for Jacques, or the mercurium cells might have burned, and then foof!—good night Canada. But the problems were never ending. We'd get the targeting system running, and then there'd be trouble in beam modulation-land. We'd tune the spectrum stabilizer, and the ni-cad core would degrade (just the smell of cadmium can still turn my stomach). Dr. Q had to invent Level IV polymers just to make the O-rings. Invent them! There was no deathray book. We were writing it.

Mulroney levered the flux controller. He tugged the ropes that opened the exhaust cowling. Certainly he was envisioning a day when brave young Ottawans picked commies off of Siberian tanks with backpack versions of our ray. But I saw the deathray as a tool for peace. We had a chance to make a difference. I mean the whole reason we were building the deathray was so that we'd never have to use it. That's what I was thinking when Mulroney's eyes landed on the big red button.

Vu looked like he was about to shout a warning as Mulroney reached to press it, but it wouldn't have done a lick of good anyway. Vu's accent was indecipherable, simply maddening.

The important thing was to stay calm. Start hyperventilating, and you're sunk.

As soon as Mulroney's fingers touched the button, the copper windings began to crackle green-blue, and Jacques jumped up from the hatch over the flash corrector. He'd been taking a nap in the overload chamber.

"Mon Dieu," Jacques said. "Attemptez-vous me morter?"

Jacques wore buckskin trapper's pants, birch bark boots, and a skunk fur hat. He was the hairiest man any of us had ever seen, and Mulroney winced at his breath, ten meters away.

I'd been feeling uncomfortable since Mulroney's arrival. Jacques was liable to begin masturbating at any moment, and the secretary was the first guest we'd had in years. Jacques called his penis "le baton de joie," which Q said translated roughly as "stick of joy." Without warning and whenever the fancy struck him, Jacques would stand, announce "temps pour le baton," and head for the Sno-Cat shed.

But there was no time to explain any of this to Mulroney. The button had been pushed, and once she was charged, you couldn't stop. What if the core degraded? What if the mercurium cells lost matrix? It was all theoretical at that point, and we weren't waiting around to find out.

There was only about twenty seconds to get a target for that beam. We had dozens of rabbits, but they weren't shaved, and we couldn't risk another fire.

Luckily Q took charge. "Scotty," he commanded, "check the shaved rabbit bin."

Normally Q wasn't much of an authority figure. People didn't take him seriously because of his grooming and posture, but as the huge platinum charging plates began to rattle, Scotty snapped to it. He plucked out the last shaved rabbit—dazed and razor-burned—and tossed it to Vu, who sent it sailing off to Jacques. You could hear the rabbit's teeth chatter as Jacques caught it by the scruff. It is a haunting sound, if you know it.

Jacques moved with deft perfection. He climbed the aft transducer and wormed his way through the hatch until we could only see his tiny feet above the fire wall. Jacques was born to load the rabbit hopper. He was the only one small enough to squeeze into the parabolic targeting chamber. On top of that, he could tolerate incredible amounts of radiation. One time, Scotty absentmindedly left a dish of strontium 90 on the counter, and Jacques, thinking it was table salt (we iodize our own), sprinkled it on his meat. Afterward, Dr. Q scoped his chest, and the rads were off the chart, but Jacques was unfazed, felt nada.

The deathray was warming to full charge, and I knew what was next. Honestly, there was something cold and brutish about the deathray that I didn't like. When her pink power tube heated up and began to vibrate, it gave me the chills. Then there was what lay ahead for the bunny. The first rabbit fire was a real wake-up call. I'd been telling myself the deathray's subjects would just "disappear." But the animals were terrifying when they burst, simply pyroclastic. Someday the subjects would be human. Were a man, sufficiently hairy, to be subjected to that beam—I shuddered at the thought. As for the fire, Q calculated that we hadn't been adjusting for the fur resonance, a frequency that always eluded us, and we were forced, finally, to begin shaving them, which I took as a kind of defeat. You can't shave a man on the battlefield.

The ray let out a brief, piercing whine, and then we all winced at the ghastly sound of our erupting subject.

Mulroney, semi-impressed, got back to business.

"Gentlemen, you have been in scientific seclusion for some time now, and it has become necessary to inform you that a couple years back, the communists launched a fixed orbiting vehicle into the upper atmosphere. Canadian Intelligence believes they named it 'Studnik.'"

We all looked at each other. Mulroney continued.

"Now, gentlemen, our remote Saskatchewan sensing station is picking up high levels of iridium emissions in the upper atmosphere."

We all paused in reflection.

"Iridium?" Vu asked.

God, his accent.

"I bet it's blowing in from Russia," I said.

Scotty, ever the critic, dismissed it as a solar anomaly. "It's just a corona playing hell with the Van Allen belts."

"Ya, but that's about a heck of a place to find iridium, don't'cha know," Vu countered. "We're talkin' about some pretty big dispersion forces, eh."

We all looked at Dr. Q. He closed his eyes and lifted a hand. It made me stop breathing.

He began patting his pockets, searching for a slide rule. I gave him mine. His thick fingers worked feverishly before me, his class ring winking in the moonlight. He asked me to remember the polynomial $VX^2 - 5VX + 3V^2$, and I repeated it over and over in my head, lucky to be the scratch pad of greatness. At last, Q stopped, turned grave. He and Secretary Mulroney exchanged a dark look.

"These are venting particulates from spent fuel," Q said. "The Russians are testing a new engine. A tremendous engine."

"Our worst fears have been confirmed, gentlemen," Mulroney said and then raced out into the cold to deliver the news to Ottawa.

I didn't have much of an appetite at dinner that night. Scotty's pot pies weren't even worth the meter of floss they cost me, and Vu was driving me crazy that danged puck. Dr. Q, my polestar, was lost in thought.

I grabbed my storm overalls and thermos and went for a walk on the ice fields. A man wouldn't last ten minutes up here without a thermos. It must have been minus fifty Kelvin out. Many nights, too many, I would get lonely and walk the vast sheets of ice that swept up to the abandoned meteorology station where we worked. There was something wrong with me, but I didn't know what. Months of continual dark and cold would get me turned around. I'd ask myself, did I graduate top of my class for this? For my dissertation, I created the world's first Gas Amplified Stimulator of Emissions of Radiation. And here I was, in the cold and dark. I mean, one day I wanted to get married and settle down. I've always loved casserole, and Vu was continually screwing up the laundry. A base of operations would free me up to do lots of pure research. For now, though, Q needed me.

That night, I crunched through the drifting banks with my head leaned back. I stared into the night, imagining a whole sky full of Russian studniks, their brassy chests shining boastfully down on me, and I wished I had a GASER big enough to blast every one of them.

On the horizon, I spotted Jacques dragging his traps toward the glaciers, and I trudged after him. He and I had sort of become pals over time. Jacques had been using this old station as a base camp for trapping, and when our team arrived, I was the one who discovered him sleeping among the rotting weather balloons. He leapt up with a thin knife, and in his third-grade French, boasted that he was five feet tall, that I had better look out. I thought he was a barbarian because he seemed to have little knowledge of the metric system. Though he was clearly lying about his height, it was his breath I will never forget—a yellow cloud of vibrating spirochetes rising from the tarry saucepits of hollow tooth sockets.

Hygiene aside, Jacques and I sort of fell in together. True, he was a trapper, and I was a man who needed lots of small animals, but it was more than that. I didn't know a dang word of French, yet we had an amazing ability to understand each other. We had both lived in the dark and cold, knew what it meant to be cut off from mankind, from warmth and companionship.

Ahead, Jacques's snowshoes went still in the ice drifts.

He turned and beckoned me. *"Bon soir, mon grand ami. Allons-y."*

Jacques handed me the bunny sack, and we set off into the dark, tromping side by side through snow so new it squeaked under us. How Jacques found his way, or even his traps in this absolute and featureless dark, I'll never know, and tonight I didn't even try. There was a beauty to this region of Canada that you came to know only through exile, and as we walked, I tried to look no further than the ghostly flicker of our little subjects struggling ahead. It was easier to focus on the little things—the rusty springs, the hempy smell to the burlap bag—because if you let yourself feel the shock of the snow around you, the depth of the black above, you'd be forced to consider the degree to which you truly belonged to this universe. Jacques, with his knotty arms and racked torso, would muscle open the iron hinges of a trap, I'd unwrap the bunny sack, and we'd stave our new guest home before moving on.

I needed to relax, but couldn't. The thought that the Ruskies were up to some new monkey business really got my mind spinning. The deathray was about to take a great leap forward, and as the beam man, it all rested on my shoulders. The next step was to ditch our relatively weak thorium 232 fuel and begin processing the most theoretical of elements. We were going to push the edge of the periodic table. A demon lurked out past the end of row seven, beyond nobelium and lawrenciuim, beyond the mere unstable and volatile theoretical elements. We called this demon saturnium, and Q's calculations showed it would burst into phenomenal radioactive decay the moment it was created. It would be my job to harness this bitch.

On certain nights, when the moon was full, Jacques would bait his traps with salt. This we did tonight, and the whole world appeared elemental: the driven snow was unbonded calcium, the sky was dark as manganese. Our shoe prints filled with somber cobalt the moment we moved on, and ahead, the moraines of receding glacier heads seemed to glow with the lithial blue of radium. We worked slow and sure, measuring our breath between traps, places where we'd chip the old, frozen blood from the pressure plate before Jacques trigger-set a chunk of rock salt that, in this platinum light, was ten shades whiter than snow.

Of course, Jacques got all the salt he wanted from our supply shed, but in years past, when he could scrape no sodium from the thermal vents around Terminal Geyser, he would ejaculate on his traps, letting the semen freeze to the trigger pan. With this *sel d'homme*, or "man salt," he could catch any minx or fox, even the elusive arctic beaver—all specimens sure to carry nasty diseases, if you asked me.

Using my hands, I gestured to Jacques that, because of sodium's single electron valance and limited oxidizing potential, it was impossible for it to produce a smell that might be detectable by an animal. How could an odorless element work as bait?

The old trappers, Jacques gestured, still say the moon is made of salt. He pulled a salt lick from his pack and held it aloft. Animals can live alone in the cold and dark, he continued, but this they need. This is what makes them howl for the moon.

It was difficult to understand him with those mittens on, but it didn't take much to get across the idea of "need" to me. Love felt like some cruel Canadian joke. The bunnies were white. The ice-fields were white. The sky, endlessly aflurry, was blind with white. Through a kind of pantomime, I asked Jacques how the heck animals even found each other in such a place.

"Dans le froid absolu de l'Arctique, avec le cammoflage parfait?" He shrugged. *"Je ne sait pas."*

I wondered, where was my casserole? Where was my slice of the Canadian pie? Wind howled through my parka. I shook my head. "Sorry, but *no parlez*," I told him.

It was a long walk home in the snow, and I arrived to find Q asleep in front of the thermal circulator. I felt the urge to sit with him in the warmth, imagine his dreams as I'd done on so many nights, but it was late. I spread a quilt over his lap, and with my little finger, wiped a faint line of dribble from his cheek.

Even Vu was snoring peacefully as I laid out my long johns for the morning and lined up my prebreakfast vitamins on the edge of the dresser. The last thing I saw before sleep was Jacques through my bunk window, half-naked out on the tundra, murmuring softly to the moon as he masturbated. His shoulders and chest, even through mats of hair, were perfectly defined. Neck craned, head back, he stroked himself in the lunar glow, a light just bright enough to illuminate the pearls of his semen, already half-frozen into globes, as they arced toward the snow.

In the morning, I decided it was best to ignore my feelings toward the studniks and get to work. Jacques could barely keep the hopper loaded. We were a dang fine team on average days, but now we were like mad robots. *"Encore des lapins,"* Dr. Q would yell to Jacques, as Scotty shaved for all he was worth.

Of course, it was hard to brag about the ray, considering we'd soon be needing human-sized targets. Privately, I saw the deathray as a necessary first step in the creation of a liferay. I had a theory about the true state of our universe, a theory so elegant and terrifying that I couldn't even tell Dr. Q.

Basically, it goes like this, and stop me when you disagree: Matter doesn't exist. "Things" are made of energy; atoms are really tiny packets of vibrating waves. The appearance of substance— of "weight" and "shape"—is simply a product of fluctuating frequency. Gravity also is a myth. Popular science would have us believe that bodies are magically attracted to each other by this invisible force. Don't make me laugh. The real force at work here is something I call sympathy, an affinity between energies. In school, you may have been taught that love includes a rubbing of the genitals. Life, however, has hopefully proved this fleshy dance a lie. Love is our clearest manifestation of sympathy, a pulling of equal and opposite spirits. The moon is held in orbit by sympathy. The dancing poodle rolls a ball with sympathy. A man, finally, is only a beautiful, unwavering band of energy. If you could only harness this force.

That night, Secretary Mulroney was back.

"Gentlemen," he said, "follow me."

We tromped out to the Sno-Cat shed, a path Jacques shoveled by hand. The cold made me stiff and weary.

"Behold," Mulroney said and rolled his eyes skyward. "What do you see?"

We turned our goggles toward the dark night above.

I didn't get the point of the exercise. All I saw was our breath rolling upward in a column, my steam mingling with the others', with Q's.

"I don't see a damn thing," Scotty said.

"Ah," Jacques said. *"La lune."*

"Through these lenses," Q said, "the moon glows a ghostly pink."

The moon did seem pink. A shiver went through me.

Mulroney continued. "A communist moon looms, gentlemen. Our Yukon team believes the Reds are building giant engines in preparation for a moon launch. I don't need to tell you the grave military implications of that."

I pulled my collar up. There was no wind. A nameless feeling rose in me. Everything had changed, but I did not know how or why. The Canadian starscape above seemed foreign and strange.

"Naturally, we've had our own secret moonshot team," Mulroney said. "Alpha team has been testing experimental fuels in the Arctic. Yesterday, however, a blue flash was reported in northern Canada, and then communications were lost. We fear the worst. As of now, the deathray is shelved. Men, you are the new Alpha team."

"We'll have to rise to the challenge," Q assured Mulroney.

Jacques could tell by our faces that everything had changed. He looked to Dr. Q. *"Voulez-vous encore des animaux?"* he asked.

"Non, mon petit ami," Q told him. *"Nous sommes fini avec les animaux."*

Jacques eyed again the heavens. *"Quel noir,"* he said. *"Quel infini obscurité."*

And thus began our nine-week odyssey to beat those Russian

faggots to the moon. We upgraded to Level 5 Security, which meant an eleven-hundred-kilometer move north to a remote glacier tracking station. Now our supplies would be dropped at night by black parachute, and we were only allowed to bring one personal effect. Scotty was torn between his bagpipes and the veterinary shears he had come to love. Vu had no such qualms. He spent his last night before heading north to cold country ironing his Edmonton Oilers goalie uniform, while Jacques polished his grandfather's giant bear trap, an iron contraption with jaws big and menacing as cross-inductor struts.

Dr. Q stared endlessly at his bookcase before deciding on a leather-bound edition of *Wuthering Heights*. For me, there was no question. How could I leave my flatworms behind? I didn't really have a plan to revive them, but there's no shortcuts in science. I figured I'd put them in a bowl of warm water and give them lots of love. If that didn't work, I'd switch to liquid hydrogen, and, as a last ditch, I could always go back to *E. coli*.

We were like kids, wide-eyed as we kept saying *the moon* to each other. We were making a *moonshot,* I thought as I funneled my mixture of worms and liquid nitrogen into a thermos for the trip. I almost didn't notice Jacques ducking out through the side doors that led to the thorium dump.

I followed him, walking a few paces behind, on the same course we had taken the night before. Something was bothering him. We walked single file, silently, Jacques dragging his grandfather's enormous bear trap. What struck me was the cold. In the name of freedom and peace, we were going to beat the Reds to the moon, yet it was just as cold as the night before. It occurred to me suddenly, like a calving glacier, that my years of work on the deathray were over, and without result.

We wandered aimlessly, it seemed to me, from icefield to icefield, until Jacques felt somehow satisfied and stopped. He began digging and clawing his way through the permafrost. One patch of ice looked like any other in my book. A storm was rising from the northwest. That's what I was thinking about, the cold ahead.

Jacques dug a sack of moose jerky from the tundra. Then he uncovered his speed sled, something I hadn't seen him on in a while. Most trappers I'd read about in the *Encyclopedia Canadia* used dog teams, but Jacques rode a tiny sled he called a "luge," which you drove with your feet. It was more like a cookie sheet mounted on knives. Up and down the hills, it was the fastest thing you ever saw, simply a blur.

Jacques placed his bear trap and jerky on the luge, and we moved on. At the first of the traps we'd set the night before, Jacques crouched down before a rabbit. He let the little guy go, saying *"au revoir"* as it hobbled away.

Jacques only came to my sternum, but traces of pain in his eyes made him appear large and noble. The wind blew him down. He stood up again.

What was making him so sad, I wanted to know.

"Au revoir," Jacques said to each of the animals he freed. When we reached the edge of the glaciers, where the crevasses made trapping impossible, Jacques turned to me. *"Au revoir,"* he said.

It sounded like he was saying "old river," but with French, you never can tell. I tried to approximate his mother tongue as best I could. "Are you leave now? Go you where?" I asked.

Jacques nodded toward the ice behind him, while his hands described the outlines of mountains beyond. I figured this was where he'd look for that old river. Jacques was born to be an explorer, and I'll admit I was jealous of the way he'd brave the world on his own, how he took years of loneliness and cold until, by chance, he stumbled upon the path of another human heart. I wasn't made of such strong elements, it occurred to me. It sparked another little truth to rise. The reason I was so happy about the moon project was because now, I wouldn't have a chance to screw up the next phase of the deathray. I'd made a small string of mistakes, early in my career, including one that made a real mess of things at the Saskatoon Linear Particle Accelerator. Some equipment was damaged, and it still haunted me. There was a reason I was working out here in a desert of cold, instead of at prestigious labs like the Manitoba Institute of Technology.

"Vous aimez votre voyage à la lune," Jacques said. He climbed atop a block of ice, placed his hands on his hips.

"Je suis fini avec petits animaux. Je desire le grand et savage loup polaire, ou le tigre du Siberia, qui est blanc est musculaire. Tres feroce. Tres violent."

Jacques hopped down and gathered his traps. I stood dumbly as he mounted his "luge." I closed my eyes when rocketed off into the dark and cold.

We determined that Dr. Q was too fragile to make the eleven-hundred-kilometer trip north. He was dropped in by black parachute with a CIA advance team, while Vu and I towed the enrichment gear and mercurium cells on a special sled Scotty had welded. Scotty followed in the Sno-Cat behind, pulling the giant magnets.

The journey was long and painful. Vu kept reliving hockey's great moments, and he didn't spare the glory. If he said "ya betcha" one more time. Deep down, I think something else was upsetting me. I half hoped I'd encounter another little fur trapper when we reached the Glacier Lab because I already missed Jacques.

From the Sno-Cat, I called Dr. Q on the scramble phone. The encryption caused a lot of static, so Q sounded like he was out in the middle of nowhere. It was clear we'd have to enlarge the team to make a moon shot. We needed to build a flight simulator, and that was no easy feat. You had to configure all your own ergonomic systems, devise lots of small controls, as well as be a wizard with an eight millimeter projector.

"The best simulator person out there is Nell Connelly," I said. Nell was a wild prototype theorist who was prone to bursts of emotion.

"I know, I know," Q said.

"Any team would be proud to have her."

"Certainly," Q acknowledged. "Of course."

I was in near whiteout conditions, the mercurium we towed kept melting the ice right out from under us, and Vu had only made it to the '36 Olympics, in which the Nazis cheated their way to hockey gold by freezing the rink's ice out of sugar water, a move whose syrupy result was to slow any skate not made from superior German steel. It was dark, the phone was crackly, but I sensed Q and I were communicating on that higher level Jacques and I sometimes achieved.

"In my gut," Q said, "I feel Nell's red hair might be a distraction to the team."

"I second that motion, sir."

So it was that by the time I reached the Glacier Lab, Q had chosen Mansoor, my nemesis from the Saskatoon project, to come aboard as the new simulator man.

Mansoor was the first person I saw when we arrived at the tiny outpost. I barely knew I'd arrived, the cab windows had so sheeted over, but I could smell his Royal Lyme toilet water in the air.

"Ah, brilliant to see my old chum from Saskatoon," he said, opening my door.

Mansoor had been raised under British rule, which was why he wore those hideous blue socks. I eyed his thin mustache, dark brows, and took his hand to help me down. Mansoor fancied himself a ladies' man, and though you couldn't help finding him devilishly handsome, he was forever going on about exploits with coeds from Calgary to Moosonee.

We trudged toward the warming hut, Mansoor patting my back the whole way, but before I had a chance to tell him to keep his distance, I noticed something, out in the snow. There was a large, shiny crater in the darkness, and I suddenly knew the Alpha team had met its end, here, in a cone of blue vapor.

At Q's planning meeting, we all sat at a large table that had once acted as the nerve center for the Canadian Emergency Glacier Tracking Network, or CEGTN, for short. Color-coded thumbtacks were everywhere. Seven clocks, each set to a Canadian time zone, ticked on the wall above us.

We decided Vu would switch from targeting to navigation— he'd build those tricky atomic gyros. As a thermodynamic specialist, I was the natural choice for propulsion. Q would sew the re-entry parachutes. With Mansoor building the flight simulator, and Scotty hammering out the capsule, we figured we'd finish ahead of schedule.

As far as the launch strategy was concerned, a sustained burn would, ideally, be the way to go. You couldn't argue with liquid fuel; it gave you control and timing, though it also bogged you down with a huge, multistage fuselage and some real headaches in the engine department. In the end, it wasn't worth it. We were going rocketless, and we'd need to cook up that nasty load of saturnium after all. This was going to be a proton elevator to the heavens, governed by nuclear gyroscopics.

Dr. Q stood. He'd been doing a lot of math lately, I could tell. There was a glow about him that hypnotized me. He announced his initial calculations: the launch was going to take out much of central Canada, and depending on the winds, northern Manitoba and Saskatchewan. The EMP alone was going to knock every duck out of the sky for twenty-five hundred kilometers. Q also predicted an eighty-five percent chance of a tsunami off the coast of Chile, something we'd just have to accept.

Mansoor didn't wait long to rear his ugly head. I drew up the cooking schedule, and in an effort toward nobility, I gave myself KP detail the first night. I wanted to try my hand at Italian, and maybe wow the guys. It was just Scotty, myself, and our new Urdu brother.

Folding a napkin, Mansoor said, "So how have been your days since Saskatoon?"

I wasn't sitting for this treatment. "You mean since I broke the Linear Accelerator by loading fluorine instead of bromine in the atom smasher?"

"I thought Boris Kladnikov broke the atom smasher."

"You know dang well it was me."

"An honest mistake, I'm sure," Mansoor said. "All halides look alike to me."

"As project engineer," Scotty butted in, "I need to know if you've got a problem with bromine."

Oh, that scorched me, it scorched me. How could I hate bromine? I even kept a sack of it handy as a fire retardant. In a pinch, it also makes a good pesticide, and a quick mixing with any isolinear alkali yields a whopper of a tear gas.

"You just watch your back," I said to Mansoor.

Vu arrived late, grabbed a bread stick, and looked suspiciously at the Chianti. He said, "Pass the cacciatori, could'ja, and some-a them there noodles, eh."

I lost it. "It's *Mac-a-ro-ni*, an ancient food product invented by the Venetians."

Scotty had to add his. "Yes," he said, "the Venetians also invented grapeshot, land mines, and the incendiary grenade."

"They gave us syphilis, too," Mansoor threw in.

"Speak for yourself," I told him.

In these early days, Dr. Q developed a device to perform long arithmetic. He called this box an "algebrator," and with it, the nodule would basically fly itself. No more working a steering wheel with one hand and a slide rule with the other.

The time came for me to begin preparing the nuclear propulsion assembly, which required long hours in a full-containment suit. I used a lot of tongs. Loneliness was my worst enemy, and whole days would pass in which I saw no one—I'd emerge from the nuclear shed to find everyone asleep. There was no remedy. But the work was too dangerous to cry-baby about feelings. Most of weapons development is monkey see, monkey do, but the party stops when you get to the actinide series of the periodic table. If you could simply whip a rhombohedral element like samarium into an orthohombic like proactinium, then everyone would be doing it. You don't just sprinkle protons around and slap on electron shells. Try dicking with the fusal enthalpy of a polonium isotope and see if it will let you tiptoe out of the room when things go south. The ol' lead apron won't save you then.

Late at night, I'd sneak into Dr. Q's room and warm my hands over the algebrator's tubes, breathe deep its ozony breath. Whispering, I'd ask, what lay ahead? Did happiness wait for me? Regarding my fate, the algebrator held its silence. The fastest mathematical device in the world would not say. I'd admire the neat rows of toggles, let the copper coils ionize the hair on my arms, and then wander off to my quiet bunk.

The command nodule was the first hardware component to be finished, and when Scotty debuted it, we drank Mooseheads all the way around. Dr. Q put some Latin music on the reel-to-reel, and Vu killed us with his cancan. I did a merengue with Dr. Q, and I tell you, I was zany, I wasn't myself. It must have been the bubbles in the beer. Palm to palm, we held our arms high, poised and steady, while below, our hips flashed like solid-state diodes—one two three, *cha*—and I was feeling quite heady. I let Q lead.

But then, in the conga line, I had to endure the wafting smells of gin and starch coming off Mansoor, while Vu's sweaty hands on my shoulders brought me down to earth. As we snaked around the heli-arc welder and acetylene torches—*cha*, our legs would fly in unison—I began to wonder which one of us would be making the moonshot. Dr. Q was too important, Scotty was prone to drink, and of course, I had my allergies. Secretly, I was for sticking Vu in the darn thing.

Just then, Mansoor led the conga line up to the command nodule and stopped in front of the canopy. The capsule was beautiful: anodized alloy frame, gold-plated com links, fireproof Perspex windows all around. The tiny nodule's infrastructure alone contained fifty kilometers of wiring, enough that Scotty had to train two snow ferrets to pull the cables through the complex web of conduits.

Mansoor opened the hatch and moved to step inside like he owned the thing, like he had just crowned himself moon pilot. Part of me really wanted Mansoor to go, except for the fact that there was an outside chance the whole dang thing might work, that he might make it to the moon and return a hero. But Mansoor couldn't squeeze in through the hatch. None of us could, not even Vu! Scotty had made the nodule too small. When we cornered him behind the central shop-vac unit, his desperate margarita eyes passed over all of us. "There must be something wrong with my slide rule," he said. "It could have happened to anybody."

Furious, Dr. Q called an emergency meeting, right there in our sombreros. Mulroney listened in on the scramble phone. "What we need," Q said, "is a candidate who can withstand intense G forces, high levels of radiation, and long periods of cold and dark. He must be able to entertain himself and also be under 150 centimeters tall."

Mulroney assured us the CIA would find our man, so there was nothing left to do but get back to work and trust in Canadian Intelligence.

Three nights later, Mulroney was back. I was shaken out of a dream about submarines: when I raised my periscope, I could see Jacques on the shoreline, racing his luge up and down the hills in a perfect sine wave.

"Gentlemen," Mulroney announced. "I present your Canadanaut."

"Canadanaut?" I asked. "What the heck are you talking about?"

"It means 'Canada-voyager,'" Mulroney said. "The boys in PR cooked it up."

Mulroney then pushed forward a tiny, emaciated man with a skin condition. He was blindfolded and probably drugged.

Dr. Q asked him his discipline. Aeronautics? Vector Analysis?

"I'm an English teacher from Edmonton," he squeaked.

I nearly laughed up my cocoa.

Vu rushed him. "Did the Oilers make the Stanley Cup play-offs?" he asked.

Such was our seclusion. But this guy didn't know anything.

I walked over and poked him in the chest. He almost fell down. What a puss. I didn't even want to know his name. How were we going to beat those Communauts into space with a bookworm at the wheel? Did I have to remind everyone of the grave military implications of failure?

Dr. Q and I decided to get right to work, right there in our nightshirts. The first thing we did was irradiate our Canadian hero with uranium isotopes. I set the dial at 500. Q shrugged, so I cranked it up to 650 rads, a dose that made our subject turn pink and swelly. The procedure also loosened his teeth, and the diarrhea would not stop. As if you could fly to the moon with a case of the dribbles riding shotgun. On the master clipboard, Q marked his radiation tolerance as "moderate."

Next, we stuck him in the centrifugal chamber, an event that pulled his arms out of his sockets, and that was it, we were back to scratch.

I was relieved that our so-called "Canadanaut" was gone, but something was still bothering me. All day, the numbers wouldn't add up, and I kept spilling the hydroxinum crystals. What I wouldn't have given for one rabbit to calm my nerves. This mission wasn't about Canada. This flight was about one man, leaving the world of men, making a sacrifice for the love of mankind. It seemed to me that our pilot should be called a "man-voyager," or Homonaut, a name that suggested fellowship and unity.

At dinner that night, it was Scotty who snapped. "I'm tired of all these military figures telling us what to do." He slammed his fork down. "The whole point of this enterprise is exploration. I say our man is a Star Jockey and should be referred to as such. In a certain sense, we're all Star Jockeys."

"I'm partial to Empyreal Cosmoteer," Q said, "but you can't fight the boys in PR."

"What about Sky Musher?" Vu asked.

We pretended not to hear him.

"If we're being open, sirs," Mansoor said, "I prefer the title 'Qamar Musafir' or perhaps 'Kaukab Tayyar.'"

Steaming, I tore my bib off and blurted, "We're Homonauts or nothing at all."

Dr. Q waved his hand. "Pull yourselves together, men."

Scotty, in a temper, grabbed his ferrets and stormed off in a Sno-Cat to hunt for possible launch sites. Vu wanted to go after him, but Q said no, "Let him cool down."

Days passed, long and cold. When would I find someone special?

I was dreaming of submarines again when I felt something warm on my chest. Dr. Q suddenly joined the dream in a gold-braided hat. In a deep voice, he gave the torpedo coordinates. But then I felt that the warmth under my covers was furry, and it was Jacques, who entered my dreamy nocturnal vision. He wore a skin-tight wetsuit, complete with a diving helmet. Jacques stuck a breathing tube in his mouth, and then launched himself out of the sub's conning tower on a secret mission to mine an enemy harbor.

I woke suddenly and found myself alone. When I came to my senses, I realized Chilly and Willy, Scotty's snow ferrets, were under the covers with me. They had climbed in through a storm window that Vu had accidentally left open. I had a bad feeling. Scotty wasn't in his bunk, so I woke Vu, who knelt down to the ferrets.

"Is something wrong?" he asked them. "Is Scotty in trouble?"

Chilly and Willy just gave us stupid chatter. I knew a couple ways of getting ferrets to talk, but that would take precious time, and we needed to find Scotty.

"This is no use," I said. "Come on, Vu. Let's mount a rescue."

We hopped into the Sno-Cat and headed out to scour the frozen wastelands. The narrow cones of our headlights were the whole universe as we drove and drove. Vu picked up where he'd left off last time, a chronological listing of inductees into the Hockey Hall of Fame in Winnipeg. As the night wore on, Vu described the gear—the helmets, the shin guards, the supporters—and by the time he explained face-offs, checking, and that darned icing rule, I'd begun to develop a fondness for the sport. My favorite part was the penalty box. God, if that didn't sum up life.

Ahead, we saw something in the dark, a mere white lump in a field of white. I downshifted the Sno-Cat and engaged the ice brake. Vu and I ran out into polar-driven winds to find Scotty, weak of breath, half buried in snow.

I checked Scotty's thermos. It was almost empty.

"You nearly got yourself killed out here, you fool," I told him.

Scotty's only response was to lift his leg out of the snow and show us a large trap, grappling his mangled foot. Black frost lined the wound.

I turned to Vu. "Jacques is near," I said. "I have to find him."

"Are you crazy?" Vu asked. "You won't last ten minutes out there without a thermos."

"You can't stop me," I told him. "Now get Scotty back to safety."

And so I stumbled out into the blast-freezer of the night, riven and keening with cold, in search of my old friend Jacques. My fingers thickened, my vision blurred, everything smelled like ethylene glycol. In my mind, I saw images of times when I had been petty and small—framing colleagues for my mistakes, reporting the sympathizers and sodomites in my infantry unit, borrowing phonograph records with little intention of returning them—and now, as a mere speck wandering the vast Arctic expanse, I was just as small, but it was somehow different. I felt different. Toward the horizon, I hallucinated mountains and frozen rivers. On them raced a hairy little man, lugeing up and down their steep banks. Then everything went white.

I woke in a snow cave, lit by an oil-fat lamp. I could not move my limbs.

I woke again, days later, and the numbness was gone. I focused, and there was Jacques, heating lichen soup over a small fire of dried tundra moss. I felt warm and safe, and there were no fears of Jacques pulling any funny business on me while I slept, like those guys back in the service.

"My old friend, Jacques. Where have you been?"

Looking tired and defeated, Jacques pointed in various directions, suggesting the longitudes of Kamchatski, the Bering Sea, the Klondike Plateau.

"*Il n'y a pas du tigre de Siberia,*" he said. "*Je n'ai pas cherche les loups polaire.*"

It was time I taught Jacques a lesson about life. I motioned for him to follow me. We donned our snowshoes and forged out into the bracing cold, covering our faces as we stumbled toward the edge of an ice shelf where one of Jacques's traps sat empty. We stood over its open jaws, and I couldn't help but observe how primitive and pointless this device appeared against the endless nothing of our world.

I began by explaining to Jacques that in the beginning, sixteen billion years ago, all the energy of the universe was, for a microsecond, a ball of pure sympathy. Perfect states cannot last, I continued, which is the definition of our existence. There was a bang, and as the universe expanded, energies grew dim and distant, separated by galactic cold and dark.

I spread my arms real wide.

Jacques scratched his chin.

At some point, in about three billion years, I continued, the universe will stop expanding. Then, all the energy will rush together again. The spirits of all men, animals, and things will be joined at the core. Men like us, I suggested, were just born on the wrong side of the universe.

It was like my flatworms, I thought to myself. I hated to see them tighten and curl as I introduced them to superchilled noble gasses, but then there was the moment they relaxed, when their energy left us for the great return. This was a moment of pure sympathy, the thing that thrilled and terrified me about the death-ray. Creation is fine—I'll admit it's a necessity—but its stinging backhand is felt every time one life is separated from another: child from mother, scout from troop, private from platoon. Sympathy, however, is a coming together of energies. When this was all over, they were probably going to kill us. We knew that. I just hoped I'd be able to stand next to Q, without blindfolds, so we could face the dark voyage home together.

Jacques still looked confused. I realized I had skipped the part about matter not existing, so I hit him with that, and then threw in the myth of gravity. Finally, I briefly summarized how all appearance of solidity and permanence is an illusion.

Jacques scooped up a mitten of snow. He held it out. *"Il n'y a pas de neige?"*

"Sorry, friend," I told him.

"Et le grand et noble tigre?"

I swept my hand from the glaciers to the trap at our feet. "Nothing is real."

Slowly, almost fearfully, Jacques pointed at the moon.

I shook my head.

Taking my little friend by the shoulder, I led him back to the world of men.

Sure, everyone was glad to see Jacques's return, but we were simply too busy to throw a party or anything. Dr. Q was worried about finding a Canadanaut in time for the launch, and everything was behind schedule because of Scotty's frostbite. It turned out that Q couldn't save the foot, though he did fashion quite a replacement out of fiberglass and gypsum. You couldn't tell the difference. Scotty donated the old foot to my reanimation project. I was pressed for time, but I hoped to defrost it soon, hook up a big battery, and get those toes wiggling again.

I got cracking on launch preparations. I took core samples, tuned the blast lens, and spent countless days inside a lead suit, squinting under the nuclear shed's bad lighting, while my nights were eaten up by the old pencil and protractor.

Meanwhile, the completed and launch-ready command nodule sat ghostly under a sheet in the middle of the lab, and we all looked away whenever we passed it.

I was doing some charts in the rec room when Jacques wandered in. I think he felt a lack of purpose in all our commotion, so I showed him how the compass helped me draw perfect circles and let him give it a shot. Jacques didn't recognize a map of Canada at first. Slowly, he realized it depicted his trapping range, and quite excited, he pointed at the red and yellow circles I'd drawn.

Those, I explained by drawing a saturnium isotope, were fallout zones. The red circle was the nucleic flash wave, the yellow circle showed the Rutherford zone of fuel-pile vaporization, and the dotted line represented the bombardment fallout cloud, which, depending on the jet stream, was variable.

Jacques took the pencil and drew a picture of a raccoon. Or maybe it was a skunk. I told him I was sorry, but there weren't going to be animals in northern Canada for about twenty thousand years. The disappointment was clear on his face, and I reassured him that maybe, by sweet-talking Mulroney, we could get him some free vocational training. Through stick figures, I helped Jacques understand the concepts of duct work and siding installation.

Jacques disappeared for a day and a half. We searched everywhere for him—behind the radon tanks, down in the twin walk-in freezers. Finally, we found him sitting inside the command nodule, head reclined on a proton gyro.

When we opened the door, he spoke. *"Le Canadanaut,"* he said. *"C'est moi."*

We liked his proposal, but it wasn't so easy. When Mulroney did a background check and discovered Jacques had never paid taxes, he was dead against the idea.

"What kind of example would this set for the young people?" he asked us.

"Jacques is an explorer," Q pointed out. "He's never even seen money."

"There's another issue," Mulroney said. "I don't think the boys down in PR would see many photo opportunities with Jacques, and then there's his breath."

We considered Jacques's features in the laboratory light, his curling nose hair, those wax-filled ears. For the first time, I noticed the patches of ringworm.

"At least let's see how he does in the flight simulator," I pleaded.

Mulroney shrugged. "I suppose it couldn't hurt."

We put Jacques in the flight simulator, and it didn't go well. There were precious few days before launch, and Jacques had never seen a steering wheel before, let alone a clutch.

"Would the Canadanaut please focus his attention on the movie," Mansoor would say. "Please if the Canadanaut would push each button that lights."

Mansoor was pushing it with the phony manners. Plus, he kept calling Jacques a "Cuh-nad-un-ot" instead of the obvious "Can-uh-duh-nut." The way Mansoor said it, Canada had nothing to do with it. It was like Canada didn't even exist to him.

During the exercise in which Jacques was to navigate a simulated asteroid field, he kept jerking his legs and leaning in the chair, until finally, he fell flat on the floor. Using the powers of scientific deduction, I concluded that Jacques was attempting to fly the nodule the same way he steered his "luge."

"You're going to have to rig this nodule to be operated with the feet," I told Scotty, which was the wrong thing to say. I was about to eat a crutch when Mansoor had a stroke of brilliance.

"I'll go you one better, old fellow," Mansoor said and began constructing an ergonomic navigation system based on Jacques's *"baton de joie."* On the dash, Mansoor mounted a single, protruding stick that controlled both direction and velocity. Where Jacques pointed it, in theory, the nodule would follow.

It wasn't until the day before launch that we got the green light from Ottawa on Jacques. Dr. Q delivered the news while we were transferring fresh mercurium from the minibreeder to the charging cylinders. He entered the clean room, donned a surgical mask and shower cap, and then gave us the big thumbs-up. We were glad the mission wasn't scrubbed, but nobody was going to put on pointed hats and toot horns in front of four vats of brewing mercurium. I held the containment lids open while Vu and Scotty extracted the liquid core with long-handled skimmers. Talk about trust.

But Q had another announcement. "Jacques leaves in less than eighteen hours," he said, "and I've decided, according to custom, he should receive sexual gratification before departing on this perilous voyage."

I could only see Q's eyes, so I wasn't sure if he was having us on or what. "A joke's a joke," I said. "We've got work to do."

"I've already spoken to Mulroney," Q said. "The CIA is dropping a woman tonight. I took the liberty of ordering cigars for the rest of us."

I looked at Mansoor, whose head wrap bulged strangely under his cellophane clean suit. "You had a hand in this, I'm sure," I told him.

"It's tradition," Mansoor said. "You can't send a man to his . . . to the moon, without knowing a woman."

"Tradition?" I was so excited my voice cracked. "No one's ever done this before. We launch in the morning, and you want to send our pilot into a stressful and unknown situation? Why don't we also tattoo him and teach him to fire walk?"

Vu crossed the room with an overflowing scooper.

"Easy, easy," we all said. Vu was dragging his feet on the carpet, and if one spark of static electricity were to hit the mercurium—*sayonara.*

At L-minus twelve hours, we shaved Jacques. We told him it was to reduce heat inside the suit, but honestly, we didn't know why we were doing it. It just seemed like the right idea. Science is about following your instincts, and I guess we didn't want to take any chances.

It was somber in the room. You could smell the ozone from Scotty's shears as they bogged in mats of hair. Jacques sat on a stool, occasionally raising his eyes to the ceiling as if the hum of the buzzer was the drone of propellers that were at that moment, we all knew, high over Canada on a mission to deliver her.

When Scotty was done with the straight razor, there was nothing to do but marvel. Jacques only weighed thirty-eight kilos, and he'd lost a lot of volume without the body hair, but he was grand, the most perfect male specimen I'd ever seen. Lithe and symmetrical, his pectoral muscles fanned across ribs that undulated beneath a brawny torso. About his genitals, I won't even speak.

For dinner, Jacques requested a moose patty, which he took alone, with red wine. Then we all walked out into the icefield to wait for her. The whole idea rattled me, a woman falling from the sky to take hold of one of us. Mulroney had assured us she was the leader of an elite canando unit—she was the best woman they had.

Above, the Milky Way swung its galactic fist at nothing, while the moon, searing and steamy, seemed ruled by convection. When stars twinkled, going dark for a moment, I wondered if a high-altitude drop plane was passing overhead. Under a black parachute, was she swooping toward us? We stomped our feet for warmth. Our breath plumed. I swore I heard the faint, gargly cry of a faraway wolf.

At last we heard it, the whistling of parachute cord. Then I felt the growing shadow of her black silk, and she was upon us. The canando unclasped her harness before she reached the ground, so she was in pure free-fall the last ten meters.

She hit, rolled, and leapt up aiming a red flashlight and a pistol. She wore bulky, bullet-resistant body armor and light-amplifying goggles. She must have been 195 centimeters tall! Before we could say anything, we were engulfed by a lufting cloud of black as her parachute drifted down on us.

With the gun barrel, she lifted the chute off our heads. She let her teeth show, like graphite in the dark. Her black name patch read "Lt. Braun."

"Which man is Jacques?" she asked.

We didn't say shit.

"Qui homme est Jacques?" she demanded.

We all shrank back. The poor bastard, I thought.

But Jacques stepped forward. *"C'est moi,"* he said.

"Bien," she said. *"Commençons."*

Lt. Braun holstered her weapon and then adjusted a dial on her amber-glowing watch. She reached down and unsnapped an insulated panel covering her groin. Removing this panel revealed that her body armor was crotchless, and we all stood watching her vagina steam in the Arctic night.

"Stop this madness!" I shouted.

It was too late. Jacques had seen her yeasty pubis, and was already stripping his clothes. Naked, hairless, vibrating white in the moonlight, he ran toward her. She caught him midstride. Together they climbed into the cab of the Sno-Cat and dieseled off into the distance, leaving us to hoof it home.

"Cigar?" Mansoor offered, smiling.

The next morning, Jacques walked back into camp like a gunslinger. His breath had reached a new dimension. I told Q that we'd need to initiate a complete physical and scrubdown, but Q said no, there wasn't time.

"Think of the microbes," I pleaded, but Q was right. It was go-time.

On the horizon, we saw Lt. Braun launch a large reflective balloon that hung in the Arctic night, tethered by an elastic cord to her harness. Moments later, a small jet approached. It caught the balloon with a tail hook—and snatch!—she was gone.

I did a last-minute rundown of the checklist while Jacques suited up. It seemed like we'd thought of everything: reentry was going to be hot, but luckily we had tons of old asbestos from the glacier station's insulation. As far as water was concerned, I'd developed a catheter filter that worked rather nicely. To produce oxygen, Jacques would need only drop a couple methyline tablets into a jar of hydroferric acid, shake briskly, and then get that lid off quick, or look out.

Mansoor, who was pretty handy with the brush and palate, whipped off a few watercolors to document the top-secret launch. Jacques posed with Dr. Q, both giving the thumbs-up. Then he crouched down beside the mercurium cells, where he tipped his helmet and smiled. Finally, Jacques mounted the canopy and spoke to us:

"Observez la lune. Il n'y a pas de lune. Le tigre, dans l'arctique, finelment, est une illusion. Son grandes dents ne mange pas le corps. Son attaque ne cause pas la mort. Je suis un homme. Je ne suis pas un homme."

With that, Jacques entered the capsule. Scotty armed the rotary locks, swung the door shut, and then caulked the joints.

The moment had finally arrived. I took the battery out of the Sno-Cat and we all went down into the bunker. Below the permafrost, our breath billowed in the light of the handhelds. Q gave the nod and Scotty pulled the cord that dumped the thorium 247 into the now-glowing mercurium cells. Mansoor counted backward on that fancy-ass watch of his.

At zero, I connected the wires, triggering a switch that activated the giant magnets. The positively charged protons were pulled off to the right, while the negatively charged electrons veered left, leaving a perfect beam of thorium neutrons. We're talking 10^{13} joules! Straight into mercurium! We created, for 2.3^{-37} of a second, one kilo of pure saturnium, the first production of a theoretical element in the history of the earth. For a moment of perfection, we'd echoed the creation of the universe.

There was a hell of a bang, and we knew the ground above us was molten glass. We counted to one hundred, then ran up top in our yellow suits to check things out. Everything was glowing, but when my eyes adjusted, and I turned my red goggles toward the launch sight, there was nothing. I couldn't believe Jacques was gone. We searched the sky. Nothing. I found myself thinking, was he really up there? But I knew where he was: traveling twenty kilometers per second inside a halo of flame.

Was he burning alive? Did he forget his compass? We'd sent along every gram of equipment the nodule could lift: there were twin solar-powered com links, bulky arm-mounted units that weighed nearly three kilos each, without the four-hectogram antennae. He took an asbestos-lined PCV suit with a backpack oxyrecirc unit, and a handheld echo-locator to navigate the craters, together nearly sixty kilos. We sent Jacques's favorite snowshoes (six kilograms for the pair) in case the moon's surface was unstable. There was an entrenchment tool, a rope ladder, a horizon finder, all pretty serious weight. At four dekagrams, Jacques brought a box of sixty leakproof Baggies for his elimination and masturbation. Said and done, Jacques would hump nearly ninety-seven kilos of gear with him, though this was the moon, with .165 gravity, so nothing would be a burden, really.

And, unbeknownst to us at launch time, Jacques had brought his grandfather's twenty-kilogram bear trap, which was enough weight to send the nodule seven thousand kilometers off course, causing Jacques to miss the moon entirely.

Slowly, our dread lessened, and as I saw the smirks of victory spread across the faces of my colleagues, I realized that a well-deserved elation was building. We had done it, we'd really beat those Russian fags into space.

Q shook his head. "I need a vacation," he said into the Canadian darkness.

We wouldn't be able to raise Jacques on the dictascope for another twenty-seven minutes, so we all marched back down into the bunker, where we sat upon upturned thorium drums and shot the breeze. Mansoor described the appearance of the moon, seen from the rooftops of Islamabad, on one particular night of his boyhood, an image that still moved him, yet eluded description—"not saffron, not tamarind, lighter than orange peel"—while I entertained my first notions of life after this project. Already, I could see Q and myself on vacation in Acapulco, sipping Mooseheads on the beach, while the rhythms of the swaying palms and surf blended into the singsong of Mansoor's memory, "the color of spiced butter, near melting, but textured and pewtery, like old lacquer, or perhaps the yellow base of a parrot's beak, where it disappears into the violet of its feathers."

Q started telling a story about the old days, about doing research back before fancy instruments. I hung on his every word, so rapt I didn't notice he'd accidentally lifted my thermos off the floor.

"We worked on instinct, letting our balls be our guide," Q was saying as he unscrewed the lid to my flatworm experiment. "In the days before electron microscopes, logarithms were our eyes. We didn't need particle accelerators when our guts told us that nutrinos existed." Then he lifted the thermos of liquid nitrogen to his mouth. He drank, turned blue, and we lost him, right there in the bunker.

"Give us room," I yelled as I prepared to revive him. Mansoor held back Scotty, already weeping as he reached to touch Q's sleeve. Vu was in hysterics, but they all left the bunker so I could get to work. I placed Q's body in one of the long thorium drums. Next, I filled the drum with warm water. Then I gave Q lots of love.

It didn't work. I couldn't bring him back. There was only an expression of beautiful inquiry in Q's eyes, a look suggesting he'd witnessed what lay ahead—warmth, light, acceptance—perhaps my truest proof of sympathy's existence.

Alone, I wept in a way that did not redden my eyes or crack my face. It was a sadness that expressed itself only as a rattle in my lungs, a strange twitch to my fingers, and it is a weeping that never stopped. This sorrow settled in, became such a bunk mate that I forgot its source. Convinced I had asthma, arthritis, anything, it wasn't until a decade later, when I ran across a photo of Q in a top-secret folder that I knew I wept yet. At the back of the file, I saw Q's real name: Randolph.

The guys returned to console me, but I waved them off. There was nothing to do but get back to work. In three short days, Jacques would safely float down to the biggest party Ontario had ever seen. Mulroney had already ordered the beer. Until then, we owed that little fur trapper our best. It's what Q would've wanted.

"Allo, allo," we heard over the speaker. "C'est Jacques. Dites-moi, mes amis."

We looked at each other. Dr. Q was the only one who'd spoken French.

Mansoor grabbed my arm. "Just repeat whatever the heck he says."

"Quel ciel! J'observe les cometes et le systeme solaire."

I grabbed the handset while Vu checked Jacques's position. *"Solaire,"* I said.

We all watched for Jacques's green blip as Vu fired up the dictascope.

When the screen warmed up, Jacques's blip was way off course.

"Wouldn'cha know he missed the moon," Vu said, "by about a heck of a lot, eh."

"Make you now an around turn," I said to Jacques. "U-turn."

"Oui," he said. *"Espace resemble l'uterine. L'acte du creation est tres evident."*

Vu grabbed the handset. "Look here, Jacques, you better return, eh."

"Retournez?"

Mansoor gave it a go. "Use the stick, Jacques. Time for the baton of joy."

We then lost radio contact with him for about five minutes.

Despite the unnerving radio silence, Jacques's green blip did slowly begin to turn back toward the moon, except now he was forced to land on the dark side. Scotty grabbed a slide rule for some quick extrapolation. His fingers whirred, then stopped cold. "He's used too much fuel in the turn around. He'll never make it home."

Upon landing, Jacques began broadcasting nonstop, narrating everything he saw on the moon's far side. His voice soared and plunged, was laced with awe and fever. I imagined the landscape he described, its starlit plains legioned by purple well-heads of rock, the sky above a lecture on black. As Jacques spoke and spoke, I filled the great canyons and craters with my own loss and loneliness, felt a void no rope could span.

What we really needed was a French dictionary or some type of recording device, but we'd left Q's reel-to-reel back at the Tundra Lab. All night, we listened to Jacques convey to us wholesale the pure nature of the universe. In the morning, the nodule's battery went dead, and we never heard from Jacques again.

The whole thing was a public relations nightmare for the CIA, which was forced to deny ordering over eighty kiloliters of beer delivered to Martyr's Park in downtown Ottawa. Mulroney's men confiscated all our documents, and then they began killing us. Vu was thrown down an ice crevasse, Scotty was immolated below the launch pad of a Yukon ballistic base, and rumor has it that Mansoor's last date was with our own half-working deathray. The labs were burned and the bunkers buried in an attempt to hide the embarrassing truth that the great nation of Canada could put a man on the moon, but not bring him back. The only evidence this country ever even had a space program is the total wasteland we made of north-central Canada.

Yet I survived, even though all my attempts at reanimation had failed, and I was a bad scientist. I was a career-long failure as a weapons development scientist. I toyed with anthrax a bit, to little avail, and then there was that now-famous stab I took at controlling the weather. I suppose my only success was some minor work with defoliants.

I wouldn't learn why my life was spared for some time, until the CIA approached me and revealed that they'd been doing their own flatworm experiments for years, but with less noble intentions. They were getting close to harnessing the power of sympathy, a force the CIA believed, if properly applied, could fuel the greatest destructive device ever created. All they needed was the equation I'd developed to calculate the quotient of sympathy. Naturally, I was excited and vowed to help any way possible. But when I explained this force could also join all men, without the

need for genital contact, in a perfect state of harmony, they can-
celed the project and swore me to secrecy.

But now I say, enjoy: $\Sigma\{\Delta S - E\}^2 = Q$.

There you have it. There's your moon and poodle, your falling
apples, rising tides, Keplerian laws of angular momentum, and the
attraction of all bodies in this swelling universe. There's your dang
formula—go ahead and take it. Science never brought me closer
to the brotherhood of man. I drifted from government work to the
private sector, and eventually to the university—talk about your
wasteland. It turned out I'd get that casserole after all: I finally
wed, and fate dealt me five daughters.

No, the closest I came to transcending our cruel existence was
on those Arctic nights, long ago, when we set aside our personal
needs and lived as a team. Together, we didn't feel the cold. We
were at home in the dark. Scotty would be humming over the
whir of veterinary shears, while Vu practiced slap shots with old
tuna cans, and Dr. Q knitted us leggings to line our crampon
boots. Jacques was the only one restless enough to keep leaving
our team. It was as if, like a foot in a freezer, some missing part of
him waited in the endless cold and dark, always beyond the next
glacier. On that night I lost Randolph, I felt a part of me was missing. I wandered the icefields and stared at the moon, a place
where a small man, armed with nothing but guts and rope, moved
alone under the indifferent firmament. I was no explorer, I realized. I had no stomach for real discovery.

I wish I could say the moon that night was tinged milky-bay, or
that it sang in the sky, remote as the call of a tangir parrot. But it
was only flat and white and blank, all the more reason that others
would want to print their image upon it. I understood that the
Amerinauts and the Mexinauts would one day make it to the
moon as well, but I also knew they'd stand weakly on the lighted

side, staring back at home, the place they'd just come from. They'd bring things like golf clubs and martinis, horse around with Slinkys in zero G. They'd make home movies of the smart speeches they'd fashioned and upon a safe return, spice their talk with God.

But Jacques's view spanned into dark space, into the future, which is cold when it comes to truth. I knew Jacques was already wandering from our puny nodule, into the absolute black, crossing craters and plains wiped clear of features. Moving by feel, he hunted the right location to set an iron-jawed trap for the next man with balls enough to search the heavens for sympathy.

THE EIGHTH SEA

When I arrive at my first Adult Redirection meeting, my arms are dyed rusty pink, though the color's official name is "Anasazi Sunset." The meeting is on the third floor of Tempe City Hall, a creepy building, even at night. It's an upside-down pyramid of gray glass and green steel that leans farther and farther over you the closer you get. Crossing the lot, the night air is Arizona-April perfect: lemon blossoms, freshly cut grass, a sky black enough to see the moon actually move, its hips chonga in the heat waves.

I stop when I catch my reflection in the glass doors of City Hall. My hair is black with sweat. I'm so thirsty my skin is tight, and my shoulders glow with sunburn. I hauled like ten thousand cement blocks for my father today and shoveled tons of sand. Then there were all these wheelbarrows of cement and heavy bags of Anasazi Sunset, which is black in the concentrated powder, fluorescent red when it touches water, and pink when it dries in the mortar. I flex my red biceps and check them in the reflection. *Yes.*

Inside, I drink a half dozen little cones of water from a blue cooler and begin peeling an orange, stuffing the rinds in my back pocket as I take the stairs two at a time. In conference room C, the other redirectees are seated at an oval table, around which a heavy guy circles, lecturing dramatically about something or other. He's wearing a blue, pearl-buttoned shirt that's worn thin enough to see the dark shadow of his chest hair. He makes a show of stopping his speech.

"We start at eight," he says and holds his hand out for my court docket. His name tag reads Mr. Doyle.

My red arms make him pause, but he takes the slip and reads my charge: *D&D/urinated on police horse.* His eyes flash from the docket to me as he reads, shaking his head in mock disgust. "Decision making, Ronnie," he says, then for the benefit of all, adds, "We're going to talk a lot about decision making in the next few weeks."

But I don't sit down just yet. "I know you," I tell him.

Right away, he's on my case. "Do you know what's it's like to lose a child to the ravages of alcohol?" he asks me, like it's my fault. I'm not worried, though, because if things get out of hand, I know a couple jiu-jitsu strikes.

"Have you been forced to witness," he continues, "a young, hopeful soul torn from the breast of life by booze? Then you don't know anything about me, son."

"Oh, *come now,*" says a woman in a white half-shirt.

"I know I know you," I tell the big guy and take an empty chair by the woman in white. She's not exactly pretty, but rare in a certain way, like some women you only see at the supermarket, ones in tight jeans who push carts full of steaks and import beer. She grabs my wrist and squeezes once, quick and strong, before letting go. It's the way you let a child know you are right there for him, and though I smile back at the way her look says *they're kidding us with this guy,* all I feel is the cool, lingering trace of her wedding ring.

Mr. Doyle talks on and on about why he teaches these classes, how it's his duty, after enduring the kind of tragedy most are spared, to save as many of us as he can. He tells the story of his daughter, booze, pain, drugs, whatever. I'm checking out this woman beside me, who takes long pulls from the ribbed straw of an insulated cup, when it finally hits me. I stand up and say, "I re-member now—I had you for traffic school last month. Didn't you tell us a totally different story about your daughter in traffic class, about how she died in a car crash, like from a drunk driver or something?"

Mr. Doyle closes his eyes in frustration and then glares at me like he's going to blow his top, but I look him in the eye. All the magazines I've read say that if you start looking at your opponent's strike zones—like the collarbone or solar plexus—then you lose the edge of surprise.

"She *was* the drunk driver," Mr. Doyle says.

"Oh," I say.

At break time, I walk outside to bask in the dark heat. Down the street is the Mill Avenue bar scene, where "real" college stu-dents party, and across the way, past the sorority dorms, is the Ari-zona State University Aquatic Center—the blue-tang of its pool chlorine mixing with the waxy smell of City Hall's citrus trees.

I find the woman in white sitting on the tail of a '69 Chevelle, trunk up.

"That air-conditioning was killing me," I say.

"I was about out of vodka."

Her name is Loren, it turns out, and the Chevelle is so cherry it's obviously a man's life passion. Its paint job is a custom glitter-green, deep and flashy as raw mica, giving the swept Chevy the night-shine of a desert beetle. The license plate says POWER.

She sits in white shorts on the chrome bumper, the black trunk

open behind her, pouring Sprite and Popov into the sport cup between her knees. "How old are you?"

"Nineteen."

"I got a daughter who's nineteen," she says, adding a final top-
off of vodka, some of which splashes on her thigh. She wipes it off
with her hand, then licks her palm.

"I don't act my age, though," I say. "I'm an underachiever with
difficulties facing maturity because of early instability in the
home. I also need to learn I won't get far in life on charm alone."

"Consider yourself lucky," she says. "My daughter's a
nymphomaniac."

"There's worse fates," I say, trying to be smart or something.

Loren offers me her vodka cocktail. "Like recovering alcoholic?"

My eyes sweep back to the drink in her hand.

She smiles. "That's kind of a joke."

"I've also been told I have problems with decision making," I
say and take the vodka.

She reclines a moment, resting her elbows on the black rubber
seal of the trunk well, stretching her legs wide across the pave-
ment. From down the street, snatches of salsa music reach us off
and on.

"Everybody finds their own way to deal with a tricky setup," she
says.

"Tricky, like bad?"

"Tricky, like complicated," she says. "Labyrinthine."

From the all-Greek parking lot beyond the hedgerow come the
sounds of girls talking, though I can't make out what they say.
When they laugh, it gives me a small thrill and kind of needles
me, too. Loren doesn't seem to hear them.

"Do you believe in God?" she asks and begins fixing another
cocktail, using the same method, right down to the little spill and
lick.

"Jacob wrestled the angel," I say, "and the angel was overcome." This is a song lyric from U2 that pops into my head.

"Amen," she says as she stirs the drink with a finger. She tests it, approves, then sets the vodka bottle back in the trunk, next to a stack of chrome crowbars.

"Like they say," Loren lifts her drink. "Rain falls equally on saint and sinner."

I lift my drink, too, but the sight of her lipstick, dark and smudged on the rim, makes me pause. I cup my mouth around it, get a shiver in the hot parking lot.

Back inside, we are broken into groups to play unusual board games that seem designed to teach us how to have fun without controlled substances, which is supposed to be the point of this class. In reality, however, all the games are rigged so that everyone loses, and there's something weirdly churchy about them. There's "High Times" and "One for the Road," which uses hazardous highway signs to convey its message. Loren and I join a group playing a Monopoly-style game named "Last Call." You start with plenty of money, but it quickly goes to pay the bartenders, dealers, and bookies. Once poor, you have to draw from a stack of cards called *Sobering Realities*. I keep landing on *Make Mine a Double*. Loren wraps her Corvette around a tree. I go blind and my pregnancy ends in stillbirth.

After class, I walk with Loren in the parking lot. "Sorry we went *Bottoms Up* at the end," I tell her. "Those dice had to be loaded."

"Look," she says. "You want to go for a drive? I want to go for a drive."

"A drive where to?"

Loren glances up, shrugs. "I don't want to go home just yet."

She hands me the keys to the Chevelle, and the chain weighs a ton with all sorts of trinkets attached to it, but I head for the driver's door and the 'Velle fires up with authority. The interior is mint: three-speed on the column, amber gauges, and a black vinyl bench seat that is an ad for Armor All. Out on the hood is a red-faced tachometer that glows brighter the more I rev. I don't know why they put them out there, but it's universal for tough.

On the dash is a statue of Jesus. It's not the one of him being crucified, but from before, on the way to the cross with his crown and blood and bad back. The statue's arms are uplifted, and the cheap plastic molding makes the fingers look webbed.

"Don't worry about that," Loren says and pops the statue out of the little base that holds its feet and reclamps it upside-down, so that Jesus is doing a handstand.

Somehow, when I see her do this, I'm not as nervous about driving Loren in a muscle car custom-built by her husband, a man so without fear that he's removed the seat belts.

"Let's go to the tower," I say, which is the big water tank on the side of Hayden Mountain that looks down on the university.

I ease through the parking lot, but I can't help goosing the 'Velle on the first left out of City Hall, a move that sends me sliding across the slick seat into Loren's lap, leaving the car idling, driverless, sideways in the street.

"Why don't we try that one again?" she says.

The car runs hot as we wander the backstreets of Tempe's college scene, past bars and taquerias, even the open-air cantina where I pissed on the horse, but I don't point that out. Near the old Hayden Mill, we hit a bump and there's a wild jangle in the trunk. "Christ," Loren says, "Jack and his crowbars."

Up the winding road, we park in front of the storm-wire fence that surrounds the massive tank. Loren and I sit on the hood with the last of our drinks. Under us, the cooling motor hisses and seethes to run again, and out there is the orange wash of the south valley: to the east is the floodlighted Sun Devil stadium, and

south, beyond Tempe, Chandler, and the Heights, are the Mari-
copa Mountains, while west sit the Papagos, circling the dark
Phoenix Zoo.

Around us is a rocky shelf of beer cans and cigarette butts, and
then a steep drop-off down to the lights of the university, whose
cement walkways and hard-angled courtyards tremble in the heat.

"Have you ever been to Mexico?" Loren asks, and I realize she's
looking a lot farther south than I am.

"A few times," I say, but she wants to hear more, I can tell. "It's
not so different, really. You can go twenty minutes outside of
Tempe and you'd think you were in the desert outside Guymas or
Hermasillo."

Loren begins running her hand over my thigh, tracing her fingers along the muscle, absently pulling out bits of mortar that
have hardened in the hair. The little pricks of pain give me an
erection so fast and sure I get light-headed. I describe the smell of
Mexican creosote after rain, the wicked look to a yucca planta-
tion, the taste of prickly pear meat.

"When you said things were complicated," I say. "Complicated how?"

"You're young. You'll get older, you'll see." She rattles the ice in
the bottom of her cup, then she chews a piece, her voice throaty
through the plastic. "There's a point of overconnection in life.
Everything's suddenly strung together, like with fishing wires you
can't see."

I don't really get what Loren's talking about, and she sees it on
my face.

"Earlier tonight I got a glass of water," she says. "Plain water.
But from somewhere in the house, Cheryl hears the ice crusher
go off in the fridge door. Maybe the ice crusher makes her think
of the cold packs for Jack's tendons, my vodka martinis, or the
fishing bait coolers Jack fills whenever he feels a 'relapse' coming

on. Either way, Cheryl deals with things by blasting the Christian rock. And then here comes Jack, all red and worked up, concentration shot, stomping in from the garage where he's been shadow-boxing Jesus. The wires go a thousand places from there."

An El Camino pulls up a couple car lengths away, and I give it a good look over while I try to wrap my brain around what Loren's saying. The car's seen some rough trade. Its panels have been blasted and primered, and there's a pattern of Bondo rings consistent with the repair of damage from automatic gunfire. There is a homemade hood scoop large enough to funnel every bad idea in town into the motor's smoky maw.

"Forget about all that stuff, though," she says. "You don't have to worry about that for a while. Maybe that's why I was drawn to you. That and your hands. Soon as I saw your hands, I had a feeling about you."

She takes my palm, touches all the little nicks from my trowel. She rubs the patches of red on my wrists. "My daughter has this," she says, "on her neck, though hers is a softer red. I think it's beautiful. Jack hates it. He thinks everything's a sign."

"This is just dye," I tell Loren. "I lay block for my father. We buy colored block and then dye the mortar. It saves the cost of painting the wall later."

"I still like it."

Loren cups my hand, working her thumbs deep between the bones. Her breath is sweet with alcohol and Sprite, and over her shoulder I absently watch a man and woman exit the El Camino, come round to the front bumper, and unbutton each other's jeans.

I touch her neck, running the back of my hand along that tendon there. I trace the underside of her jaw, smooth her brow with my thumb. She closes her eyes a moment, the outlines of her pupils roaming beneath the lids, and looking at her features, it hits me all of a sudden who her daughter might be: Cheryl, a girl I sometimes sit near in my Civic Responsibility class at Tempe Community College, a girl with a red mark on her neck, a locket-shaped pocket of red.

Behind Loren, the man and woman start going at it on the grill of the El Camino, humping with the bland monotony of a sump pump, while the hollow throat of the hood scoop exhales waves of heat from the motor. The guy's around my dad's age, fifty maybe, and though I've done the nasty at least three different times, I guess it kind of weirds me out to see older people doing it. I mean, they don't even take their clothes off.

"Let's sit in the car," I suggest.

As soon as we're in, Loren's like a gymnast the way she sidles on top of me, straddling my lap, despite the close quarters.

Up close, the light coming in sideways, I notice the faint lines around her eyes, her mouth, a few gray strands in the hair that clings to my arm. But something seems to radiate from her, too, and it's like I can see those fine wires she was talking about, extending out, connecting to a maze of things, like all those objects on her key chain. And now one wire strings to me, which makes me feel mature somehow, adultlike for once.

I kiss her, and we begin making out with enough fury to froth up a sweaty milk of Armor All from the vinyl seat. We finger gums, ears, cheek hollows, let our teeth run zippery down neck ridges, across clavicles. We revel in friction, fabric, hair, and then I discover something dangling from the key chain in the ignition that I hadn't noticed before: a laminated photo of young Cheryl, the Goody Two-shoes in Civic Responsibility who gave her oral presentation on "Loving Thy Neighbor."

I reach for the belt buckle of Loren's shorts.

"Easy, tiger," she says. She pulls back and grabs my shoulders, holding me at arm's length.

I lift my eyebrows. "The night is young," I tell her.

"Oh, that's precious. A line from a movie." She laughs. "You're dangerous. You could really cause some problems."

I drop by my father's place on the way home. He only lives two blocks from my house, and I try to hang out with him when he gets down on himself. He refuses to have a phone, and after a running argument with the Postal Service, they stopped delivering his mail. So you deal with my father in person. He also doesn't believe in things like licenses, bonding, registration, or insurance, which is why they impounded his four-ton flatbed truck last week, the reason I have to haul so much block by hand.

In the driveway, I park next to his Dodge, and our trucks are like twins with beds full of sand and pink block. Crossing the lawn, I move through the weepy branches of eucalyptus trees I climbed as a kid. I grew up in this house, and it's always strange to see my old home as a bachelor's place—bare couch, blank walls, a crate of motorcycle parts in the corner.

Mom got this place in the settlement, and then she and I moved to a new, "memory-free" house down the street so I could go to the same school. She kept the old house as an investment, and then, in a twist of fate, leased it to my father. Mom took some psychology courses in college, and she believes a male influence is important for me to have around. Providing this, in her opinion, is a good investment.

Before I'm through the gate that leads to the backyard and the kitchen's sliding door, I hear my father's rip saw and smell hot sap and green pine. Inside, I find him sawing lumber, which is generally a bad sign. In the dining room where we all once ate our meals together, he has positioned a lone table saw, and he smokes a little Mexican cigar called a *rojo* as he feeds the pitched blade.

He is shirtless, and the sawdust frosts the hair on his chest and arms, obscuring his old navy tattoos.

"What'cha building?" I ask, and the board he's mitering bucks back.

"Jesus," he says. "Give me a heart attack."

He kills the saw and gives me a big smile, even though I know he's been real negative on himself lately. He's gotten to a strange place these days, and I don't even know what to call it. He's a worker, however, and whenever he gets like this, he remodels something, though I don't tell my mother about the skylights he cut into her roof or the bunks he built so he could sleep the way he did on the navy boats.

He grabs us two beers and explains his plan. "I've been think-ing about building a breakfast bar," he says, sweeping his arm. "Over here, so it catches the sunlight when I eat cereal and check out the paper. Breakfast is the most important meal of the day, right?"

There's some sarcasm in his voice, but the gesture is sincere— a blue-panthered bicep, coated with sawdust, shows me the only way it knows to fix things.

"I think they're calling them nooks these days—breakfast nooks," I tell him. "Because of how a bar makes you think of alcohol."

Dad grabs two folding chairs and considers this. We open the chairs and sit with our beers on either side of a masking tape outline on the floor, which is in the general shape of the future breakfast nook.

We both sit quiet a minute and imagine, I guess, that it's morn-ing, sun shining and some birds chirping maybe, as if Dad and I are reading the paper with coffee in a house we used to share. But it's beer we're drinking, and when I was living here, I was the kind of kid who mostly ate by myself, in front of the TV.

"I don't know," he says, smoking. "I don't think I'm a nook kind of guy. What about a breakfast bench. We could call it that."

"What about this idea," I tell him. "How about we get the flatbed truck out of the impound yard? We could scrape up the money to make it legal and get it back on the road."

"Forget about the flatbed," he says, shaking his head. "The flatbed was an experiment. The flatbed's over."

I take a sip of beer and a memory comes to me from when I was eight, and my father came through this door, home from a naval tour to announce that he hated the smell of metal, of insulation, and paint. He hated galvanized grating, he said, and red light bulbs and he was never going to take another order again as long as he lived. Even as a kid, I knew his heart was never really in the navy—we lived in the middle of a desert, and it didn't seem like serious sailors would commute to the ocean. But my father became serious about being an ex-sailor and serious about his hatred of authority.

I try a different angle. "Are we going to let them get away with taking our truck?" I ask him.

He puts his *rojo* in his teeth and hunches sideways so he can dig in his pocket, where he finds his keys. He twists a key off the chain and tosses it to me. "Here," he says. "It's your truck now. You take care of it. Treat it like a baby."

When I leave, I set the key on the edge of the table saw. I don't want anything to do with it.

When I'm finally home, there's a car in the driveway I don't recognize, one of those slanty-shaped Saabs. The house is dark inside, and I strip naked by the sliding door, before heading out to the backyard, where I masturbate on the lawn. The sprinklers have run, and my bare feet leave dark prints in the misted grass. I have a lot on my mind, so it takes a long time. Above, birds wrestle their wings in the tight nests of a palm tree. The grapefruit leaves are thick, waxy, as I stare up through them.

In the morning, I come downstairs to find a man in slacks and an unbuttoned dress shirt eating in our kitchen. A loose tie drapes his shoulder. There is a little TV on the counter, and he's watching "Shark Week" on the Discovery Channel while thumbing through some papers.

"Hey," I say. His briefcase sits open, and he wears reading glasses, though he looks too young for them. He's really going at the cereal.

"Hey," he says. "I'm Greg. We met at your mom's office party."

"I remember," I say and grab a bowl.

"No, wait." He points at me with a spoon. "Maybe it was at that awards thing."

"Sure," I tell him. "That sounds right."

When I pick up the box of Cap'n Crunch, it's empty.

"Isn't this stuff great?" Greg asks. "God, I haven't had this stuff in years."

"Yeah, that's why my mom buys it for *me*."

Greg kind of coughs, but it might be a laugh. "Sorry," he says.

Mom comes downstairs. She's wearing a black suit with a bright scarf, and she's in a pretty good mood. She is fumbling with an earring and heading for the coffee when she grabs one of my hands. She turns it back and forth in the light. It's still a faint pink. "You better graduate college," she tells me, shaking her head. Then she hands me some pamphlets. "Here, I got these for you."

The pamphlets are about depression. One's entitled "Warning Signs," which features a big, yellow *Yield* on the cover. The other features a lamb, bright-eyed, gazing out from where it is cradled, in the great paws of a lion. This one's named "Last Call." Crucial to my mother's idea of my father is that there is something really wrong with him, because if there isn't something wrong with him, then he left us for no reason.

"Where'd you get these?" I ask her.

"City Hall. I filed a petition there yesterday, and they had all these sitting out on a table."

Mom kisses Greg, grabs her briefcase, and then kisses me before heading out into the garage, leaving the two of us.

The theme music from *Jaws* is on the TV.

"So, are you just going to hang out?" I ask.

"Well, I got to finish this report," he says, "and my show's not over. Shouldn't you be in class or somewhere?"

I shrug and take a stool across the counter from Greg, who makes being a county judge look pretty easy. "Shouldn't you be married or something?"

"I was," Greg says, "but I got a little condo now."

When I graduated, my friend Terry Patuni asked me to move in with him, to get our own place, and I said no, like an idiot. Mom was like, "stay at home and live for free," but she works a lot, and I do all the stuff like mowing the lawn and don't get shit for it.

I check out the pamphlets to the sounds of thrashing fish. The big warning sign in the depressed person's behavior, it turns out, is a sudden mood shift to peace and happiness, even elation. This can often mean a final decision has been made, and the weight of all earthly troubles has been lifted.

Sharks have limited feelings, I also learn, and they never sleep.

In Civic Responsibility class, I sit behind Cheryl. She wears a long dress with thin straps and sunflowers all over it. A fine gold cross has worked its way around the back of her neck, so it faces me, and there are running waves of goosebumps across her shoulders and the backs of her arms. I've never really said anything to Cheryl before, but I begin to wonder what she's thinking to cause them. I lean forward to smell her hair—apples. They use the same shampoo.

We watch a movie on land conservation, and I realize two things. One, by the light of a video, Cheryl's hair takes on the exact blue my swimming pool casts into the bougainvillea on nights when I lie on the diving board and masturbate toward the stars. Two, my father was born to be a U. S. park ranger. He has a deceivingly breezy manner that would be good with tourists, the military marksmanship to cull herds from the open door of a helicopter, and the disposition to spend weeks on end in solitude.

After class, Cheryl and I file out the door together, and I fall in with her as she heads toward the Snack Shack.

I put my hands in my pockets and try to be smooth. "Pretty lame video, huh?"

"I don't know," she says. "I kind of liked the part where they tagged the bears."

"Bears can be troublemakers," I say and watch as she digs through her woven shoulder bag. She balances it on the jut of a hip, and I check our the red marks on her shoulders from her bra straps, smile at the way her sunglasses start to slide off her nose, and she lets them fall in the bag as she digs around. But I don't really see anything nymphomaniac about her.

She pulls out a pack of menthols. "Smoke?"

"I didn't know you guys were allowed to smoke," I tell her.

"What are you talking about? Allowed by who?"

"Aren't you all Christian?" I ask. "I mean, the body's like the temple, right?"

"I'm not even going to respond to that," she says. "First of all,

Jesus doesn't even care about the body—he's into your soul. And besides, nobody ever told Jesus what to do."

"Jesus doesn't care what you do with your body?"

Cheryl takes her time lighting the cigarette. "I make my own decisions," she says and then heads off, walking all cool because she knows I'm watching.

When she's gone, I take the long way to the student parking lot, past the south lawn where the cheer team usually practices this time of morning. I like the way their skin flashes through those blue and gold outfits, and I sometimes hang my fingers in the fencing and stare. Today, though, the high kicks and girl tosses seem different. Today their uplifted arms and bright smiles make them look falsely optimistic, and according to my pamphlets, possibly suicidal.

I drive to the gravel pits, where I have them dump a quarter ton of sand in the bed, and then head to our job site in Chandler, my rear tires rubbing the fenders the whole way.

The neighborhood we're working in has only half walked out of the desert, and the house is one of those sprawling adobe numbers with fat, curved sides and wooden hogan ladders. The guy who owns the place is some hotshot named Treen. I don't like him, but he wants three hundred feet of pink wall around the lot and a strange, yellow decorative wall out front. This is enough work to carry my father for some time.

I mix mortar while my father, in an open khaki workshirt, eats a doughnut, smokes his *rojo,* and butters block at the same time, tapping the rows into level with the butt of his trowel. I shovel sand, cement, lime, and dye into the mixer, then polish off a grape soda as I fire the hose nozzle into the spinning drum. It's funny how the ingredients always refuse to mix for a while. Gray, red, brown, and white flop, clump and clot in the tumbler before finally blending into a smooth, pink mortar.

I crumple the soda can and drop it in the half-finished wall, listening as it jangles its way to the bottom. We throw snack wrappers, smoke packs, fast-food trash, and Hamms beer bottles into the hollows in the wall formed by the holes in the block. I tossed a broken wristwatch into a wall once, and another time, I ditched a stupid paperback I was reading called *Battlefield Earth!* And somewhere in the city of Phoenix is a wall that holds a lost set of my father's car keys. Sometimes I imagine people in the future tearing down our walls and trying to figure out who we were by what they find inside.

We both start laying block, and we find a groove, working on opposite sides of the waist-high wall to move faster. We don't usually work face to face, and for some reason, I start inventing stories, one after another, to try to crack my father up. He must know I'm making it all up, but he keeps laughing, and I can't fully explain my need to lie. I say I heard on the radio that they switched two monkey's heads in a lab in Switzerland. I describe how a cocky filmmaker was eaten on "Shark Week." Leonard Nimoy is secretly buying the space station Mir. There's a cult of Christian nymphomaniacs recruiting in Tempe, I tell him. They all smoke menthols.

At lunch, we spread our shirts on the ground in the shade of our freshly jointed wall, and we are leaning back to eat burritos and drink beer when Treen comes over. It's clear he's been lying on pool furniture by the red lines across the backs of his legs and arms. He's wearing swim trunks and a sweater in the heat, one so thin and loose I know it costs hundreds of dollars.

Treen eyeballs the beer but says nothing. I can tell he's more nervous about my father's tattoos—the red lantern on his shoulder, the blackbird fanning his back, a string of foreign characters down his spine. From here, Treen stares at the golden burst of what is supposed to be a Chinese dragon's head on Dad's chest. It always looked more like a goldfish to me.

But there's not much for Treen to be wary of. My father's a pretty nice guy who sat on gunboats for about ten years, where he probably battled some serious boredom, engaged the enemy's tattooists, and then surrendered in general before returning home to leave my mother and me.

"Look," Treen says and points where we are to build the next section of wall. "My neighbors are shit-heeling me. They said they would pay for half the cost of the wall, and now they're backing out."

I try to visualize a shit-heeling.

"They know they've got me," Treen says. "They know I'm going to build the wall anyway. I'm wondering if there's a way we can make their side of the wall crooked or crappy or something."

This appeals to my father's sense of justice. "Sometimes," he says, "the joints on a wall come out looking smooth and clean. Sometimes they're uneven and messy."

"Can you do that, make them crappy?"

"Can do," my father says.

I think this idea is a mistake. Our walls are solid and true, built to last, not like most you see today, cracking from lack of rebar, skimpy mortar, or thin footings. You only get one chance to build a wall right.

"Was it the color?" I ask Treen.

"What?"

"The neighbors," I say. "Did they hate the pink?"

"It's not pink," Treen says. "It's called Anasazi Sunset."

The rest of the day, my father and I work quietly, on opposite sides of a wall we are on tiptoes to finish. I groom my joints, while Dad lets the mortar slop where it may, the two of us running rows until the wall completely outgrows us, and all I can make out of my father is the pitched blade of his trowel. There's a strange comfort to spending the afternoon a few feet from someone you cannot really hear or see, though I can't quite explain it. You just know they're there, even when they don't seem to be there.

On Thursday, I sit by Loren in City Hall, and we play more games.

Mr. Doyle has us pull words from a purple velvet bag that looks suspiciously like the kind that come with bottles of Crown Royale, and play a kind of charades. The words begin simple enough. There's "friend" and "goal." A man in a suit acts out "share" by holding imaginary objects close to his heart before giving them away to each of us. We receive our invisible gifts with two hands, to prevent spilling.

But the words start to get weird—next come "sacrifice," "testify," and "redeem." My word is stupid. I reach into the fuzzy bag and draw a folded slip that reads "hope." I have no idea what to do with this.

I walk to the head of the table, and unable to think of any way to convey hope, just stand there in front of those creepy, outward-slanting windows that invite you to fall into the parking lot below.

"Balance," the old woman shouts.

"Sober," someone says.

I wave these responses off, but with the sight of my lifted arms comes "wings," "soar," and "guardian angel."

I decide to divide the word into two parts, "hoe" and "pee." I begin to work my imaginary hoe through crop rows, emphasizing my elbows and the straightness of the tool. I get "garden," which prompts "grow" and "blossom."

Loren shouts "weed."

I try the "pee" part of the formula by tracing an imaginary arc of urine with my little finger, extending it from my crotch out toward the confused redirectees.

The old woman shouts "police horse," and Mr. Doyle says my time is up.

When it's Loren's turn, she sets down her sport cup and comes to stand before us with her word. She looks down at her feet, concentrates, then works her lips as if she's evening her lipstick. What she does next makes everyone lean back and inhale. She bends down, throws her legs high, and executes a perfect handstand—palms pressed wide on the tan carpet, spine curved hard, legs together.

No one takes a shot at what this might mean, except me. "Jesus," I say.

Like that, she pops back up, and is shaking her hair straight before anyone can react. "Beautiful, Ronnie," she says.

Clearly troubled, Mr. Doyle comes to check the piece of paper. He opens the folded square, eyes the two of us, then puts it in his pocket. "This is a good time for a breather," he announces.

At break Loren and I take off, heading south toward the Maricopas, the closest thing I know to Mexico on a Thursday night. My truck is full of block and tools, and when we reach a certain speed, sand whips in the windows and bites us.

To the east, the moon is swollen, rising, so that it is framed in the truck window past Loren's face, which is fixed somewhere just short of regret.

"I should tell you," she says. "My husband can tear a phone book in half."

"Are we talking Rural or Metro?"

"We're talking about the Yellow Pages."

I laugh, and with that, some reservation leaves her face.

Loren opens lukewarm wine coolers for us and tunes the radio to a Mexican station. I point out the snakes that appear in the edges of our headlights, sprawled across the shoulders of the road to warm themselves on the asphalt. The road begins to bob and switch, and where the foothills of the Maricopas rise, we pull off the main road, the tires moaning through the sugar sand of an arroyo until I shift into four-wheel.

To the south are cliffs that appear obsidian, and the distant heat lightning they reflect seems to flash from deep within them. Loren's eyes are drawn to where we came from, to the orange dome of Phoenix. I wander through rolling hills and washouts until we are deep enough into the dark carpet of the desert that the faint *whoosh* of cars on the road vanishes.

I park near an outcropping of black rock that rims the swell of several dunes. There is silence when I cut the motor, and Loren is wide-eyed at what lies before us. Chollas stand fuzzy and glowing against the indigo sand, and saguaros look cut from smoky, purple-green glass.

The sand hills loom ahead, and after climbing out, we move through the crumbly, pink chalkstone and caramel-colored joshua trees that lead the way. From somewhere, a light breeze brings the clean, dusty smell of wet granite. Smoke trees waft in the dark, stirring elf owls and their strange double calls.

"It's like a whole nother world," Loren says.

"This is happening every night out here," I tell her.

We move on into the desert, taking deep steps up the moonlit faces of the dunes, and sliding down their bluish, shadowy backs. We sink and climb, sometimes on all fours, our hands and feet moving through a cool layer of air that hovers over the sand. When there is nothing to be seen but dunes, we lie at an angle along a crest, the stars overhead seeming to wobble and migrate, shifting design as easily as the high, formless clouds that cruise below them.

Loren rolls on top of me, straddles my midsection.

"I've done some things," she says, "and Jack's done his share, believe me. But I'm not really one to run around, alright? I'm just telling you that."

"Do you love him?"

She puts a hand on my chest to support her weight, and with the other, touches my cheek. "What do you know about love?"

She smiles, but it's a little bitter, too. I shrug.

"Do you ever think about leaving him?"

"That's not so easy."

"I don't know. My dad left us at the same time he left the navy. Then he moved in down the street, and I saw more of him than ever."

"Oh, tiger," she says. "I'm not sure if that's a sad story or not."

My shirt and pants are starting to fill with sand. I touch Loren's side, feel the last, stunted ribs of her cage. "It's the only story I got."

In the morning, I wake to the whine of my mother's hair dryer across the hall and the phone ringing downstairs, so I head down to the kitchen in my boxers, where I find Greg, in his undershirt, hair wet, talking on the phone and peeling an orange.

"It's for you," he says when he sees me. He passes the receiver. "Some woman, maybe your teacher."

"Morning, sunshine," Loren says when I answer.

I cup my hand over the phone. "Maybe it's none of your business," I tell Greg and head out the front door to stand in the driveway for some privacy. But lots of women in the neighborhood are out working in their yards. The fire station is two blocks down, and this is the time of the morning when the young firemen go jogging down our street.

"What's going on, is something wrong?" I ask Loren.

"I can't just call you?"

"It would be kind of weird if my mom answered. How'd you like me to call and have Jack pick up?"

"Would you like to speak to Jack? He's in the next room eating his protein flakes. I'll get him if you want."

Across the street, Mrs. Goldwyn is raking leaves in her sweats and next door, Mrs. Sekera prunes in polka-dot gloves. They both look at me in my boxers.

"You know what I'm saying," I tell Loren.

"I just called to say I want to see you. Jack's got an exhibition and then a late-night revival."

The firemen come by, five young men in tight blue shirts and nylon shorts, trotting with radios in their hands.

"Okay, I'll pick you up at eight," I tell her. "What did that guy say to you?"

"What guy?"

"The guy who answered the phone."

"He asked me if I was your girlfriend," she says.

"What'd you tell him?"

"I told him to go write 'I will not be nosey' a hundred times."

The garage door opens, and my mom comes out, lugging the big briefcase.

"Who are you talking to?" she asks.

"Nobody."

"Nobody, out here in your underwear?"

"A girl."

"Okay now, a girl. That's more like it."

Mom spots Mrs. Sekera. "Did I miss them?"

"Boy, did you," she answers.

In Civic Responsibility class, Cheryl passes me a note. We are watching a video on being nice to animals. The teacher apparently forgot that we'd seen this one before, and during the part where the man in red suspenders throws the chickens into the pit, Cheryl lifts an arm, as if scratching the red spot on her neck, and holds a folded paper out for me. I almost have to reach into her hair for it.

The note is really a flier for the Power Team, a weight-lifting group coming to campus today. The posters are all over school: four muscle-bound men hold the corners of a Volkswagen Beetle, while another reclines in a folding chair beneath.

Cheryl turns to me in the dark. Backlit by the video, her eyes and teeth are extra white. "The other day, were you just messing with me?"

"You mean, about the cigarettes?"

"Because I was serious about not letting people tell you what to do."

"I wasn't making fun of you," I say.

"If you're serious about finding the strength to do your own thing, you should come check out the Power Team."

"The Power Team?"

"Yeah," she says. "They cut through all the hype. My dad is on the team, and he's living proof of how much someone can change."

"So your dad's like a weight lifter?"

"More of a motivator. Can I count on seeing you there?"

"Sure," I tell her. "You bet."

We all still gasp when the video shows footage of "retired" racing greyhounds.

After class, I run into my old friend Terry Patuni at the fence where the cheer team is practicing. There are several guys there smoking. I stand next to him, and we put our fingers in the mesh. The team is making a pyramid by kneeling on each other's backs.

"Why don't they ever line up the other way," Patuni asks, "so we can see their asses?"

"Yeah, what's with that?" I say, and it feels kind of good to just hang out with him. We used to be better friends, but I wouldn't move in with him, and then I was kind of a prick once at the end of our senior year. My dad needed extra help one Saturday, and I brought Patuni along. His father is dead, and for some reason, I kept guffing it up with my dad, making it look like we were best pals.

We go eat a discount lunch in the Food Studies kitchen, which is kind of unnerving because they watch you eat it. Today it's lasagna, and I'm no expert, but it's either overcooked or needs more sauce. There's always something wrong with the food that we can never pin down, but it only costs a dollar fifty, and it's better than those sixty-forty soy burgers and vitamin-fortified tater wedges they pawned off on us in high school.

Patuni is pretty worked up about the Power Team, going on and on about it. We eat on metal stools above a Formica island, and he keeps showing me the flier. "Look at the pecs on those guys," Patuni says. "Think of the babes you'd pull." He keeps leaning his stool back on two legs, which is against the rules in the Food Lab.

"I think I'm going to check out this Power Team thing," I say, acting like there was never anything weird between us. "You want to do it together?"

He squints at me, shrugs. "Sure, yeah."

On the exit ballot, I rate the meal an 8.5, while Patuni cuts them with a 6.

In the gymnasium, we sit on retractable wooden bleachers and wait for the exhibition. Only about thirty people show up, mostly guys, but Patuni points out that there's nobody from the college here, and we take this lack of official endorsement as a good sign.

There are several weight sets on the basketball court, including a bench press on the free-throw line with black plates stacked deep enough to bend the bar. We're trying to act cool, but really, we can't take our eyes off all that iron.

In the front row I catch Cheryl looking back at me. She waves.

Suddenly, "Eye of the Tiger" by Survivor plays over the public announcement system. Five guys in tight, red wrestling suits come running out. They jog circles around the weight gear, clapping in an exaggerated manner meant to make us join. Nobody does.

The Power Team doesn't really say much. They just start lifting incredible amounts of weight, which is how we like it. An enormous man in a flattop ducks his head under the bar of a squat rack and takes the weight on his shoulders. He backs up in slow, staggering steps while the other guys crowd around, chanting, "feel the power." He looks at the ceiling, chugging air, and dips down until his ass touches the ground. His rise is so slow we can't take it. He braces his teeth, snatches great gasps of air, iron plates trembling.

"My God," I say.

"Jesus," Patuni says. He keeps spitting on the floor between his knees and rubbing it out with his foot, a habit of his when he's excited.

The weights slam back on the rack, and the other guys ask him how heavy it was. He looks out to the audience. "I didn't feel a thing," he announces.

Patuni and I look at each other. "There's cocky," Patuni says, "and then there's pissing in people's faces."

Another Power Teamer does a tremendous military press while the others jog in place and chant "yeah, uh-huh" over and over. When the bar is over his head, and his elbows lock, he manages to stutter, "I used to be weak. Then one day I found strength." He drops the weight, which visibly moves the hardwood floor. They all high-five.

"Is this like a skit or what?" Patuni asks.

"I think they're gonna try to sell us weight sets," I say.

The black Power Teamer lies down on the bench.

The flattop Power Teamer asks him very loud, "Do you want a spotter?"

"No thanks," he answers. "I've already got one." He goes ahead with the press alone, and now we know they're running some kind of scam. But the lift is magnificent. It has us. The iron rumbles like storm drain covers, the floors moan, and we are left gripping our own elbows. Cheryl looks back at me. We shake our heads in disbelief.

Another man presses a nail into a block of wood with his bare hands, and then, in what is the most terrifying thing I have ever seen, he blows up a hot water bottle. It takes forever, veins throbbing, tendons straining, and you can hear the dry hasp of his throat rattle through a balloon that now matches the color of his reddened skin. The sight has the same life-threatening grip as the natural childbirth video they scared us with back in Health and Hygiene.

Finally, a man steps forward with a chrome crowbar, and I know this is Jack. He is older than the others, with a thick mustache and blue eyes that scan us all. His tanned skin runs loosely over his muscles as he grabs the hook and spade ends of the crowbar in his fists. He starts the bend by wrapping it around the back of his neck, but then does the final crunch, elbows out, right in front of his face. It looks like he is bending it with his mind, and when the bar starts to fold, the chrome plating crackles off into mist of sparkly flakes.

"How did you bend that?" the black Power Teamer asks.

"I didn't bend it," Jack says. "Jesus did."

You can tell it took a lot out of the guy.

Then Jack goes for the grand finale, a long, boring struggle with a phone book, and it is only the white pages, from a town the size of Tucson at best. The process involves a lot of folding back and forth, and mostly it looks like he is giving the book a massage. Afterward, Jack can barely breathe. "You don't need a phone to dial up Jesus," he says, and then leans over, hands on his knees, panting.

"Such bullshit," Patuni says. "What are we, dupes?"

"This is such a lie," I say. "Everything is so rigged."

Yellow pamphlets entitled "Yield to Jesus" file down our row and as soon as the Power Team opens things up for Q&A, I stand up.

"Answer this," I say. "Wasn't Jacob stronger than the angel?"

The Power Teamers look at one another.

"Forget the Old Testament," the black Power Teamer says. "Jesus is where it's at."

We all wait for one of them to expand on this, but they don't, and we're not sure if things are over. What's clear is that Jack is beat. I wonder if he maybe strained something. Cheryl is down by him, running a hand over his back, and even bent over, his lats are like Corvette fenders.

Toward the early afternoon, an unusual weather front moves in. It sweeps up from the Baja and stalls in the Phoenix Valley. Cloud heads rise, threaten, and dissipate, leaving the city overcast and hot. The mugginess gives my father a considered mood as he works quietly in the heat, finishing the last pink panels that will seal us into Treen's back lot. The blocks flow with method and precision—he tamps down a row, steps back, eyeballs the line, hefts another block. Already, I have a mixer of bright yellow mortar turning for the curved, decorative wall out front, and as I feed him the last of the pink block and mortar, I keep thinking about Jack, about how much that phone book meant to him.

Halfway through the yellow wall out front, my father loses his steam. He does not like the weather, he says, and we take a late lunch. We search the back roads of Chandler for a Burger King, but we are forced to settle for a tavern that in some way appeals to my father. There used to be an air force base out this way a long time ago, and the tavern is called The Lazy Jet.

We sit at two empty stools in the center of the long bar and order drafts and a microwave Tombstone pizza. Everyone in the bar watches TV, including the bartender, whose wild, choppy hair looks like it was cut in an emergency room. Four or five people to the left of us look up to a TV that shows *One Life to Live*, while those to the right watch a documentary on Africanized bees.

The TVs are loud, especially all the buzzing, and we don't really talk much. The tavern's air-conditioner struggles to keep the place cool in this humidity, and when the pizza comes, I am hungrier than I thought, even after eating earlier. Dad lets me have the extra piece. The bar phone rings, and the bartender answers in front of us. He mutes the TVs with the remote.

"Yeah," he says. "Yeah, okay, yeah, when?" He looks at his watch and hangs up. "The caller said there's a bomb in here," he announces. "And it will go off in five minutes."

Nobody makes to leave, and neither do we.

Dad uses plastic tongs to help himself to a pickled egg, which he eats whole.

The bartender sets up a silver shaker and follows a scoop of ice with a clear stream of liquor. He shakes it with two hands, and the muted rattle of ice sounds like the rocks inside the rotating drum of the cement truck when my father and I pour footings. But with the smell of chilling alcohol, I think of Loren, try to picture the inside of her house. I see a refrigerator at the center, hear Christian rock everywhere, but other than that, I mostly see objects—sports cups, crowbars, protein cereal, a hot rod in the garage—and I can't really get them to come together, get them rolling like a movie in my head.

Dad orders two more beers. "I wish it would hurry up and rain," he says.

I'll confess I'm also thinking about the bomb, which is getting to me a little.

A guy at the end of the bar asks if the caller's voice was a woman's, but the bartender doesn't answer him—instead, he just turns the TVs up again.

"Enough with the bees, already," I say and get some dirty looks.

Back at the job site, Treen shit-heels us. I load up the trucks while Dad finishes the yellow wall by himself. I hose out the mixer, shovel sand, and pack the leftover cement and dye. I spray down the walls with the hose, and I like the feeling of the water coursing through the nozzle. The slower the mortar dries, the harder it gets, so this is the last part of every job, and I'm on the west wall when Treen comes out with a check that's only half of what it should be.

Treen points to a crack in his driveway he claims wasn't there before we stacked block on it. "I'll have to repour the whole pad," he says.

"Driveways crack," my father says. "That's how it works."

"Nobody cracks my driveway and gets away with it."

"Your driveway was probably cracked long before I came," my father says.

"Look, this isn't about you," Treen says. "It won't cost you anything. You're bonded and insured. All you have to do is file a claim."

"This is a bad idea," Dad says. "You've come up with a real mistake of an idea."

"You're bonded and insured, otherwise you couldn't get a license. We all know it's a crime to contract without a license. I know it is because I'm a member of the county commissioner's board."

"You can barely see that crack," I say and point, but they don't even hear me.

My father considers Treen very carefully and then walks to his truck.

Deep down, I know my dad isn't going to hurt anyone, but I want it to happen, I do. "You better start running," I say to Treen, and the two of us watch my father stride toward his truck like he will return with a bazooka.

Instead, he comes back with a push broom. He sweeps out the crack to show its age, which begins a long, futile debate with Treen that leaves my father exhausted and angry. At the end, Treen holds a light check in one hand and a cordless phone in the other, threatening to call some public agency I've never heard of.

My father will not take the check.

I'm looking at Treen, and his collarbone is right there. I am so ready to lay some jiu-jitsu on him that I start bouncing up and down on my toes. "Come on," I tell Dad, "let's take him out."

"Go wait in my truck," he tells me, and I just do what I'm told.

It's only a minute later that my father is behind the wheel, and without really speaking, we're driving to a gas station to buy a twelve-pack of Coors. Then we return to the job site, where we find Treen's gone inside, the check sitting under a rock in the driveway. Here we drink in the hot cab for three hours, until sunset, looking at the blue kachina symbol painted on Treen's garage door. It is a rainbird.

My father starts talking and he never really stops. He talks about everything, most of it I've never heard before, and though his mind goes all over the place, it's like he's only telling different parts of one big story. He tells me that when he was a boy, he had a half-wild sheepdog named Bone that killed the mayor's son's prize boxer in front of the Bijou Theater. He tells me I was named after his great uncle Ronald, who was rumored to have seen an angel, underwater, when he was drowning in the Atlas River—the angel said *breathe the water*, but Ronald knew the angel was lying. I hear that Dad enlisted in the navy on a bad impulse, and regretting it, stole a horse from a ranch in Kingman, rode into the hills to decide whether to report for service, and when he returned nine days later, no one had noticed the pony was gone. I was conceived at a drive-in feature of *The China Syndrome*, he tells me, a movie that kind of rattled him because it was a true story.

We sweat beer, and the adrenaline settles into a dull ache in my stomach. While Dad talks, he lets his arms hang on the steering wheel, so that it seems like we are driving to a place we know so well there is no need to watch the road. The illusion is ruined only by Treen's head popping over our pink wall from time to time to view us with eerie concern. But my father does not seem to see him.

"You know," my father says, "by the time I was your age, I'd made it through shark survival school, dengue fever, and a magazine fire. I've made it through the seven seas of the world." He lifts his hands. "Now where am I?"

"Let's go home," I say.

Looking tired, he says, "I suppose," and puts a smoke in his lips that he doesn't light. Then he steps out of the truck, walks up the driveway, and bends down to grab the check, which he folds and puts in his shirt pocket. "I've got a repair job for us tomorrow, at the end of Ocotillo Street," he says and clamps a hand on my shoulder, squeezing the way he used to when I was a kid. Then we part.

My legs are cramped when I climb into my own truck. Pulling away, I can barely work the clutch. In the rearview mirror, I see my father pausing to light his *rojo* before he, too, heads out. His face flares orange as he lifts the glowing lighter, smoke curls from the cab, and then comes a faint clang as his shifter finds reverse.

Loren's house is across from the Presbyterian Youth Center, and at eight, I pull into its parking lot. Under this low cloud ceiling, the moon, if involved, casts no glow, and it is absolutely dark. The church's perfect lawns crawl right to the asphalt, and my headlights set to glowing a row of white-trunked orange trees.

I find Loren sitting on the curb, the way her daughter might between classes. Right away, I can see she's been crying, and when she climbs in, a shiner is clear under the dome light.

"What happened to your eye?"

"Don't say anything, please. Jack had another relapse. Let's just leave it."

"Is this because of me?" I ask. "I mean, I got a look at his power thing today."

"Don't worry, tiger. He's more likely to try to baptize you than kill you."

"I'm worried about you," I say. "I can take care of myself."

Loren laughs once, a little too hard, and has to blow her nose.

"Look, I don't want him to ruin this, too," she says. "Let's just go to the desert again. That's all I want right now."

I put the truck in gear and swing south toward the desert, but as soon as we hit the two-laner that crosses the Indian reservation, we get stuck behind a semi rig pulling an open trailer of onions. The papery skins snap into the wind and flutter in our headlights like snow. Our eyes water as they whip in the cab, do loops, and leave.

The onions make me sniff and tear up, but what I really feel is pissed.

"What a hypocrite," I say. "Does he think Jesus is just going to forgive him? I wouldn't forgive him if I were you. I say don't do it."

"Please," Loren says. "Let's just drop it."

I can't drop it though. I'm getting all worked up out of nowhere.

"Who does he think he is? Why doesn't he pick on someone his own size? That's what these Christians do, they—"

"You ever stop to think about the kind of problems you'd have to have to want to be born all over again?" Loren asks me. "I suppose other people become marines or wind up in jail. But before this church thing, Jack was raging all the time. All the time. My daughter, Cheryl, was completely out of control."

The city lights dim with the curving road, reducing the flurry of skins to two cones of mothlike flutter in our high-beams until the highway finally divides, and we can pass the rig. It's so dark that it's hard to know how fast we're going—creosote and palo verde appear in flashes, leaning over the road's tight shoulders, and then are gone.

As I swing into the new lane, I ask, "How come you didn't join the church? I mean, what kept you in control?"

"I can cope with lots," Loren says, bracing a hand on the dash. "I can roll with just about anything."

The trees start to disappear in the west, and I know we have taken up with the SanTan rail line beside us, though the only sign is the rise and fall of a purple shine that paces us in the power wires that follow the tracks.

In the dark, I find a turnoff that looks like the one we took before, but I can't tell, and we're pretty much committed when we hit the soft sand. We wander through a web of scrub brush, the lights casting stark shadows that wheel and bounce through all our wrong turns and back-outs.

We wallow down a dry arroyo, and the virgin desert we'd hoped for isn't in the cards. We come to a halt before some old drums and a pile of blackened bedsprings left from a giant mattress fire. I switch off the dome light so it doesn't blind us when we open the doors, and even making the few steps to the tailgate in such dark is like negotiating the cold ass of the moon. In the Chevy's work bed, we make out for a while under a low sky, staticky and featureless. I scatter the tools, throwing shovels and trowels over the side, and then I peel back a plastic tarp to reveal a half ton of cool, wet sand, into which we sink our shapes like snow angels.

Loren lays her body on mine, and as our clothes come off, our breath alternates, hard, in each other's faces. She pulls me inside her, then presses her thumb hard behind my scrotum. The feeling is deep and weird, and I am erect forever. For a while, about six degrees of the moon, I am outside of myself, I am a part of someone else, and it doesn't feel like flying, the way you might think. It feels like landing, maybe the way a jet comes down out of the clouds, or a ship steams all the way around the world and finds its slip.

I drop her off in the church parking lot, rolling in with my headlamps off. Across the street, instead of seeing the green-black Chevelle in the driveway, the garage door is open, with all the lights on, and we make out the distant figure of Jack, leaned-back on an incline bench, smoking a cigarette with one hand while his whole other arm soaks in an orange cooler.

Loren kisses me quick, climbs out, and then leans in the window. "It's been a night," she says to me. "You've joined the ranks of the complicated."

I look over at Jack. "I don't think the night's over."

"Don't worry about him. He's harmless for now."

"I guess I'll see you at the Redirection meeting tomorrow."

Loren turns and walks away, but as she nears the streetlamp, she slows, then underneath it, stops. She stares at her arms, leans over to examine her legs. She looks back at me with astonishment, and I start to realize what has happened.

I put the truck in gear and creep forward into the light of the streetlamp. I stick my arm out the window and it's splotched with patches of fluorescent yellow.

"Shit," I tell her. "It's dye. We got mixed up with it in the bed."

I climb out of the cab, and she shows me her hands. "What the hell is this?"

"It's yellow dye. It won't come off for a while, a couple days."

She rubs her hands on her jeans. "This is some kind of joke, right?"

"Come on," I tell her. "Let's try to get you cleaned up. This dye is strong stuff."

"Forget it," she says and turns to leave.

I grab her arm. "You can't go in there. *Jack's right there.*"

"You don't get it. He's so guilt-racked right now. He can't even look at me while my eye's like this. I could punish him all week, if I had the spirit to, but I don't anymore. I really don't." She pulls her arm back and then uses it to touch my shoulder, squeezing it once, before letting go. "That's why I'm with you."

Then she walks down the street, following the neighbor's lawn and garage, and turns up her driveway. She ducks into her own garage, where she passes a hanging speed bag, stacks of iron

plates, and a husband who lifts his head to watch her before reclining again when she's gone inside.

In the morning, I drive to the end of Ocotillo, a quiet street with
small, thick-walled houses. I didn't sleep well, so I'm early and my
dad's not here yet. I park in the alley and unload tools for a while.
The job is to repair a backyard wall smashed by a car that didn't
stop when it reached Ocotillo's dead end. Two whole panels of
block lie in a pile of rubble. There's glass and motor oil everywhere, and one thing's for sure, whoever cracked up was on his
way back from the grocery store. As I sift through the block, I find
a potato, a thing of Aquafresh toothpaste, and a can of creamed
corn. I drop these things in the holes of the wall that still stands.

I upturn a grout bucket to sit on and start chipping the old
mortar off the blocks with a mason's hammer, throwing cracked
and oil-soaked block to one side, and stacking the ones I chip
clean to the other. About half the block looks okay, and I set out to
save as much of it as I can. Where the old block will meet new,
the wall will look patched, but there's nothing else to do. I come
across a broken cassette tape called *Aloha, Elvis* in the pile and
then an onion. I toss this junk in the wall. There's also individual
grapes everywhere, and it's pretty amazing that there was enough
force to pull the grapes off the bunch, and yet the grapes are still
not squashed.

An older man comes out of the house to watch me work. He
stands a little bit away, on the grass, with his arms folded in a
brown suit, and I don't figure him to speak English until he says,
"Enrique has departed to his occupation."

"Yeah," I say to the guy. "Enrique probably talked with my
dad."

"Concerning the payment, you must dialogue with Enrique."

"Sure," I tell him. The old cement's really hard to chip off the blocks, which means they used plenty of lime in the mortar.

There's a pack of Breath-O-Fresh gum, still good, in the pile. I undo the wrapper and stick a square in my mouth. The gum has a liquid-flavor center, and it's perfectly okay. I offer the old guy some, but he kind of backs up. Under the next block I move is a Volvo emblem. It looks like silver, but you can tell it's really made of plastic. That sucks because those cars are supposed to be real safe. I picture some guy spending a lot of money on a Volvo—he's a regular guy who likes his corn and potatoes and rock 'n' roll— and then *bam!* Here's this wall.

I notice some sheared bolts and cut metal on the ground, which means the fire department has been here. I pick up a cracked Gerber jar of strained carrots, and the old man and I look at it. I drop it in the wall, where it falls with a *thuk*.

"Horribly accidental," the old man says.

"Hey, what happened to these people?" I ask him.

The old guy doesn't say anything. It's like he can speak the lingo but not understand it. I stand up and walk through the broken wall to the sidewalk, and there's no skid marks in the street that I can see, only patches of kitty litter, which the tow truck drivers spread around. That's a bad sign. Maybe the Volvo guy just fell asleep or something or maybe his brakes went out. I take a closer look at the exposed wall, and it's just like one we would build—deep footings, mortar-filled pilasters, and extra rebar—not a very forgiving thing to hit.

For some reason, I think of Mr. Doyle's daughter, the one who was killed, and the whole thing starts to give me the willies. I look for my old man's truck coming down the street, for the familiar way that he smokes and drinks coffee and drives all over the place with his knees, but the street is empty.

On the ground I see a package of condoms, and I pick them up. They're ribbed.

The old guy crosses himself.

Then I notice these assorted kid-size boxes of cereal, from a variety pack, and it makes me spit out the gum. When I start to think about this Volvo guy's story, I feel awful, just horrible. Here's this guy, he's got a kid and a new baby, and he likes music, but things are not going so good for him at his small stereo shop. His wife wants another kid, but he's like *let's wait a while,* and maybe things aren't so good between them right now, what with his long days at the music store, and she's going nuts with the kids, and he doesn't even get off work until dark, when he has to go to the market, but maybe tonight things are looking up for him, you know, he's bringing home the bacon, got some Tony Tiger cereal for his son, and he's got some Rolling Stones playing in his Volvo with a moon roof and he's cruising down Ocotillo, feeling tired and mellow, tapping his fingers on the wheel. He's just driving down the street, and he's got no idea, no clue at all.

ACKNOWLEDGMENTS

These stories have appeared, in slightly different form, in the following publications: "Your Own Backyard," *Sundog: The Southeast Review*; "The Death-Dealing Cassini Satellite," *New England Review*; "Trauma Plate," *Virginia Quarterly Review*; "Cliff Gods of Acapulco," *Esquire*; "The History of Cancer," *Hayden's Ferry Review*; "The Canadanaut, Part I," *Harper's*; and "The Canadanaut, Part II," *Paris Review*. Several of these stories also appeared in *Scribner's Best of the Fiction Workshops*, *Best New American Voices*, and *Speak*.

I am indebted to the support of the Kingsbury Fellowship at Florida State University, the Stegner Fellowship at Stanford, and the generosity of my mentors: Ron Carlson, Robert Olen Butler, John Wood, Janet Burroway, Virgil Suarez, Mark Winegardner, John L'Heureux, and Tobias Wolff. I also wish to recognize the various experts with whom I consulted while researching these stories: I'm grateful to Dr. Todd Pierce for advice on the behavior of exotic species; for his expertise in African folklore, Dr. George Clark will always enjoy my gratitude; concerning coastal meteorology, Dr. Russ Franklin proved invaluable; and thanks to Professor Neil

Connelly for access to his archives and for his vast knowledge of the early days of Canadian space exploration.

Special thanks go to Warren Frazier, the prince of literary agents, and to my editor at Viking, Ray Roberts. Thanks to Julie Orringer, ZZ Packer, Angela Pneuman, Ed Schwarzschild, and, of course, Gay Pierce. Thanks to Michael Knight.

My mother, Patricia, always believed and was always there. My father, Donald, gave me his ear for stories. And nothing is possible without my wife, Stephanie—you are my satellite, my white flash, my outside heart.